THE
UNWELCOMED
THE CURIOUS CASE OF CLARA FOWLER

INSPIRED BY A CHILLING STORY
OF DEMONIC POSSESSION

RON FELBER
AWARD-WINNING AUTHOR OF *MOJAVE INCIDENT*

Black Rose Writing | Texas

The author grants the final approval for this literary material.

First printing

This is a work of fiction. Names, characters, businesses, places, events, and incidents are either the products of the author's imagination or used in a fictitious manner. Any resemblance to actual persons, living or dead, or actual events is purely coincidental.

ISBN: 978-1-68513-419-8
PUBLISHED BY BLACK ROSE WRITING
www.blackrosewriting.com

Printed in the United States of America
Suggested Retail Price (SRP) $20.95

The Unwelcomed is printed in Garamond Premier Pro

*As a planet-friendly publisher, Black Rose Writing does its best to eliminate unnecessary waste to reduce paper usage and energy costs, while never compromising the reading experience. As a result, the final word count vs. page count may not meet common expectations.

To WPB friend and mentor

"The greatest trick the Devil ever played was convincing the world he does not exist."
–Charles Baudelier

THE
UNWELCOMED

Dear Prince,

You will hardly believe me, I fear, but I have only just attained to the reading of your 'Dissociation' book.

Not only is the case destined to be historic, but your exposition is a perfect masterpiece of lucidity and narrative art.

But who or what is the "demon"? That is a dark point.

Ever truly yours,
William James
September 28, 1906

PROLOGUE

Central Station
Court Square
Fall River, Massachusetts

January 8, 1886

Marshal Rufus Hilliard, who everyone called "Bassett", was born in Pembroke, Maine, not Fall River, but the local politicians and business leaders took to him right away. Perhaps it was his rugged good looks: jet black hair, handle-bar mustache, and strapping six-foot-one physique. Or, as likely, it was his seriousness. Dressed in a vested suit and steed derby with spit-shined boots, he exuded iron-willed determination.

Most knew his background. A tough one. His mother died when he was two. His father passed away three years later when he was sent to live with an older sister, then another sister after that. At age fifteen, he enlisted in the army, where he rose to the rank of captain. Once discharged, he traveled to Fall River, where he joined the police force. Three years later, he was promoted to sergeant. Four years after that, he was appointed Fall River City Marshal.

Perhaps he was thinking about his career or rise in social stature since his engagement to Judge Thomas Clark's daughter, Nellie, as he sat silent behind a desk at Central Station. But it was neither of those things. It was a report he'd gotten at 3:05 p.m. about a disturbance at the Fowler House.

He rose slowly from his chair and put on his long coat and derby, bracing for the bone-chilling bluster of Fall River winter.

"Are you headed to the Fowler's place?" Officer William Medley asked, looking up from his copy of the *Boston Telegraph*.

"I figure it's my turn since Harrington made the last trip. Besides, I know John Fowler."

"Will you be takin' the wagon?" he asked with an Irish brogue.

Bassett thrust a wry smile across the room.

"Not today," he answered, opening the door to leave. "I thought I'd give Hunter that distinction."

By 3:48 p.m. the Marshal had hitched his horse, Hunter, to a wooden post and was trudging through a blanket of snow. His warm breath spun out into the freezing air like a ghostly vapor as he approached the crude, slat-wood home of John and Mary Fowler. He huddled into his long coat and tugged his steed derby down on his head remembering when, as a young deputy, he was first-on-scene to investigate the mysterious death of their son, Charles. Now, he was back in similarly wretched circumstances, the death of Bessie who, like her brother, was four days old.

Stepping onto the ramshackle porch, he could hear the screams of John Fowler, drunk and spewing curses, punctuated by the rages of his wife, Mary, crying out in horror at her loss. He pushed the door forward. It creaked open to reveal Doc Landry, a full-bearded man in his mid-sixties, bent over the sullied sheets of an unmade bed to examine Bessie's body.

Bassett entered the roiling gloom. His eyes flicked to a young nurse comforting twelve-year-old Clara, the oldest of the Fowler children, who swayed back and forth in a rocker humming a nursery rhyme to the invisible infant nestled in her arms. He turned toward John, her father, stalking up and down the room like a madman, his curses rising above the undercurrent of his wife's shrieking. It was a scene that even the grizzled lawman, who would soon bear witness to the carnage of the Lizzy Borden ax murders, could hardly make sense of. Where was God when abominations like this happened, he anguished, with no rhyme or reason, no hint of motive?

Doc Landry's eyes raised from the infant's corpse. He frowned and shook his head. The Marshal nodded, then turned to the young nurse who'd volunteered to help with the baby.

"Would you like to tell me what happened?"

"I was asleep upstairs," the nurse began, "and did not hear nothin'. Well, the baby crying, yes, but I was too tired to get up and knowin' Mrs. Fowler was sick figured Clara would tend to Bessie."

"Did she?"

"Yes, sir, but then lyin' there half-asleep, I noticed there was no cryin'. No," she said, shaking her head solemnly, "not a sound and that's when I knew somethin' was terrible wrong."

"You went downstairs—"

"That's right, officer, that's just what I done and come to find Clara standing in the middle of the room—right there where you're standin'—the baby in her arms. But there was no sound from Bessie, not a whimper and Clara was singin' a nursey rhyme, eyes wide open and glittery-like, but she was not seein' anything, sir, not of this world anyway."

"What was she seeing? Did she tell you?"

The nurse looked down at the floor, gathered her thoughts, and raised her eyes to him.

"She was lookin' at the Virgin, sir. The Virgin Mary, who she said was standin' in front of us."

"The Virgin?"

"Yes."

"And the baby?"

"That's the point, sir. I reached out to touch Bessie and her body was stone cold. She was dead, sir," she blurted, tears streaming down the sides of her face. "The baby was dead!"

He pondered her words, then turned to Doc Landry.

"Better check on her," he suggested, casting a sidelong glance at Mary Fowler, "while I try to sober the husband up."

Landry got to his feet, "Mother's no better," he croaked, walking past him. "Puerperal infection. Ghastly condition. Lots of filth. Lots of pain."

The Marshal's steely gaze locked on Mary Fowler, sweat-slicked with fever, tongue blackened with contagion, alternating between low moans and nightmarish screeching. Then, she bucked up in her bed, looked straight at him and rasped, "It done it for spite."

"What? What did she say?" he asked, but Doc waved him off.

"She's burning up with fever, Bassett. She does not know what she is saying."

The Marshal held the woman's gaze. The hair prickled on the back of his neck.

"You're right, Doc. It's the fever," he murmured, turning his attention to John Fowler.

"Get hold of yourself, John," he began, cautiously approaching the raging madman. "I know what a terrible turn this must be—"

"Cockchafer! The French pox on ya!" the Irishman swore, eyes glaring. "My baby's dead," he said, backing away from him. "Dead! And my wife Mary? Look at her. Good as dead and Doc knows it!"

"I'm sorry, John," he cajoled, walking him back toward the wall, "truly I am."

"Yea," he laughed scornfully, "you guards, always tryin' ta help, are ya?"

Fowler inched toward the wall until his back lay flat against it, then let loose a roundhouse punch that Bassett caught with his left hand, snatching the .32 Colt revolver he carried on his hip with his right and slamming it across the side of Fowler's head. A thin line of blood seeped from the gash above his right ear. He sank to his knees, the Marshal taking hold of his arms, twisting them hard behind him.

"This is not what I wanted, John," he swore, slapping a set of handcuffs on him.

"Jesus fuck!" he cried out. "You're the guard, for Chrissake. Have you no eyes? Can't you see? It's her!" he screamed, raising his cuffed hands in his daughter's direction. "Ask her mother. She knows. It was she what killed our babies!"

Bassett craned his head around to find Clara staring back at him, eyes vacant and clouded, still see-sawing in her rocker, humming a lullaby to her dead baby sister. *Haunted* was the word that passed through his mind then. The room. The house. If there was a Hell beyond this life, he was thinking, this is what it looked like.

"It wasn't me that hurt Bessie," she said dazedly. "How could I? I loved her. I love my baby sister."

The Marshal's gaze flitted from Clara back to John Fowler, wife-beater, child-abuser, monster.

"You, John Fowler," he concluded, pulling tight upon the cuffs behind him, "are a drunk. And a nasty one at that." He shoved him toward the door. "You near finished here, Doc?"

"*Laudanum* for the pain, which will be excruciating," he answered without looking up from his patient. "Change the sheets if I can find clean ones."

"Fair enough," he agreed, pulling the front door open with his free hand. "I'll let Brady down at the morgue know." Then, about to step out onto the porch, he stopped. "Nurse," he asked, swiveling around to face her, "was there anything else Clara said? When she was holding the baby?"

"Just what I told you—about the Virgin," she answered.

He nodded, then turned to leave.

"Oh, but wait," she called after him. "There was one thing. She looked at me and her eyes. They seemed to change, cold-like, and she said 'squalid little thing'—just like that. Then she looked down again and started singin' that nursery rhyme. The one she was always singin' to little Bessie."

Bassett let the words settle in his mind for a moment. Then, he buttoned his long coat, pressed his derby down onto his head, said 'thank you,' and left.

Walking onto the porch, he felt something beneath his boot and stopped to retrieve it. It was a wooden icon, demonic, with ragged wings, clawed fingers, taloned feet, mouth stretched into a feral grin. He contemplated its significance, shook his head, and slipped it into his pocket.

Three days later, Mary Kavanaugh Fowler would succumb to puerperal fever. By all accounts, it was a horrible passing.

I: INFESTATION

"One day men will look back and say
I gave birth to the Twentieth Century."
–Jack the Ripper
The "Whitechapel Butcher"

ONE

Rooming House
15 Blagdon Street
Boston, Massachusetts

TWELVE YEARS LATER, April 14, 1898

Clara Fowler turned the lock on the door to her room, nervous about the term paper that was due for her "Literature of Shakespeare" course at Radcliffe college. The thought of being accepted into such a prestigious school made her giddy. One of the Seven Sisters, no less, and they had chosen her! In her heart of hearts, she knew she would have the paper submitted on time. Still, she worried. It seemed she was always anxious about something these days, but soldiered on, working mornings as a stenographer for a law firm and attending classes in the afternoon.

She entered the cramped room, proud of herself as she surveyed the "grand abode" as she referred to it in jest during conversations with the widow Kerr, who managed the boarding house. Her eyes scanned its interior: a scaled-down gas stove, desk with St. James Bible atop it, battered oak-wood dresser, toilet-sink-mirror—and oh, yes, a row of nails lining the back of the door to hang coats. It wasn't much, but it was hers and she took care to keep it clean and neat with specific places for everything.

She shed her wool coat and hung it on the third nail from the left, her mind flashing back to the times when her life was not so orderly. When she was forced to quit her job at Children's Hospital because of erratic behavior, then Massachusetts General Hospital and two after that. She wasn't sleeping well nor was she eating. These were the symptoms that signaled the onset of a breakdown, and she never wanted to go through that again. Deep depression. Unanchored dread. The unrelenting sensation of free-falling into a fathomless abyss.

She undressed and slipped into a nightgown. The paper could wait since tomorrow her schedule was open except for an afternoon appointment with Dr. Morton Prince, whom her physician, Dr. Putnam, had recommended she see. Yes, that was it, she calculated. She would lay out her clothes for her meeting with Prince, get a good night's sleep, and begin writing first thing in the morning.

Since Clara believed first impressions were important, she chose her best outfit, a blue cotton trill skirt with a white pleated blouse. She placed each carefully atop the dresser, then padded bare-footed to the desk, taking the Bible in hand. It was her habit to randomly select one passage and read it before going to sleep each night. She moved the lamp closer to the bedstead, opened the Bible, and closed her eyes. She ran her finger down the page. Tonight's reading was from *Ephesians 6:10*. She sat on the edge of the bed and read:

> *"Be strong in the Lord and in His mighty power.*
> *Put on the full armor of God so that you can take your*
> *stand against the devil's schemes. For our struggle is not*
> *against flesh and blood, but dark forces of evil that live*
> *unseen among us."*

Not exactly a warm glass of milk before bedtime, she pondered, shivering as memories of Charles and Bessie knifed their way into her thoughts. Mamma blamed her for their dying, but it wasn't so. Couldn't be. She loved them more than anything in the world, she reasoned, suddenly noticing the room was cold. Freezing. A shadow streaked across the room. Her head whirled around to look. But there was nothing. With unblinking eyes, she stared into the ticking darkness. "Hello?" she called out. No answer. "All right now, Clara," she whispered, trying to calm herself, "it's true. You are not well. And nervous. Extremely nervous. But tomorrow you'll see Dr. Prince, who Dr. Putnam believes can help you. As for the cold? It's winter and, yes, the room is cold, but you have a blanket to keep you warm," she rationalized, bunching her long legs and torso into a ball beneath the covers, eyes wide open, still unsettled. A strangeness was in the room, she thought, body quaking beneath the sheets—invisible— but undeniably present. These were her last thoughts before plunging into a deep and harried sleep.

In the twilight between sleep and wakefulness, she felt its coming. The mattress depressing as it lowered itself down onto the bed beside her. The sulfurous smell. The sound of its breathing. The feel of its long-fingered hand upon her chest. Every instinct in her body told her to lurch from the bed and run, but that is not what it wanted.

Clara Fowler's dreams that night, were bone-chilling.

She is walking through a long, deserted hallway when she sees a huge cat glaring at her. Heart pounding, she stares into its eyes. They are dark wells. The cat springs on her, tearing open her breast.

She awakens to find herself lost in London surrounded by a mob of women who push her to the ground, hurling curses at her as a priest, with a Catholic missal, looms over her reading prayers, not to God, but to Satan.

She dreams she is dead in a coffin lined with hands clutching at her. Half-awake, she buries her head in a pillow but the pillow bursts and long worms wriggle out of it, covering her head to foot. She shrieks in terror. When she tries to escape from the worms, the hands clutch her. When, finally, she breaks loose from the hands, the worms bore into her flesh!

Clara bucked up in bed, nightgown soaked with perspiration, screaming. Mrs. Kerr and Sylvia Griffin, the boarder, stared down at her, panicked.

"Are you all right?" Mrs. Kerr exhorted, holding a lit lantern to her. "You had a nightmare. You were screamin'."

"No," she cried out, "there was someone in this room!"

The ladies' eyes raked every corner.

"There's no one," Miss Griffin said, turning around a second time to look. "No one," she repeated.

"The door," Clara spouted, pointing, "he came through the door!"

"My poor child," Mrs. Kerr comforted, "I used my key to get in. The door was locked."

Then, as if by precognition, Clara's eyes darted to the window, partially open, the wind whistling past the broadcloth curtain.

Mrs. Kerr charged toward it.

"It's open all right," she gasped. "And look. The roof leads right up to it. We must have just missed him!"

Mrs. Kerr slammed the window shut and fastened the lock with New England resolve.

"Let this be a lesson to you, little Missy," she chided. "Because you're here on the third floor, don't think a man can't get in. From now on, lock your window," she cautioned, walking away, Sylvia Griffin in her wake. "I'll be calling the police tomorrow to make a report."

The two women shambled to the door and left. Clara, frightened to the marrow, walked to her desk and sat. She put her hand to her forehead, feverish with confusion. What had triggered the nightmares? The shadow streaking across the room? Her gaze drifted to the window, then to the pillow on her bed and, finally, to the dresser. Rising like a ghost she drifted toward it, shocked to discover the skirt and blouse she'd put aside for her meeting with Dr. Prince were ripped to shreds as if by a maddened animal.

"My-dear-Lord in Heaven," she gasped, retrieving a handwritten note left beside her ravaged clothing.

> 'How do you like your clothes? It's a new fashion I made just for you, Mistress Clara. You are such a sweet child. I hope you may enjoy your life very much indeed during the coming days. I am going to make it just as interesting for you as I can and you know that means a great deal when I say it.
>
> Does your fancy conjure up all sorts of visions? You shall have all of my thoughts and attention to keep you from

brooding, My Dear. Think of it. I will not spare the rod for
by it you may be saved even yet.
   With much love,
   X'

Clara cringed in the corner of her room, too afraid to close her eyes for fear of what might happen next. Then she saw it. The faces of Charles and Bessie, floating mid-air above the bedstead.

TWO

Prince home
458 Beacon Street
Boston, Massachusetts

Morton Prince sat behind his desk in the second-floor office of his Beacon Street townhouse studying Clara Fowler's medical records. Dressed in a three-piece suit with high-collar shirt and four-in-hand necktie, he was as he appeared: a hale, cinnamon-haired, Boston Brahmin, standing 5' 10" tall with piercing gray eyes, refined features, and Imperial-style mustache.

His steely gaze fell on the 'patient biography' section of the file Clara's physician, James Jackson Putnam, had provided, pondering the obvious. Clara Fowler was, by all measure, his antithesis in background, each a product of what Theodore Roosevelt called "times of unstoppable forward motion." The 20th century brought with it sweeping changes in technology. Electric lighting and telephones found their way into everyday life; H. G. Wells wrote about time travel in his visionary novel, *The Time Machine*; the Great Houdini electrified audiences with daring feats of escape, an apt metaphor for modern man's emergence from superstition to scientific advancement.

For men like himself, if the past was bright, the future coruscated with promise, Prince reflected, settling into his chair, lighting a cigar. As a student at Harvard University, he rode horses, played golf, tennis, football and studied in Vienna where he first met and instantly disliked Sigmund Freud, before graduating from Harvard Medical School with honors. Two years later, he married Fanny Lithgow Payson, a descendant of the Lithgows of Scotland, securing his position among the "sifted few" who populated Beacon Hill.

Though ardent and sometimes brooding, he and Fanny hosted dinner parties once per week, marked by spirited debate, often violently argumentative. It was true, Prince conceded, he did not suffer fools gladly whether lecturers, politicians, or physicians, like himself. Perhaps it was his insistence upon studying an illness until it had been clinically established that led Dr. Putnam to refer Clara Fowler to him. Could it be a cure demanded the fortitude of a man who would not compromise with the truth no matter where it led?

If this was Prince's life in Fall 1898, according to her medical records, Clara Fowler was the product of the gloaming underbelly of Bostonian progressivism. Along with the mid-century influx of immigrants into Boston, came poverty and familial dysfunction. Alcoholism, incest, and wife-beating, all fell below the line that separated public from private behavior where achievements were vaunted and dirty laundry shoved into the black hole of "family matters." Certainly, the doctor discovered, Clara's childhood provided fertile ground for the onset of the *neurasthenic* condition Dr. Putnam tried to treat and given up on.

Prince's eyes dropped to the 'patient biography' section of Putnam's report, the title on the page pulsing like a heartbeat, **Case File: Clara E. Fowler.**

BACKGROUND

"Clara F was born in Beverly, Massachusetts to John Charles Fowler and Mary Kavanaugh, July 20, 1873. When Clara was seven, her mother gave birth to non-identical twins, a girl named Tara, and a boy named Charles. Four days later, Charles died suddenly, his death certificate listing 'congenital debility' as the cause of death. In a horrible coincidence, on January 8, 1886, a girl named Bessie was born to the Fowlers but died like

Charles, four days after birth, the cause of her death listed as 'convulsions'. According to testimony given by the attending nurse, the infant "died in Clara's arms."

"Bessie's death was another psychical blow to Clara F, but an insurmountable one for Mary, her mother, who contracted puerperal fever and died three days after her infant daughter. With her mother's passing, the patient tended to her younger sibling, Tara, as well as standing up to her father, a violent alcoholic, who sexually abused her. Her saving grace was the entrance of Richard Forest, a family acquaintance, into her life. Forest, twenty years her senior, protected her from her father, whom she both hated and feared. At fifteen, Clara F eloped with Forest to San Antonio, TX. where they married. She returned to Massachusetts three weeks after her marriage without him, registered at Beverly High School and matriculated graduating first in her class, September 1889.

"We know little about the patient's life during the immediate years that followed. What we can verify is that she tried to work as a nurse on four separate occasions, having failed each time due to "erratic health." In 1895, she lived at a Boston rooming house and worked as a stenographer while attending classes at Radcliffe College."

The doctor puffed his cigar, contemplating the emotional tumult from which his newest patient had emerged. A life born from a cauldron in Hell, he was thinking, his gaze shifting to the 'diagnostic observations' section of the Fowler file.

DIAGNOSTIC NOTES/OBSERVATIONS

"Clara F is a highly intelligent twenty-three-year-old student. Morbidly shy, nervous, and loath to talk about herself. When pressed for information about her current situation, her instinctive response is "I have never been in the habit of talking about my private affairs." Patient is *neurasthenic* of the extreme type. Symptoms include headaches, insomnia, persistent fatigue. These physical maladies related to feelings of guilt and a self-effacing, near saintly, disposition."

He stabbed out his cigar in an ashtray and moved on to the next paragraph.

"Since she was a child, patient has experienced Visitations from Jesus Christ and the Virgin Mary and believes she has interacted with them. In times of trouble, she prays for tangible help, and Christ or the Virgin come to her aid. Attacks of *somnambulism* are not uncommon. When she was fourteen, she walked into the streets of Beverly at 3 a.m. in her nightgown and was brought home by a police officer, unaware of where she had been or what she had done.

"Patient describes presence of a contemptuous 'thing' inside her that prevents her from eating, drinking, sleeping for days at a time. After violent convulsions, accompanied by a grotesque change in facial features, she speaks in a deep solemn voice claiming to be the 'real' Clara F. 'Cursed be God,' she growls, eyes gleaming, 'Cursed be the Virgin,' 'Cursed be Jesus Christ,' then in a higher voice—the voice of Clara F with eyes full of tears, 'It is not my fault if my mouth says these horrid things,' she swears, 'it is not I—it is not I!'"

NO FURTHER ENTRIES

Prince's gaze dropped to the handwritten note at the page's bottom.

> *Dr. Prince,*
> *I shall go no further with my observations for fear it will prejudice your considerations. As discussed, your expertise in the field of abnormal psychology is sin qua non to a clinical diagnosis of—dare I say it?—an encounter with what in medieval times would be branded 'demonic possession.'*
> *I leave the final word to you.*
> *Sincerely,*
> *Dr. James Jackson Putnam,*
> *Neurology Department*
> *Massachusetts General Hospital*

Prince furrowed his brow. At the fringe of his awareness drifted a warning about the Fowler case. Had he seen this before? Where? When?

"Papa—"

The doctor's head lashed up, startled, to find his nine-year-old daughter, Claire, standing in front of him.

"Blast, child! Have I not told you time and again to knock!"

"I...I'm sorry, Father," she stammered. "Here," she said, handing him a sealed envelope. "Someone delivered it to the door for you."

"Someone? Who?"

"I don't know, Father. A man. It was mamma who opened the door to him."

"Very well," he said, nodding as she turned to leave. "Oh, and Claire—"

She turned.

"I'm sorry for raising my voice."

"I understand, Father," she said with a timid smile and left.

He unsealed the envelope and examined its contents.

"Newspaper clippings?" he whispered, spreading the spate of articles across his desktop. The headlines glared up at him like the flickering film of a slow-motion nightmare.

FALL RIVER HERALD
SHOCKING CRIME!
A VENERABLE CITIZEN AND HIS WIFE
HACKED TO PIECES WITH AN AX!

"The Lizzie Borden murders," Prince whispered.

BOSTON DAILY GLOBE
SECOND HORRIBLE MURDER IN FALL RIVER
MAN MUTILATES BODY OF
BERTHA MANCHESTER WITH AX!

"The Fall River farm worker, Jose Corriero, who butchered his boss' wife four years ago," he recognized.

CHICAGO TRIBUNE
H. H. HOLMES CONFESSES TO 27 MURDERS,
BLOOD-CURDLING ATROCITIES
ARCHFIEND'S 'MURDER CASTLE' DISCOVERED!

"America's first serial killer," breathed the doctor.

THE GUARDIAN
TERROR IN WHITECHAPEL
FIFTH BARBAROUS MURDER
OF WOMAN IN EAST LONDON!

"Jack the Ripper!"

The name shot through him like a jolt of electricity as he thought about his wife and daughter one floor below and the stranger who had brought these reports of murder and mutilation into his home. He jumped to his feet, bounding from his office, down the stairs, to the first floor. "Fanny!"

"Yes Morton, what is it?" she asked, confused.

"The man who delivered this envelope," he said, raising it in front of him, "do we know him?"

She shook her head. "I don't think so. Why?"

"What did he look like?"

"I don't know; I'm not sure," she answered, bewildered.

"Short, tall," the doctor rattled off, "fat, thin, what was he wearing?"

"It was a man, Morton, just a man," she faltered. "Tall with a handlebar mustache and hat. A steed derby, I think. Why, Morton? Why do you ask?"

Prince took a deep breath, about to answer, when his daughter, Claire, hearing the commotion, stepped from the sitting room into the foyer.

"What is it? Have I done something wrong, Father?"

Prince lifted his daughter's hand; smiled fondly, kissed it.

"No, Claire," he answered, "you've done nothing wrong."

The Grandfather clock in the sitting room chimed 3 p.m. Clara Fowler would arrive any moment.

THREE

When Clara Fowler knocked at the door to 458 Beacon Street, Prince answered instead of Cody, their houseman. His first impression was of a prim young woman, pale and thin, with a winsome face and light brown hair, conservatively dressed in a black gored skirt with pleated white shirtwaist. If there were two adjectives that passed through his mind upon seeing her, they were "wholesome" and "anguished."

The two exchanged introductory remarks before Prince escorted her to his office. The room was smaller than most in the house, comfortably furnished with a heavy wool rug, cushioned armchairs, leather sofa, and fireplace.

The doctor noticed her rigid posture as she took a seat across from him.

"Miss Fowler, please," he remarked, "I promise this is not an inquisition."

Clara squirmed uncomfortably. "I'm sorry. It's just that—"

"Just what?"

"It's Dr. Putnam with whom I generally speak."

"Yes, but soon you shall know me and I promise you'll feel equally at ease."

She passed him a diffident smile and sat back in the armchair while the doctor perused Putnam's notes. He put them aside and reached for a pen and notepad.

"Dr. Putnam tells me you're having trouble sleeping."

She nodded.

"Does your insomnia persist?"

"Yes."

"And eating? I understand that is something you've become averse to?"

"No, I don't sleep or eat well."

"Do you know why?

"For fear of visions," she explained, eyes darting around the room, "—ugly, horrid."

"Visions?"

"When beef or mutton is put on my plate, I see dead meat crawling with maggots."

"What else do you see?"

She shivered. "I cannot describe it."

"Please try, Miss Fowler, I am not a man easily frightened."

"I see 'things' that used to be people in my room at night," she said, gathering her courage. "Monsters and demons, hooded creatures dressed in dark robes, marching in long processions," she explained, eyes fever bright, "and, Dr. Prince, I am walking with them!"

"Go on," he said, jotting a note onto his pad.

"But those that I described are not the ones that frighten me. No, it is the One. A kind of leader. He sits alongside me on my bed and I pray—I pray to Jesus and the Virgin with all my heart—and sometimes my prayers are answered."

"Can you describe what the 'One' looks like?"

"I cannot."

"But you say you can see him, is that not so?"

"That's just it. He is not just one. He is many within one. He can take on the appearance of anyone—a man, a woman, a child, so he could be anyone."

"But in these dreams—"

"No! They are not dreams. They are real!"

"Very well," he allowed, patient and controlling, "but at night when he's alongside you, do you not see him?"

"Because I pray so ardently, he comes at random. But there was one time," she said, straining to remember, "just once, when I saw him as he really appears."

"Yes?"

Her chin quivered.

"He is not human!" she erupted. "His eyes are red as hot coals, his face savage-looking as if a maddened animal—a jackal or pig—and a human were combined. And the scent—" she said, shaking her head as if trying to dispel it, "—I can tell when he's near by the scent of sulfur that precedes him!"

The doctor appraised her with a calculating stare.

"You're in a safe place here so, please calm yourself," he comforted, offering his handkerchief. "We cannot make progress unless we're both honest with one another."

Behind the tears, a tense smile returned. She drew a deep breath.

"I understand," she said, dabbing her eyes. "I shall try."

"Very well," Prince agreed, resetting the mood. "Is there anything else you'd like to tell me? Anything that makes you nervous or uneasy?"

She reached into her purse, pulled out the note she'd found beside her shredded outfit.

"Last night after the demon came, I found the clothes I put aside for today's appointment torn to pieces as if by a wild animal or madman. Beside them was this," she said, handing the note over.

Prince studied the words, roughly scribbled in large, hard-pressed letters.

"The handwriting. Is it yours?"

"No," she demurred, "it's nothing like my own."

He digested this for a while, "May I keep this?" he asked, putting it aside.

"Yes, of course."

The doctor searched her tragic eyes. They were brimming with something. What? What was it?

"Miss Fowler, I've studied Dr. Putnam's notes carefully. To be frank, he was concerned about your health. One's habits, what you eat and drink, how you sleep, the exercise you allow yourself, can affect an individual's mental disposition. But what these notes tell me," he said, holding the case file up for her to see, "is that his recommendations haven't taken hold: weight loss, poor nutrition, chronic insomnia. This cannot continue and with your permission, I'd like to try something else—hypnosis. Oh, it's not like something the 'Great Houdini' would perform on stage. No," he said, emphatically, "just another way to encourage good habits, the healthy ones. Do you understand?"

"Anything, Dr. Prince," she pleaded. "I shall do anything to regain my health."

Prince began putting her into a hypnotic trance. His strategy was bilateral. As an immediate result, he hoped to relieve her physical distress using *hypnotic suggestion*. His long-term goal was to use *retrogressive hypnosis* to uncover and treat the root cause of her condition, leading to a permanent cure.

Once begun, Clara went into a deep hypnotic state. The doctor gave the instructions:

"You will sleep well at night."

"I will sleep well at night," she echoed.

"You will maintain a healthy appetite."

"I will maintain a healthy appetite."

"You will feel strong and refreshed during your waking hours."

"I will feel strong and refreshed during my waking hours."

These suggestions she repeated, then stopped, abruptly. The doctor watched, bewildered, as she squirmed in her chair, hands balled into fists, digging them into her eyes.

"'She' will not sleep well at night," Clara rasped in a voice totally unlike her own. "'She' will not maintain a healthy appetite. 'She' will not feel strong and refreshed during her waking hours."

"Why do you say 'she'? It is you to whom I'm speaking."

No response.

"Miss Fowler," he demanded, "why do you reject my commands?"

Slowly, she withdrew her clenched fists. Her eyes flashed open. No longer Clara's gentle blue eyes, but another's, dark and malevolent, prowling the room corner to corner.

"I am n-not Miss Fowler!" she said, scowling, and the hairs prickled on the back of Prince's neck because the voice was an impossibly deep bass, thick with menace and power.

He leaned forward in his chair. The eyes that met his glinted back at him.

"Who are you?" he asked, warily.

Again, no answer. Just that sardonic grin frozen like a mask molded onto her face.

"Where is Miss Fowler?"

She drilled her eyes into his with an unblinking stare.

"You th-think you can control me b-because you c-control her," she blasted in a treble voice that rang out like an explosion, "but you c-can't. I sh-shall do as I p-please!"

He pulled back from her, shaken.

"What is your name?"

No response.

"Why do you say you are not Miss Fowler?"

"Because I h-hate her," she spat back, seething, face alternating between the newcomer's own hideous expression and Clara's as it struggled for control of the body.

"Why do you hate her?"

"She is all that I d-despise—holy, h-holy, holy—h-hate, hate, hate—" the voice croaked.

"You say you are not Miss Fowler yet you share the same arms and legs as she, do you not?"

Silence.

"If you share the same arms and legs, how can you be someone other than Miss Fowler?"

She sat back in her chair, rage mounting, until finally she spoke.

"It w-would be easier for you to be f-friends than to try to f-fight me."

A chill ran up his spine. The doctor inched forward in his seat.

"Who are you?" he asked in a harrowed voice.

"I am Sp-spirit," she blasted in a thunderous roar that shook the room. Then, sitting up like a Royal on a throne, proclaimed, "I am the Devil!"

"What do you want?" Prince breathed.

"To educate my d-dear Clara on the s-subject of m-murder." She grinned, eyes glistening. "Did your d-daughter enjoy the newspapers Bassett brought her?"

Prince's heart froze. He looked at the eyes. They shone with triumph and spite.

"What?" he asked. "What did you say?"

"Chaos rules in this corner of the earth!" she warned in a haunted whisper, a heart-stopping shriek bolting raw from out of her.

Then, silence.

Moments later, when the doctor took her out of trance, Miss Fowler was herself again with no memory for anything that happened.

FOUR

The startling transformation witnessed by Prince left him shaken but never more determined to treat Clara Fowler's disorder. Sitting alone in his second-floor office, he felt a thickening coil of darkness. Every turn of the furnace, every creak in the oak flooring seemed to divert his attention as he sat at his desk, tie unfastened, shirt sleeves rolled up, medical studies strewn across his desk like a scattered deck of cards. The smoke from his cigar swirled ghost-like toward the ceiling as he sipped from a mug of black coffee between the pages he scoured.

Immediately following the April 15 session, he ordered his protégé, Dr. George Waterman, to research case histories involving the splitting of a single consciousness into two or more (multiple personality) and Richard Hodgson, president of the Society for Psychical Research, to gather accounts related to the phenomenon whereby a malevolent consciousness invades the body of another (demonic possession).

Prince unfastened his pocket watch and placed it on the desk, 10:58 p.m. He perused the medical histories Waterman had selected starting with the case of George Lukins. According to the local pastor, Lukins "screamed blasphemies in various voices, made barking noises, sang the *Te Deum* backwards, and became dangerously violent when in the presence of priests, crucifixes, or religious articles." He was eventually hospitalized, his condition studied by a team of physicians, before being pronounced "incurable." Finally, the doctors resorted to exorcism. When confronted with the ritual, Lukins "spoke in voices not his own and contorted his body in ways no human could configure, screaming blasphemies against God, until at last he exclaimed, 'Blessed Jesus!' and was cured." But the ultimate verdict came when it was discovered that Lukins suffered from epilepsy and had once made his living as a ventriloquist. Clearly, a case of an undiagnosed physiological disorder, Prince concluded, and outright fraud!

Moodily, the doctor plucked his cigar from the ashtray, passing over familiar documentation, finally stopping at Marcel Camuset's study of Anna X. Anna X was sexually assaulted by a neighbor as a child and, in later life, literally *became* her attacker, assuming both his personality and physical characteristics. She spoke in a man's voice, dressed as he did and grew facial hair, losing her breasts with upper torso expanding to masculine proportions. She was finally cured when Camuset confronted her with her attacker. Anna X, the doctor determined, had undergone a *hysterical conversion reaction*, choosing to become her attacker rather than face the trauma of her assault.

Now, here was a study with similarities to the Fowler case, Prince ruminated, marked by changes in voice, appearance, demeanor; but also marked differences. Unlike Anna X, who underwent a transformation from herself to her attacker's identity, Clara struggled against the so-called demon's coming. Beyond that, Anna X's two personalities were corporal, while the demon claimed to be "Spirit," knowing—and hating— everything about Miss Fowler. Still, the outcome was the same. Anna X was no more her attacker than Clara Fowler was the devil incarnate.

The forty-four-year-old doctor glanced at his pocket watch, 12:05 a.m. He rubbed a tired hand over his face. His eyes were burning. He jabbed his cigar into the ashtray, stood up, walked to the window, and looked at the sky. It was overcast and gray. A stinging wind shook the bare branches of the elders lining Beacon Street where a covey of wassailers wended their way home after a night at the taverns. What was it that so troubled him about the Fowler case? Was it about him? His obsession with fame and a legacy beyond that of arch-rival, Sigmund Freud? He slid the window open, gulped the cool winter air and stood there, thinking. Yes, there was that, but more, something poignant and unsettling. What had the so-called demon said about someone named Bassett and the envelope? "Did your daughter enjoy the newspapers Bassett brought her?" How could that 'thing' know about the clippings? Why the reference to his daughter enjoying them? The connection between the two made his blood run cold.

Prince walked back to his desk. He scoured his mind for the take-away from Waterman's research and it was this: among the dozens of cases Waterman had collected, not a single instance of demonic possession held up under scientific scrutiny.

He sipped bleakly from his cup of coffee shuffling through the files that psychic researcher, Richard Hodgson, had collected. A student of history and medicine, Prince understood that abnormal psychology stood at a crossroads that would see it accepted into mainstream science or dragged into oblivion by the riptide of Spiritualism. For a man of science, like himself, it was anathema to think that people like Conan Doyle, Charles Dickens, Pierre and Madame Curie put stock in mediums. Yet, like enamored adolescents, they attended seances even after the Foxx sisters admitted they were frauds and Hodgson, himself, uncovered spiritualist Etta Wriedt's "trumpet voices" were nothing more than a chemical reaction induced by potassium and water!

Still, the preternatural aspects of the Fowler case could not be ignored from Visitations from Christ and the Virgin to encounters with Satan. No, the doctor pondered, he didn't believe in spirits or demonic possession, but was open to the possibility that paranormal phenomena existed as an unexplored capacity of the human brain.

He reached across his desk for Rev. Johann Blumhardt's "A Conflict with Satan" delving into the case of twenty-eight-year-old Gottliebin Dittus. At night, neighbors heard strange noises coming from her house. When her physician called on her, he could not explain the banging sounds or the startling changes in her physical appearance. A week later, when Rev. Blumhardt visited, he became convinced she was possessed based on violent convulsions, the ability to speak languages she could not possibly know, and the capacity to move objects—books, lamps, the bed she slept on—telepathically. Rev. Blumhardt performed the Rite of Exorcism during which she screamed blasphemies in a guttural bass voice, vomited glass, iron nails, and knitting needles, along with copious amounts of blood. The possession ended at 2:00 a.m. when with "a roar of which one could hardly believe a human capable, the angel of Satan left." Afterward, Dittus was restored to good health with no memory for anything that had gone on during her possession.

'Vomited iron nails'? Prince winced. *'Sewing needles'*? Why would a respected theologian like Blumhardt lower himself to such obvious chicanery? Why did even he admit that "it seemed a horror story made into true life"? It made no sense, unless—was it possible Blumhardt's story was true?

The doctor pressed digging fingers against his brow as he studied the case of Anna Eckland, a sixteen-year-old girl whose treatment was ongoing. Anna began displaying signs of possession at the age of eight, snarling like an animal, singing religious hymns backward, divulging intimate secrets about people that she had no way of knowing. According to doctors, she exhibited superhuman strength with the ability to run up walls and cling to them, defying gravity. She would levitate in her sleep, eerily floating above the bed, and had to be tethered to it for her own safety. When priests entered the room, Anna's voice dropped to a guttural rumble threatening physical violence until other distinct voices began popping through with one demon bragging about its vast powers in perfect Latin. The most frightening occurrence was a vision of Lucifer standing in the room while a priest prayed over her.

'Puzzling' was the word that crossed Prince's mind, contemplating the research Hodgson had brought him. He curled the corner of his mustache between his thumb and forefinger, pensive, as he glanced at his pocket watch, 2:10 a.m. One hour had slipped into two; three hours to four. He got up and drifted to the window. He raised his eyes to Beacon Street. Rain slashed at the chancel window. Thunder exploded in the darkness. Flashes of lightning cracked open the sky.

A sudden rap at the door shattered the doctor's reverie. It was Cody who entered, trailed by Fanny, his wife, holding a lamp in front of her.

"Beggin' your pardon, sir, but Miss Fowler needs your help. Mrs. Kerr is askin' that you come to the roomin' house, urgent!"

The doctor took a moment to absorb what Cody told him.

"Morton," Fanny said, sternly, "you're not—"

"I am, Fanny," he answered, grabbing his medical bag. "It's vital that I see her for her own safety," he explained, making his way to the door. "And Cody! I want you to wake Hodgson. Go to his home, if you must. Tell him to meet me at 15 Blagdon Street now!"

FIVE

Prince scrambled from the livery cab, not knowing what to expect. Would it be a replay of the radical personality change he'd witnessed earlier or something else? When he arrived at the front door, Mrs. Kerr was waiting, rattled to her core.

"It was suicide, is what it was," she bawled, rushing him up the three flights of stairs. "Miss Griffin, in the room next to her, was first to notice. Gas it was, doctor. Miss Fowler—Clara," she amended, "must have locked the door, turned on the stove, and gone to bed knowin' she'd not awaken. But it was Miss Griffin who smelt the gas comin' from under the door. She knocked, but there came no answer. So, she called me to unlock it." The square-bodied landlady stopped at the third floor landing, spun around to him. "This wasn't the first time. There's been trouble before. But nothin' like this—never like this," she added, motioning him toward the door to Clara's room.

Prince, too concerned to inquire beyond what she'd told him, charged in front of her.

"—and doctor—"

He swung around.

"That 'thing'. It was askin' for you. Laughin' like Satan, himself," she warned, tracing the sign of the cross onto her breast and forehead. "It said it wanted to see you, particular."

He nodded, took a step forward. A heart-stopping shriek blasted from the room. He stopped to listen. In the breathing silence, he could hear distant murmurings like an undercurrent beneath the quiet, an old woman cursing, a choirboy singing, a man laughing.

"Is Miss Griffin in the room with her?" he asked.

"Yes."

"Who else?"

"No one," she answered. "Just her."

The doctor gathered himself. The smell of rotting flesh swept like a blast of fetid air from the room into the hallway. He covered his mouth and nose with an open palm, marched forward, then stopped at the edge of the doorway. His heart wrenched. Sitting up in bed—with Miss Griffin on her knees praying beside her—was Clara and the demonic entity alternating with inconceivable rapidity.

"Doctor Prince, please help me!" Clara pleaded, the bone-chilling expression that passed over her face transformed near-simultaneous into the demon's, eyes bulging out of hollowed sockets. "The body is mine!" a treble voice boomed. "I am the real Miss Fowler!"

A dresser drawer flung open. The door to the room slammed back and forth like some physical entity was struggling to enter or leave. Prince watched in disbelief, fear for the first time gripping him by the throat.

"Our Father who art in Heaven," Sylvia Griffin prayed, "hallowed by Thy name—"

"All glory to god, the father of Shitdom!" the voice erupted, eyes raging, Clara's visage flashing through like a woman pulled out to sea by a riptide. "They are burning me from the inside! They are cutting me to pieces!" she screeched, unknown faces and voices appearing and disappearing too rapidly to comprehend. "What god doesn't want is ours!" a woman snarled in a voice that multiplied into a chorus of discarnate rumblings. "Yes, I know Judas," a man bragged. "He sits beside me in Hell!" "Do I know how to pray? I shall shit down your neck!" croaked another. "If we had the power, we would turn Heaven and Hell upside down!" the voice of an old woman screeched, until the room was brimming with dissonant squalling.

What in God's name was happening? Prince's mind churned amid the chaos as Hodgson burst into the room.

"I came as soon—" he began, but never finished the sentence. "How long has she been like this?"

Prince waved him off, took a step forward, "Look," he whispered to Hodgson. Was it possible that Clara's facial structure was remolding before his eyes? He flung around at the sound of a glass shattering against the wall, then to an empty chair, its legs rattling on the hardwood floor. *Psychokinetic action*, the phrase shot like a bullet to the forefront of his mind. He had read about the phenomenon as an isolated event, but never in concert with the sounds, the voices, the change in facial features!

"Thy kingdom come, Thy will be done," Miss Griffin shouted, her prayers ringing out above the mayhem, *"on earth as it is in Heaven—"*

The doctor's first instinct was to sedate Clara, *chloral hydrate* or *paraldehyde*, but he couldn't do it, his tortured gaze transfixed on the bed where she sat upright, eyes burning with intelligence, grin sickling her lips upward, until like a monster surging from out of the depths, the demon erupted.

"To Hell with you!" a massive voice commanded, eyes glowering with contempt at the sight of Sylvia Griffin praying.

For a second or two, she continued, *"Give us this day our daily bread—"* until no words came.

A deadly silence filled the room. She reached up to her eyes with both hands.

"I cannot see," she quavered, grinding closed fists into the sockets, slowly rising to her feet. "I'm blind," she murmured. Then, with a terrifying jolt, the realization struck her. *"I cannot see! I am blind!"* she shrieked, twirling around in stunted circles.

Mrs. Kerr scrambled toward her, taking Miss Griffin dumbstruck into her arms, clutching her in a smothering embrace, screaming crimson-faced at the 'thing' that was Clara Fowler.

"What have you done?" she thundered, the words flung like bolts. "Go back! You are not welcome here! Filth! Scum! God has damned you and you do not belong here!"

Then, the response, ever succinct, viscerally pernicious, "My creatures must suffer as an example to others," the demon seethed, that same cunning grin creeping onto Clara's face.

The sight of it ignited a blind fury within Mrs. Kerr, who charged the bed clutching Clara by the shoulders shaking her, hands moving up toward her throat, until Hodgson wrenched her away.

"It is an evil thing come into this house!" she stormed.

"Take hold of yourself!" Hodgson shouted. "Don't you see? It's Clara that you are hurting!"

The tension dissipated amid the stony silence. Everyone in the room stood rooted to the floor, eyes riveted on Clara, except Sylvia Griffin, who gazed blindly at a spot mid-air near the foot of the bed. Clara had become herself again. Hands folded in prayer, face radiant, eyes raised to the exact spot Sylvia Griffin's was fixed upon.

"Yes, I do—with all my heart," she pledged. "No, he will never do that, but I stand weak before him—"

Hodgson whipped around to Prince. "What is she doing?" he asked. "Who is she speaking to?"

"A hallucination—both visual and auditory," the doctor speculated, eyes fastened on her, "but after all that's happened, I doubt anyone could know for certain."

"She's talking to the Virgin," Sylvia Griffin's voice rang out, head lifted upward, face beaming with wonder. "She's telling Clara to stay strong, that she will go through trials that test her faith, but Jesus will protect her."

"How do you know that?" Hodgson asked, urgently. "How do you know what she's saying?"

"Because I see her, too!" she answered, eyes glazed over, dropping to her knees. "The Virgin is surrounded by light, brighter than I've ever seen. Her face and eyes, the tenderness in her voice, give Clara—would give anyone—comfort. That is the way the Virgin wants Clara to know her as a 'comforter,' someone she can always count on."

Hodgson leapt forward. "Does she speak in words?" he implored. "Is her communication telepathic?"

His questions went unanswered. There was no sound, only the disjointed phrases Clara spoke, eyes glistening with fervor.

"Thank you," she said to the apparition standing in front of her. "I love you—yes, I will do as you say."

For long, troubled seconds Prince, Hodgson and Mrs. Kerr were still; no theories were put forward, no discussions followed, their every thought and emotion twisted and turned in on itself.

Moments after Clara awakened, Sylvia Griffin regained her vision. What Prince would later diagnose as *hysterical blindness* subsided and was never experienced by Miss Griffin again.

SIX

Prince Home
Boston, Massachusetts

Canceling all appointments, Prince arranged a meeting with Hodgson, neurologist Dr. George Waterman, and Harvard psychologist William James the next day. For him, the symptoms Clara displayed were unsettling, as they were intriguing. The radical changes in personality and facial characteristics, the intermingling of voices, and mind-bending power of—what to call it? —the "demon's" presence! A host of known diseases could account for her behavior—*angst-neurose*, being terrified of imagined dangers; *delirium*, the existence of both an aberrant and sane consciousness; *brain lesions*, frequently the cause of abnormal behavior and hallucinations, but beneath the surface, Prince was convinced lay a rare psychological disorder that he was determined to cure.

"Good morning, gentlemen," he welcomed, stepping toward Waterman, a newly appointed Harvard professor who, like him, eschewed Freud's theories of psychoanalysis. Prince shook his hand, turning to Richard Hodgson, the psychical researcher. Vocal in his disbelief of mediums, Hodgson famously exposed psychic Madame Blavatsky and others, until he became enamored with Leonora Piper, a medium, who he believed was a channel between the living and the dead. Prince clutched Hodgson's hand before shifting his attention to psychologist William

James, whose interest in abnormal psychology rivaled his own having taught the first class of its kind at Harvard University Medical School. He acknowledged James, then motioned the three of them to sit.

"Dr. Waterman," he said, nodding in acknowledgement, "I trust Mr. Hodgson has briefed you on—" he searched for the word,"—the *curious* events that took place yesterday."

"He has," the twenty-six-year-old neurologist answered, "and I'm not sure what to make of it."

Prince took a chair in front of them.

"Head trauma," he offered tentatively. "A brain lesion could account for it." His eyes scanned the faces of the three men. "Perhaps a combination of conditions leading to a single disorder—"

Professor James, sitting on a cushioned chair, full-beard, with long legs crossed, turned his deep-set gaze on him. "Putnam's therapy failed by that logic," he interrupted. "Labeling her condition the result of a physiological anomaly barely scratches the surface. Clearly, the root of her disorder has both a physical and mental etiology. Considering Freud's writing on the power of the unconscious mind many of the symptoms I once considered physiological I now believe are psychological."

Prince bristled at the mention of Freud, a sworn adversary since he'd branded his practice of psychoanalysis "scientific rubbish" in an article published in *The Journal of Abnormal Psychology*.

"Underneath every mental act there is a physical catalyst," Prince argued. "With every thought, sensation or emotion comes a physical change in a material entity, namely the brain. Miss Fowler's cure doesn't lie in her dreams or sexual fantasies, but by redirecting her brain functions, setting her on a course whereby the normalcy of life becomes a practiced habit."

Hodgson, tall, broad-shouldered and handsome, spoke with a conviction that left a vibration in the air.

"Perhaps Freud doesn't go far enough."

"What?" Waterman asked, leaning forward in his chair. "What did you say?"

"Why must we insist on the physical or psychological nature of diseases? If the unconscious mind can cause an ulcer, for example, why can't it facilitate a cure?" He rose from his chair, eyes brimming with ardor. "Consider Binet's experiments in hypnosis where after being put into a hypnotic state, the doctor told his subject that the pencil he was holding was a hot poker. He then touched the pencil to the subject's hand and watched a blister form exactly as it would had he been burned by a fire iron!" He shook his head in wonderment. "Gentlemen, there is so much about the human brain we don't understand, more than even Freud suspects. Imagine the unconscious mind as a gateway to another invisible world as real as the one we occupy and you will fathom the singularity of Clara F's condition."

Prince dropped back in his chair.

"Madame Blavatsky, is that where you're taking us?" the doctor asked irritably. "A séance with Miss Leonora Piper, perhaps?"

"It's one thing to respect the tradition of scientific orthodoxy," Hodgson shot back, "and quite another to be bound by it. So, yes, I'm proud to have unmasked Madame Blavatsky and others like her, but equally proud to have discovered Miss Piper, a genuine practitioner of mental telepathy and, yes, communication with the dead."

"I'm sorry to say this, Richard," Prince lamented, "but this woman has wrecked your mind!"

"To the contrary, she's opened it to the possibility of a 'spirit world,' separate from our own, where the souls of the dead—angels and demons— exist. I know. I've seen her communicate with them."

"Demons?" Prince asked, incredulously. "What will be next, exorcism? Is that what you're recommending?"

"There's nothing absurd in the notion that there may be non-human spirits, good, bad and indifferent. Nothing compels us to believe that the only intelligences in the universe are those connected with the bodies of human beings. If the evidence for a God and an afterlife is accepted, then we must allow there may be non-human intelligences, either discarnate or associated with cosmic energy in ways we don't yet understand."

"We're all Christians here," William James piped up, "isn't the existence of God, angels, and devils core to our Christian beliefs? Aren't these, by definition, 'non-human' intelligences?"

"Precisely!" Hodgson exclaimed. "And wasn't it you, Professor James, who investigated the case of a girl in Watseka, Illinois, who underwent a personality and identity transformation, claiming to be the reincarnation of Mary Roff, a sixteen-year-old who'd died in a state insane asylum years before. What was the conclusion of your study?"

James answered in a hushed whisper, "That the Spiritualist explanation was the most plausible."

"You see," Hodgson concluded, "even in our own experience, the possibility of a spirit world exists!"

Prince turned to Waterman, still sitting, and Hodgson, standing a few steps away, eyes pinning them.

"Throughout the ages, diseases of the mind have been falsely labeled demonic possession by those who would have us believe supernatural entities creep into the natural world. Ghosts! Witches! Devils! Have we learned nothing from the work of Charcot on the pathology of *hysteria* and *epilepsy*? Think for a moment about the poor souls subjected to unspeakable tortures. Women burned at the stake here in Massachusetts, no less, in the name of religion and belief in evil incarnate when, as Gilles Tourette proved, the symptoms associated with *Tourette's Syndrome* have nothing to do with demons and everything to do with a chemical imbalance in the brain!"

"Listen, please!" Hodgson urged. "We have a set of symptoms manifested by a second consciousness. As proved by you, it takes possession of Miss Fowler's body, claiming to be 'Spirit,' despises her, threatens her, and has driven her to the brink of destruction. Given these facts, one can label her disorder anything one chooses, but a name doesn't explain a phenomenon that's existed in every corner of the world for thousands of years: Gregory of Tours who reported the possession of a young girl who took on not only the voice but the appearance of a Persian man who'd died decades before; the seventeenth century case of Elizabeth Knapp who read her exorcists' thoughts, predicting future events through messages spontaneously erupting on her body; and today, the anthropologist Junod's account of a possessed woman in Africa who vanished from her home one night, and was found the following morning on top of a tall tree. Afterward, she glided down, head first, flicking her tongue in and out like a snake. She then hung suspended for a time and began to speak in a language later identified as Aramaic! How do you account for these?"

"Anecdotes, that's what you're putting forward, Hodgson! Where are the doctors? Where are the clinicians? Scientists who would document these stories? Without that, we have what we always have in Spiritualist arguments: hearsay, fraud, misunderstood symptoms leading to misdiagnosis and mythology. To that I say, angels, ghosts, hobgoblins, show me your face!"

Hodgson stepped up to him, pleading.

"Don't you see, Morton? Can you not bring yourself to understand the Great Mystery we stand on the threshold of solving? I beg you, consider at least the possibility that here at last, in the city of Boston, 1898, is tangible evidence of transcendence. If there are demons, there must be angels and probably a God and a life everlasting. You ask where are the doctors and clinicians? Dr. Prince, we are the doctors. We are the clinicians!"

Prince stared deep into his eyes, the glow of belief glimmering behind them. A hard-nosed practitioner of behavior-based psychology, he was also a caring man and Hodgson's words touched him.

It was Will James' sententious baritone that broke the thorny silence.

"Objectivity is the mark of credible science, is it not, Morton? It would be unwise to shut the door on any diagnosis—psychological, physiological, or spiritual—at this stage of our investigation. By God, I agree with Hodgson!"

The doctor heaved a weighty sigh, "And what would you have me do, Richard?"

"Make me party to your investigation! Let me work alongside you, you from a scientific perspective and me from that of a believer. Together, we can study every aspect of the second consciousness. Does it eat? Does it feel pain? Are there memories it possesses beyond those of Clara F? If it's

'Spirit', as it claims, perhaps we can retrogress it to a time before Clara's birth, to the place from which it originated."

All eyes shifted to Prince, who, nodding slowly, turned to Waterman, eighteen years his junior.

"George, you heard Hodgson's proposal. What do you have to say about it?"

Waterman, face flushed and diffident, spoke from behind his horn-rimmed glasses.

"I'm not sure what to believe, but I think we should take whatever resources are available. Frankly, I've seen Clara F during one of her episodes and it scares the hell out of me."

"Well stated!" Prince laughed. Then, extending his hand to Hodgson, said, "Very well, my friend, you've convinced me. You, Waterman, and myself will form a team and solve life's Great Mystery together!"

"Bully, bully!" James exclaimed, lighting a cigar.

"Bully, bully," Waterman repeated, vowing to work the Fowler case along with them.

II: MIND-TEAR

"Possession has by no means become obsolete;
only the name has changed to *neurosis* or *unconscious complexes*."
–Carl Jung
Founder of analytical psychiatry

ONE

Our Lady of Perpetual Hope
Roxbury, Massachusetts
September 12, 1898

Clara knelt in a pew surrounded by parishioners attending mass at Our Lady of Perpetual Help. The church, with its iconic shrine dedicated to the Blessed Virgin, held special meaning since she, like thousands before her, was praying for a cure to an illness, hers too horrible to contemplate. The pile of crutches left behind as testimony to healing at the behest of the Virgin inspired her pleas for intercession. But what crutches could she leave behind? What tumor to disappear? What vision to be restored? No, hers was not an illness visible to the eyes or even a doctor's scrutiny. Her cure, she believed, lay in something beyond medical treatment or psychology. The disease? She dared not contemplate the darkness that lay dormant inside her, but understood it had something to do with the episodes of "missing time" she was experiencing.

A week before, while walking in the Public Garden, knowing it was 3 p.m., she awoke forty-five minutes later drifting aimlessly in the middle of Arlington Street with no memory for what she'd done or how she'd gotten there. The same happened during a class at Radcliffe College, 9 a.m., two days before. Starting out on campus, she awakened three hours later walking the railway tracks outside the city, hair undone, dress torn and shoeless.

The priest made his way from the sacristy to the altar.

"*In nominee Patris, et Filiet et Spiritus Sancti,*" he canted in Latin, facing the congregation and making the Sign of the Cross.

Clara rose to greet him, missal in hand.

"*Amen,*" she declared, blessing herself, in chorus with the other parishioners.

She opened her missal to the *Ordo Missae* and glanced down at the page.

"*Introibo ad altare Dei,*" the priest exalted.

"*Ad Deum qui laetificat—*" Clara read from the missal, but the words had barely left her lips when she felt a dagger of pain jab at her side from within.

It was happening, her mind raced. She could feel it rising like a river overflowing its banks, the One making its presence known, slashing, as with a surgical blade, through flesh and sinew from mind to body to soul.

SLASH! Clara is tumbling head over heels in a vast cold darkness, spinning in the void, helpless!

The missal she was holding slammed shut.

"*Judica me, Deus, et discerne causam meam de gente non sancta—*"

The missal flew from her hands, crashing down onto the floor with the crack of a rifle shot.

"Mary, Virgin," she uttered, thoughts disjointed, adrenalin bolting through her body. "Help, help!"

Teeth gritted, she reached for a Rosary in her purse, seizing it with both hands.

"Hail Mary, full of grace—" the words choked out of her, fingers threading through the black beads.

SLASH! She is adrift in a boundless abyss. Dread permeates her soul. Is she dead? Is she in Hell?

The rosary exploded in her hands, its beads hurled in every direction.

"Are you all right, Miss?" a man behind her asked.

"Goddamn you, Fucker, to Hell!" the demon, now emerged, growled, teeth bared like a cornered animal.

Clara battled for control of the body, bizarre images flashing through her mind—the face of the man behind her turned monstrous; the priest at the pulpit transformed to the One screaming its own Gospel of hate; the gleaming red eyes of the congregation transfixed upon her like lasers.

Finally, coming to herself, she sprung up amongst them. "There is only One, and that is Jesus Christ!" she proclaimed, shoving her way to the center aisle, emerging from the church like a swimmer breaking water.

She needed to catch the trolley, she told herself. She needed to get home to something familiar, somewhere safe—was that the word? No, there was no 'safe' place, she anguished, looking over her shoulder as she made her way to Tremont Street. The 'thing' inside her was getting stronger by the day!

Worn out and depressed, Clara turned the key to her room and entered, surprised to find a package wrapped in gift paper with a red bow tucked neatly beside her pillow. She trembled with delight. A gift for her? She took it in her hands, eagerly unwrapping it. Was it a "get well" gift from Mrs. Kerr? Miss Griffin? Heart racing with anticipation, she opened the box and fell back in horror at the sight of it: a dead rat, eyes wide-open, staring back at her! She felt a tingling sensation skittering over her skin. Spiders, dozens of them, emerging from the box, swarming up her arms and legs! She let loose a howl of rage and disgust, frantic, as she brushed the spiders away, staggering to the opposite side of the room, her wide-eyed glare falling on the dresser top where a letter waited.

Chest heaving, she tore it open.

You little wretch! I suppose you've killed all my nice spiders and tossed out my rat. I hope they've bitten you all over. It's good for you, you know; you must always remember that, Dear Clara. 'Soul of honor indeed!' 'How the mighty have fallen!' There are more spiders, and snakes, too, that will amuse you in bed at night. But I know you're not the

least bit grateful—but you will be before we have finished our
course together.
  With much love and caring,
  X'

Clara searched the room for an intruder. Someone was playing a deadly
game with her, hellbent on undoing the progress she had made in her life,
but it wouldn't work, she vowed, noticing a chill breeze coming from the
open window leading to the roof.

Knowing she'd locked it, she dashed to the corner of the room, craned
her head outside in time to see the silhouette of a man slip into the
shadows beyond the glow of a street lamp.

"Say, you!" she screamed, "You there, I see you!" but it was too late, the
person she suspected was behind the savage prank was gone!

Where to go? What to do now? Clara agonized, Doctor Prince's name
flashing from subconscious to conscious reverie. She would write Prince a
letter describing all that happened, every detail, she resolved, hoping that
he could fathom the horror of the existence she lived each day.

Vertiginous with fear, she stumbled to her desk, sat down pencil in
hand, and began writing, then stopped to consider what was happening.
She tried to write, but could not. Seconds later, her hand began moving on
its own. The letters were large and unaligned. 'B,' 'A,' 'S,' they began
appearing in a burst of fury until, finally, the pencil snapped, her eyes
dropping to the words she had written.

BASSETT
BASSETT BASSETT
DIE! DIE! DIE!

TWO

Prince Home
Boston, Massachusetts

Recently arrived from London, artist John Singer Sargent was annoyed.

"Please, Doctor Prince! Could you try to stay still?"

Prince, dressed in a high-collared shirt, sable brushed vest and brown cutaway sack coat, was no less irritable having succumbed to Fanny's insistence that his attire "reflect the spirit of the 20th century." Yes, he thought sourly, a century presaged by the Gibson Girl—well-educated, independent, sexually liberated—who graced magazine covers marking the emergence of the "New Woman"; zealous psychoanalysts like Freud who refused to engage evidence contrary to their beliefs; and Boston streets overrun by bicyclists, disliked by both horsemen and car drivers alike, the horse people claiming the cyclists spooked their horses and the car enthusiasts fuming that cyclists were unanswerable to traffic laws!

"The portrait was not my idea, Mr. Sargant, but my wife, Fanny's, who seems to think years from now people will have an interest in what I looked like, but that I doubt."

Sargant said nothing, applying paint strokes, pallet to canvas, while Prince mulled over his day and the evening to come.

A fastidious man, demanding of himself and others, Prince's daily regimen began with an hour of exercise, 6:00 to 7:00 a.m.; breakfast, 7:30

to 8:30 a.m.; a dive into the morning papers—*Post, Telegraph, Globe*—then consultations, 10:00 a.m. to 4:35 p.m. when Cody would accompany him to the Boston Riding Club where he'd engage in a spirited gallop atop Garland, his prize Quarter Horse, until 6:00 p.m. when he'd return home for dinner.

But this day was nothing like that, he brooded, perched on a highchair set before the bay window in his living room, posing, book in hand. Instead of tending to patients, he'd spent his day engrossed in *The Varieties of Religious Experiences*, a book Professor James had written based on lectures he'd given at the University of Edinburgh. The accounts, specifically of M. Alphonse Ratisbonne, James suggested, could provide insight into the Visitations Clara Fowler experienced.

Prince opened the book to the dog-eared pages documenting Ratisbonne's religious conversion and began reading.

> "'Coming out of a café, I met the carriage of Mssr. B., who invited me for a drive, but first asked me to wait whilst he attended to some duty at the church of *San Andrea Delle Fratte*. Instead of waiting, I entered the church. I can remember only a black dog which went trotting before me, then, in an instant, the whole church vanished. I no longer saw anything or, more truly, I saw, o-my-God, one thing alone! Oh, indeed, radiant with grace, it was She! The Virgin standing before me!
>
> I did not know where I was. I did not know whether I was Alphonse or another. I felt myself changed and believed myself another me. At the bottom of my soul, I felt an explosion of the most ardent joy, and in a flash of blinding light, all became clear to me. The Virgin's face told me that had been saved!'

Immediately following the Visitation, Ratisbonne converted to Catholicism and joined a monastery. The effect of his *spontaneous religious conversion* lasted his entire lifetime."

Wrapped in thought, Prince placed the book on the coffee table in front of him, trying to draw comparisons between Ratisbonne's experience and Miss Fowler's.

"Doctor Prince, please!" The artist protested. "Can you not sit still for even one moment?"

"Blasted, man! You said I could read!"

"Read, yes, but read in stillness!"

"I shall try, Mr. Sargant," the doctor retorted, casting his razor-sharp mind back to his most recent notes about Clara's Visitations.

NOTES, November 27th

Patient has a constant sense of Christ or the Virgin near her. In one vision, she saw the Virgin with Child in her arms. "The Virgin is about to go away," Clara recounted, "and she turns back and looks at me. It was dear!" She describes the encounters vividly, using her hands to point out the spatial relations of the visions and their surroundings, as if the personages were standing before her.

Though Miss Fowler does not have a religious upbringing, it is impossible to ignore her compulsion toward religion. It is also a stubborn fact that while Clara, in her normal state, exhibits behaviors—chastity, self-sacrifice, prayer—routinely associated with "saints," the second consciousness—arrogant, hateful, violent—appears the opposite, exhibiting behaviors associated with "demons."

Hence, the dichotomy of selves had become a perplexity for Prince, on the one hand, loath to entertain a notion so idiosyncratic as demonic possession; on the other, unable to ignore its divergence from conventional theories of *hysteria, retrograde amnesia*, or *multiple personality*. In his opinion, none adequately explained what was happening to his patient.

Then came the *coup de grace*, delivered to his home by courier that afternoon. A packet of notes wrapped in a handwritten letter from Miss Fowler, signaling what he feared most. The demon's attacks were becoming more pernicious by the day.

> *'Dr. Prince,*
> *I am sending you this with such notes as I have been able to find. There are more, doubtless, scattered about and I shall be glad to send these too as I come across them. Oh, Dr. Prince, save me from this 'monster,' from myself, from whatever is so absolutely merciless! You cannot imagine the torture I have endured in these last days—no one could—no one has the slightest control over this Evil that possesses me. Promise you won't leave me to its mercy!*
> *Most sincerely,*
> *Clara Fowler'*

The doctor's eyebrows knitted together, pensive, as George Waterman rushed into the room.

"You wanted to see me?" Waterman asked.

Prince held out the sheaf of letters.

"Read these at your leisure, but now I need you to check on Miss Fowler. I'm afraid something terrible has happened."

Waterman took them, blue eyes wide and inquiring.

"Of course, I'll tend to it right away," he promised, turning to leave, but thought better of it. "Is there anything else I can do to help."

"No, nothing. I would call on her myself if I could."

Waterman nodded and made his way to the foyer, Fanny Prince sailing past him as she stormed into the room.

"Morton, do you have any idea what time it is? Do you realize there are guests waiting?"

With that, Sargent threw his hands in the air.

"That's it. I'm done for the day! Mrs. Prince," he said, aggravation spilling over, "I have rendered the likeness of author Robert Louis Stevenson, the legendary actress Miss Ellen Terry, the politician Theodore Roosevelt, but I have never collaborated with a subject as exasperating as Dr. Morton Prince!"

Fanny turned to her husband of eighteen years, stared at him, and shook her head.

"Go now, the two of you!" Prince chided before she could say a word. "John, your wife, Mary, is waiting. Fanny, I shall join the festivities momentarily."

Her eyes narrowed, a playful twinkle in them. "As you wish, Doctor Prince, but you must promise not to get lost in your work and forget about us."

Arm-in-arm, the two left for the second-floor reception, leaving Prince to his solitary reflections about Clara Fowler's condition and the violence the demon had leveled against her. Was he up to dealing with a life-and-death situation like the one he'd undertaken? Success was more than a tradition in the Prince family. It was their heritage. His father, Frederick O. Prince, former mayor of Boston, had cast a long shadow. His four brothers were powerhouses in fields ranging from industry to finance. But success on a grand scale had so far eluded him, he was forced to admit, making his way to the staircase spiraling up the four floors of their townhouse.

He chuckled to himself, thinking about what Sigmund Freud said when asked by a reporter about him. "Ah, you ask about Prince, the Boston physician? His intellect is stilted. Besides being a prude, he is a self-righteous blockhead." Yet, behind the veil of self-assuredness, the doctor's mirth was accompanied by a welter of humiliation that nothing short of success beyond Freud's accomplishments could vindicate. And perhaps now, at last, he had found the vehicle to do it. Imagine a rare psychological disorder—misunderstood for the millennia—whose ambiguity he, and only he, could penetrate with the sanctifying light of scientific analysis!

Passing the second-floor landing on his way to the third, he could hear peals of laughter spilling over from the reception where champagne flowed and guests waited, but first there was a young lady to see—his daughter, Claire, in her pajamas and under the covers by now, waiting for a "goodnight" kiss from her Papa.

He paused at the third-floor landing. From behind the closed door to her room, he could hear the static-laced voice of George W. Johnson, coming over the gramophone's horn-speaker, singing "The Laughing Song."

> 'As I was coming 'round the corner
> I heard some people say, here comes the darky dandy, here he
> comes this way,
> Ha-ha-ha!
> Ho-ho-ho!
>
> His heel is like a snow plod, his youth is like a trap, and when
> he opens it gently, you'll see a frightening gap, and then I
> laughed.'

Prince crept up to the closed door, rapped on it gently and pushed it open, delighted to see his daughter sitting up in bed, laughing along with the recording.

"Ha-ha-ha! Ho-ho-ho!" She sang along, then, noticing her father, opened her arms to him. "Oh, Papa, you caught me singing—"

"Nicer than that, my Dear," he said, gathering her into his arms. "You were laughing! Did you think I was too busy to give a kiss goodnight?"

"Oh, no, I knew you would be here. I was waiting!"

He laid her down on her pillow and pecked her on the cheek.

"Now, you're ready for sleep."

"Can we talk for a while?"

"No, not tonight. Our guests are waiting."

"Okay," she coaxed, "but a story tomorrow?"

"Without fail," he swore, backing away toward the door, switching the light off. "Wonderful dreams," he whispered.

"I love you, Papa."

"I love you, too, my Darling," he said, closing the door behind him as the gramophone voice wound down to a tortured yawl.

By 8:15 p.m., Prince's guests were scattered around the reception room, drinking champagne in vibrant knots of conversation. The Doctor's eyes scanned the gathering, noticing familiar faces: the psychiatrist Boris Sidis and his wife Sarah, socialite Caroline Endicott chatting animatedly with Professor James and his wife Alice, the Winthrops, the Dudleys and, of course, the enigmatic parapsychologist Richard Hodgson, unattached since the untimely death of his fiancé, Jesse Dunn, who escorted medium Leonora Piper, her raven-black eyes meeting his and fastening upon them.

"Morton!" he heard Fanny calling above the laughter and buzz of conversation, approaching hand-in-hand with Alice James. "Mrs. James is enthralled with Mrs. Leonora Piper and her work in psychic science and was hoping you'd introduce her."

"Yes," Alice James said, edging toward him, "I understand Leonora Piper is here tonight. Is that so, Dr. Prince, because I would like to meet her and arrange a communication with my son, Herman, who passed last year."

"Yes, Mrs. Piper is indeed here—"

"Perhaps you've read about Miss J. J. Whitney's séance in Sacramento during which she identified the killer of a young boy," she twitted. "One might ask 'who would do such a thing', but while entranced in front of the mayor and the chief of police, she caused a detective to write his confession in chalk on a blank slate."

"Remarkable," Prince marveled, his gaze never wavering from Piper, "but, I'm sorry to say, the detective's confession was induced, not by Miss Whitney's slate writing, but internalized guilt and the power of suggestion. Will you excuse me, please?" he asked as Hodgson and Lenora Piper approached.

"No, no," Alice James protested, "there is much more to it than that!"

"Not more," Mrs. Piper suggested in a firm, gentle voice, "but less. In the end, the explanation is simple. The discarnate live in a world invisible to us. Miss Whitney tapped into that place," she patiently explained, "and the boy's rage at being bludgeoned to death. It was the boy who caused the murderer to confess, not Miss Whitney."

"Dr. Prince, Mrs. James, I would like to introduce you to Leonora Piper," Hodgson announced, standing proudly beside her, "telepathist, medium, clairvoyant."

"I've read so much about you in newspapers, magazines and, of course, from Richard," Prince said, taking her hand into his own, "now I have the privilege of meeting you."

She accepted the gesture with a wan smile.

"I've been a fervent follower of all that you are doing to promote Spiritualism," gushed Mrs. James. "My husband, the Harvard professor, William James, is considering writing a book about your 'gift.' It is a 'gift,' is it not?"

"Yes, a 'gift,'" Mrs. Piper deflected, turning to Prince, her expression tense and deliberate as if compelled to communicate something important, yet reluctant to do it. "Dr. Prince, Richard has told me about the Fowler case and I must warn you. The path you are taking is dangerous."

"In what sense?" asked Prince, taken aback.

She shook her head, flustered, a rose-color blush tinting her sheet-white cheeks, "Oh, Richard, I've already said too much! I apologize," she demurred. "I'm not a psychiatrist or even a physician. It was wrong of me to be so forward!"

"You are the nation's leading psychic," Hodgson encouraged. "Be assured, Leonora, your opinion is of great interest to us!" Then, turning to Alice James, he said, "If you'll pardon us, Mrs. James, I believe this is a conversation best held in private," before leading the doctor and the medium to a quiet corner of the room.

"Mrs. Piper, truth be told," Prince confided, "we are in search of answers, *any answers*, immersed as we are in the uncharted waters of the Fowler case."

"Dr. Prince, I don't know what you think of me," she said, speaking slowly. "Many people associate me with the occult, but they are wrong. Being a Spiritualist, I believe two worlds exist, one that we are conscious of, and the other unseen by most, but observed by me in flashes of insight. So I tell others what I see. But then, there is the occult," she said, choosing her words carefully, "and that is something different. I stay away from that, Dr. Prince, because that is where evil lives. Not evil as a concept, but as a living, breathing thing. So, I warn you. Stay away from it. Let the Fowler case take its course or risk being swallowed up by that evil, never to return to this side, the world where we humans live."

Until now, Prince considered Leonora Piper a sophisticated, if slightly eccentric, woman. Yet, something in her manner touched him deeply.

"Oh, come now, Leonora!" Hodgson protested. "We mustn't be morose about a channel of communication so new and exciting. Imagine the possibilities!"

"Yes, perhaps," she mused quietly, "but if it's the occult you've touched upon, there is the prospect of infection. A kind of contagion whereby the person coming to the victim's aid becomes possessed themselves. In Loudon, France during the possession of nuns at the Ursuline convent, four priests were sent to stem the epidemic. Three not only became possessed, but died soon after. The fourth spent the subsequent twenty-five years of his life in a lunatic asylum."

Prince's brow furrowed. The hairs on the back of his neck stood on end as he considered his response when an ear-splitting shriek from the floor above slashed through the fog of voices. His heart stopped. Its cadenced pounding let loose a quavering terror. "Claire!" he uttered, bolting from the room, Fanny, Hodgson, and Leonora Piper rushing up the spiral stairway along with him!

Prince stopped at the bedroom door and threw it open. Claire was shuddering in the far corner of the room.

"It spoke to me, Papa," she sobbed, lifting a trembling finger toward the gramophone.

"Who spoke to you, my Darling?" he asked, sweeping her up in his arms.

"The voice of the man singing."

"Claire, there is no voice," he comforted, walking toward the player, stopping dead in his tracks as she began screaming inconsolably.

"No! Don't take me near it! Don't take me near the man!"

"There is no man, my Child," he reassured her, placing her into Fanny's outstretched arms.

Prince stood watching in silent trepidation, both Hodgson and Leonora Piper planted a step away from the gramophone where Johnson's voice rang-out above the static-laced imperfections of the wax-roll recording.

> *'Ha-Ha-Ha!*
> *Ho-Ho-Ho!*
> *I could not stop from laughing!'*

"It's been a long day for Claire with school and preparations for the party," Prince said, tiredly. "A painful thing to observe one's child in the grips of a nightmare."

"Yes," Hodgson agreed, casting a sidelong glance at Piper as they walked to the open door with Prince, Fanny lying on the bed, Claire quietly sobbing beside her, "it's been a difficult time for all of us, even little Claire."

Once passed into the hallway, Leonora Piper's frame turned rigid, body shaking.

"There was a voice," she said, "deep and guttural and menacing. It did not speak in sentences that could be comprehended, but repeated three words. 'Squalid little thing,' it kept repeating as if it had some significance to you, Dr. Prince, or you, Richard, or Claire—*'squalid-little-thing,'*" she whispered a final time, jittery eyes lifted, as if staring at a distant terror.

THREE

Alexandra Hotel
Boston, Massachusetts

Fall River police chief, Rufus "Bassett" Hilliard, bolted up in bed screaming fierce, prolonged shrieks that ripped through the room's silence. He reached for the .32 Colt revolver tucked beneath his pillow. For long, terrible seconds he sat still, scanning the shabby South End hotel room for an intruder. There was none. Still, something had awakened him. What? Vaguely, he remembered the sound of massive and insistent jolts. But how could that be? There was no intruder, he realized, dropping the gun to his side, no opened door thrashing in the wind. But, sure as hell, it was the pounding that woke him, he swore, suddenly aware of his sweat-soaked nightshirt, understanding it was another 'night terror' sprung from his years-long investigation into the Fowler murders.

He blew out a breath and looked up to the wooden crucifix hung above the bed. He whispered a prayer then trundled to the washbasin. He was accustomed to the unusual, he thought, splashing water onto his face, catching a glimpse of himself in the mirror. He gazed at the reflection, understanding he had been scarred by the life he'd led, eyes red-rimmed from lack of sleep, handlebar mustache faded white, his once handsome face, tired and craggy, raven-black hair swept back haphazardly over graying temples. And, then, there was this. His mania, he thought, eyes shifting to the reflection of the room behind him, plastered wall-to-wall with crime scene photos and newspaper headlines bearing witness to the savagery of the murders.

"DOUBLE AX HOMICIDE IN FALL RIVER, Bordens Brutally Hacked To Death," *Fall River Post*; "LIZZIE BORDEN ARRESTED FOR MURDER, Slaughtered Beyond Recognition," *Boston Herald*. Then, the other's, blaring news of a second Fall River murder nine months later: "BERTHA MANCHESTER FOUND BRUTALLY MURDERED," *Providence Journal*; "BOLD ASSASSIN WIELDS BLOODY AX AGAIN IN FALL RIVER," *Daily Evening News*; "JOSEPH CORRIERO FOUND GUILTY OF MONSTROUS KILLING," *Boston Telegraph*.

The forty-eight-year-old lawman ambled to a desk set stark in the center of the room, police reports piled high atop it. He settled into a wooden chair and chose three files from amongst them—PR: C. E. Fowler, 6/1882 and 8/1888; PR: L. A. Borden, 8/1892; PR: J. Corriero, 12/1892—thinking back to how he'd arrived in Boston, shadowing a young Radcliffe student with whom he'd had no contact for twelve years.

He stretched his long legs outward, reached for a half-empty bottle of Jack Daniels and poured a drink for himself. It wasn't always like this, Bassett remembered, mind rocketing back to the day he first joined the Fall River police department. During those early years, he was "by the book" and while that never changed, after being promoted to City Marshal, his appearance certainly had. He grew his black hair long and combed it straight back, sported a handlebar mustache and dressed to his own liking in vested suits with spit-shined boots, a dapper steed derby and long coat like the lawmen of western lore. His reputation was stellar, especially after he married Nellie Smith Clark, daughter of socially-connected Judge Jordan Thomas Clark, who promptly invited him to join the prestigious Washington Club. Back then it seemed he could do no wrong, he contemplated, a sardonic smile bowing his lips upward, but all of that changed when, on the morning of August 4, 1892, daylight was swallowed by darkness.

He opened the "E. Borden" file and paged through it as he had one hundred times trying to uncover the thread of logic that would lead to answers to the questions that haunted him about the motive for the murders; about the nature of evil.

POLICE REPORT
Submitted by Marshal Rufus Hilliard
August 7, 1892
Date of Crime: August 4, 1892
Location: 92 Second Street
Fall River, Massachusetts
NATURE OF CRIME
Double homicide: Victim #1, Abigail
Borden, age 65
Victim #2, Andrew Borden, age 70
Time of Homicide: Abigail, 9:00-10:30
a.m.; Andrew, 11:00 a.m.

OBSERVATIONS
Victim #1, body discovered by Miss
Sullivan (maid) in upstairs guest
room. Struck 17 times with hatchet on
neck and head, 13 of them cut through
the skull. Victim must have turned
her head toward her assailant as 2 of
the blows were frontal.
Victim #2, body discovered by
Elizabeth "Lizzie" Borden (daughter),
slumped on couch in the downstairs
sitting room. Struck 11 times with
hatchet. Skull cleaved nearly in
half. Nose severed. Right eyeball
split cleanly in two, suggesting he
was asleep when attacked.

Bassett closed the file, brows furrowed, as he recalled the brutality of
the Borden murders. 'Sacrilege' was the word that came to mind seeing the
bodies that day. Skulls cleaved, faces bashed beyond recognition, brain
matter rising through the blood of their split craniums. "A crime against
God Almighty!" he swore in a haggard whisper, the phrase resounding in

his mind. How could a perfectly sane Sunday school teacher, without criminal history, mercilessly hack to pieces her step mother, then—without faltering—wait for her father to take a noon-day nap then savagely murder him? It was a crime beyond comprehension, yet it happened. Why?

Bassett took a gulp of bourbon, tapped a cigarette from out of his pack of Old Judge and lit it. He fanned out the match and tossed it in an ashtray. Delving into these files was, to him, like entering a dark chamber that he feared he would never leave again.

He drew deep on his cigarette. A ripple of uneasiness passed through him as he opened the "J. Corriero" file.

POLICE REPORT
Submitted by Marshal Rufus Hilliard
June 2, 1893
Date of crime: May 31, 1893
Location: Upper Boston Road
Fall River, Massachusetts

NATURE OF CRIME
Homicide—Victim, Bertha Manchester,
age 33.
Time of Death: 2:25 p.m.

OBSERVATIONS
Victim's body discovered by Stephen
Manchester (husband) in kitchen with
23 distinct and separate ax wounds on
back of skull and base. Defensive
wounds and ripped clothing show
victim engaged in fierce struggle
with assailant before being
overpowered.

Bassett took a puff from his cigarette, leaned over the ashtray and stubbed it out with quick, hard pokes. He stood, downed what was left in his glass, and walked to the window overlooking Holy Cross cathedral, Corriero's file in hand. He squinted at the silvery disk of the full moon, its edges hard and bright behind a scudding cloud. Corriero, the "Fall River Monster" was just 18 years old when he butchered Bertha Manchester. A Portuguese immigrant, unable to speak English, he was a gentle man who carried his weight as a worker cheerfully. He attended church on Sundays, cared for a stray dog he named "Pepito" and told other workers he would like to marry someday and raise a family.

Bassett recounted the events leading up to the murder. Corriero entered the Manchester house through the kitchen door and was confronted by Bertha Manchester. He raised the ax he held, leapt forward, and attacked her. A struggle ensued. The assailant threw her to the ground and held her down while bringing the ax down on her 23 times. Upon hearing her husband approaching, Corriero fled the house, leaving Bertha Manchester lying in a pool of blood.

An open and shut case, he surmised, except for one nagging truth: Jose Corriero was no murderer. Like Lizzie Borden who, composed and unruffled, denied killing her parents, minutes after slaughtering Bertha Manchester, Corriero went to town to buy a pair of shoes with no memory of the murder.

The lawman turned from the window, eyes lifting to the walls, crime scene photos, and newspaper headlines, screaming out at him for answers. He trudged back to his desk and fell into his chair, thinking. Was it too great a leap in logic to conclude that Borden and Corriero were guilty of the crimes they were charged with? True, Lizzy was acquitted, but based on the facts deemed inadmissible in court, he knew it was she who had done it.

During the trial, she showed no remorse and was inconsistent about almost everything, except her innocence. About that, she never wavered. But what if, like Corriero, Lizzie had no memory of committing the murders? That would explain her lack of emotion and vehement denials. Bassett sat back, pulled another cigarette from the pack, lit it. In other words, she committed the murders, but since she had no memory of it, believed someone else had perpetrated the crime.

Bassett took a pull from his cigarette. He exhaled a stream of smoke that floated eerily toward the ceiling, recalling testimony given by psychiatrists who theorized that both Borden and Corriero may have been in a *fugue* while engaged in the act of killing. That is, a mental state or period of loss of awareness of one's own identity. But, if the psychiatrists were right and they were in a *fugue*, he wondered, what identity had they assumed during the killings, if not their own?

Gripped by dark and solitary thoughts, he extended his hand, fingertips touching the third file marked 'C. Fowler' and, suddenly, the world was on edge. His brain flashed images. John Fowler: stalking the room, hurling curses like lightning bolts. Mary Fowler: bedridden, howling with agony and loss. The nurse: talking animatedly in a language he had never heard before. Clara: swaying in a rocker, dazedly singing nursery rhymes. Charles: dead. Bessie: dead, button eyes staring up at him.

He lifted a hand to his eyes and watched it tremble. No, he didn't need to open the file to see the morgue photos, autopsy reports, and John Fowler's criminal record studded with incidents of public drunkenness, assault and wife beating, he concluded, thinking back to a conversation he had with the county coroner. On June 7, 1882, four-day-old Charles died suddenly, the cause of death listed as "congenital debility." On January 8, 1886, four-day-old Bessie died suddenly, cause of death listed as "convulsions." But the deaths were highly suspicious, the coroner confided, and in his opinion both Charles and Bessie had been strangled to death by John Fowler, the father.

Bassett took a pencil from the desktop and scribbled a crude map and timeline on a piece of paper. First, the timeline:

Charles, dead, 1882
Bessie, dead, 1886
Andrew Borden, murdered, 1892
Abigail Borden, murdered, 1892
Bertha Manchester, murdered, 1894

Then, the map:

X Borden House
X Fowler House   X Manchester Farm

Five horrific deaths. Three of them ax murders; two, according to the coroner, infanticides by strangulation. All carried out in a five-mile radius!

He pushed the files aside, reached across the desk for the bottle of Jack Daniels, and poured another drink. A naked light bulb hanging from the ceiling cast a saffron glow on the police artists' renderings of America's first "serial" killer, **H. H. Holmes,** and victims Julia and Pearl Smythe, murdered and dissected, organs sold black-market to medical institutions, skeletal remains dissolved in a vat of acid. His glance shifted to photos of the "murder castle's" interior with sound-proof rooms, secret trap doors and maze of passageways leading to Holmes' laboratory where surgical tables awaited his unsuspecting victims. Headlines flashed before Bassett's eyes like the flickering frames of a kinetoscope: "**H. H. HOLMES CONFESSES TO 27 MURDERS, 'I Was Born with The Devil Inside Me,'**" *Chicago Tribune*; "**MORE GRUESOME DISCOVERIES AT MURDER CASTLE, The Most Horrifying Story Of Modern Times Told By Fiend In Human Form,**" *Fall River Post.*

His stare focused on the *Post's* headline, "fiend in human form," a phrase that stuck in his mind like a shiny steel pin. A suffocating feeling gripped the room as he considered the last documents pasted on the wall. Crime scene photos of **Jack the Ripper's** victims: Mary Ann Nichols, body discovered, *3:40 a.m.*, White Chapel, throat severed by two cuts, abdomen ripped open by deep, jagged wounds; Annie Chapman, body discovered, Hanbury Street, *6:00 a.m.*, throat severed by two cuts, abdomen slashed, uterus removed; Mary Jane Kelly, body discovered, Miller Street, *10:45 a.m.*, disemboweled, throat slit down to spine, abdomen emptied of organs, heart missing.

He darted an anxious glance to the newspaper headlines, the dates of the murders, bold, in black-ink print: "**GHASTLY MURDER, Dreadful Mutilation Of Woman In East-End,**" *London Evening News, September 1, 1888;* "**THE HORROR OF WHITE CHAPEL GROWS, 'Jack the Ripper' Butchers Two More Women,**" *Daily News, September 10, 1888;* "**RIPPER CLAIMS 5**TH **VICTIM, Woman Brutally Hacked To Death,**" *The Times, November 10, 1888.*

Bassett gulped from his glass of bourbon and took pencil in hand, expanding the timeline.

> ' *Charles Fowler (infant), murder by strangulation, June, 1882, Fall River, Massachusetts*
> *Bessie Fowler (infant), murder by strangulation, January, 1886, Fall River, Massachusetts*
> *Ripper Murders (5), hacked to death, September–November, 1888, London, England*
> *Lizzie Borden Murders (2), hacked to death, August, 1891, Fall River, Massachusetts*
> *H. H. Holmes Murders (27), hacked to death, October, 1892–July, 1894, Chicago, Illinois.*
> *Bertha Manchester, hacked to death, May, 1893, Fall River, Massachusetts*

Multiple murders executed with a degree of violence unlike any modern society had ever seen. All in little more than a decade as if evil, like some freakish contagion, had erupted into this world from another universe into the obscure textile town of Fall River, major cities like Chicago, London, and who knew where else?

Bassett whirled around to the white washbasin, startled. The faucet was dripping, one slow drop at a time. In the shivering silence, the sound seemed hollow and distant. Shaken by the Lizzie Borden murders, driven to near-madness by the Manchester slaying, he had come to Boston in search of Clara Fowler, the one witness to the murder of Charles, her brother, and Bessie, her sister, who could bring John Fowler to justice. Now, this—

He downed the last of his bourbon, opened the top desk drawer, and took out a crumpled letter he'd stolen from Clara's room two nights before. He smoothed the paper flat onto the desktop and began reading.

> *'Hypocrite! Whore! How I hate you! The pains of Hell shall come down upon thee. You shall find no help, no comfort, in heaven or on earth from my wrath—not till student Clara is dead and puts a bullet through her head! How long will that be, do you think? Days, weeks—no longer, surely. You shall sacrifice yourself at the earliest opportunity. Then, you shall be gone and I shall be forever!*
> *Devil! Devil! Devil! Devil!'*

A "demon" inside her? Bassett brooded. Threatening her? Demanding she put a bullet through her head? Of course, he knew she had switched doctors from Putnam, the neurologist, to Prince, the psychotherapist. But this?

He contemplated the words, "you shall be gone and I shall be forever." What did it mean? Had someone written Clara, threatened to kill her, and take over her body? It was madness, he knew, but something told him it could be true, that maybe the devil was a genuine presence that made itself known to humans, lured them to evil, and on rare occasions literally possessed them.

"'A rose by any other name would smell as sweet,'" Shakespeare wrote and maybe that is what he meant. Call the devil a myth, call Satan the product of a diseased mind, but who would deny the existence of evil in the world? Not Rufus "Bassett" Hilliard. Certainly not him!

He ran his hand across his brow. He needed sleep, but could not sleep. The steady plop of the dripping faucet seemed to keep time to a heartbeat, not his own. A tingling sensation worked its way from his spine to his neck. What he thought he was hearing, he understood, might be real. The light bulb above flickered. He whipped around at the crack of the crucifix falling to the hardwood floor. The beat grew louder. From a ticking sound inside the wall to a pounding that shook the room, ceiling to floor.

There was something implacable closing in on him, Bassett knew. He felt its presence in the dead of night when he thought he was alone, but knew he wasn't. Lizzy Borden, Corriero, Holmes and the Ripper, hadn't each felt the chill of its scaly hand on their shoulders?

Of course, it's all in your mind, others would tell him: Mayor Coughlin, who put him on forced leave; John Fleet, his deputy, who believed him mentally unstable; his wife, Nellie, who left him months ago, he remembered, the room and walls with their ghastly photos and headlines swirling around him.

He rose to his feet on unsteady legs, stepping around in circles in the middle of the room.

"*Stop it! Stop it!*" he screeched, teeth gnashing.

And, suddenly, the pounding stopped. In fact, there was no sound, none at all, he was thinking as he shambled to the bed, dropped into it, and drifted into a dark, dreamless sleep.

FOUR

Prince's eyes lifted to the clock set above the bookshelves that lined the back wall of his office, 2:05 p.m. He felt on edge, palms pressed flat atop his desk as he poured over fragments of baffling data. The narrow beam of an antique lamp flared on a clutter of scattered transcripts he'd spent hours studying for a detail that might shed light on his patient's shocking transformation from self-effacing "saint" to perfidious "demon."

Soon Hodgson and Waterman would join him for Clara's 3:00 p.m. consultation. He plucked a copy of Pierre Janet's *The Mental States of Hysteria* from the desktop, paged through it, then put it down amid the swamp of papers.

If he thought answers would come quick or easy, he was mistaken. The nightmares Clara experienced had intensified to where she forced herself to stay awake, but even that provided no respite. While lying awake in bed, she experienced periods of "lost time" awakening hours later to find herself stripped naked, frozen in obscene poses, perched atop a mountain of piled furniture. Paralyzed, it forced her to stay in that position until daybreak when, frantic and exhausted, she would begin her day.

During recent sessions, the doctor had performed tests to determine the physiology of the so-called demon. The results were remarkable, but underlying it all, the boast that it was always "inside" Miss Fowler; a haunting presence privy to her every thought, action and desire since birth.

When Clara arrived, the doctor ushered her to the consultation room where Hodgson and Waterman waited. Ghostly pale and profoundly agitated, the reason she'd missed two previous appointments was crippling illness. Her symptoms had worsened: debilitating headaches, unremitting nervousness and an inability to concentrate. Studying for her classes at Radcliffe College had become a monumental challenge, reading the Bible impossible.

The cause of the escalation, she believed, was a sermon she'd heard at Our Lady of Perpetual Hope on "miraculous healing." The instant the priest began, she felt the clawing sensation of what seemed like a scourge of nails raking the flesh of her back.

The suddenness of its onset left her dumbstruck. The missal she was holding dropped to the floor. She felt queasy and faint. Like a man who'd had a knife plunged into his back, she tried to extract whatever was cutting into her when the realization struck her. She could not move her hands, arms, or legs. She unleashed a bloodcurdling scream knowing what was to come, but not a whimper came from her. This, the start of a life-and-death struggle leading to six hours of "lost time."

Later that night, when she awakened, Clara told him, she was naked, her body on fire with pain, lacerations running down the length of her back, immersed in a bathtub filled with alcohol.

Convinced what his patient had experienced was a delusion, Prince asked to see the wounds. Modest and shy, she initially refused, but the doctor insisted, determined to confront her with evidence of her delusion. Finally, she agreed, unbuttoning her blouse and turning her back to him.

What Prince saw chilled his soul. Whether the result of self-mutilation or the demon resorting to physical abuse, a skein of long, claw-like lacerations pulsed back at him, raw and oozing.

Alarmed, Prince explored this most recent incident without further clarification or detail. His notes for the day reflect his frustration.

NOTES, December 14th

Patient connects feelings of being "possessed" with episodes of "lost time." When this feeling of "possession" comes upon her, she struggles with all her will. This conception is associated with the ethical idea of punishment (self-mutilation?) for her sins, Clara F believing that by punishment and prayer, the devil will be cast out of her.

The deep cuts and scratches represent a new phase of her disorder since she believes the "demon" is responsible. Discounting that possibility, since the lacerations cover the lower quadrant of her back, one wonders how did they get there in the first place (?)

Sensing the need for a more productive tact, Prince went back to hypnotic suggestion. As before, his demands for a healthy appetite, restful sleep, relief from physical distress, were given and accepted until, abruptly, her responses stopped, and a sullen presence gripped the room. Clara's face contorted, starting with her own panicked expression, then the gleeful expression of the demon, alternating one with the other, in stunning rapidity. "I will not!" Clara pleaded. "You will!" the demon countermanded in a booming voice. Torturously, her body twisted and squirmed as if trying to escape her own skin, the demon rubbing her eyes in a frantic attempt to take over. Finally, with hands balled into fists and body arched backward, her eyes flashed open and the demon appeared, beaming with triumph.

A chill passed through Prince as its eyes stayed fixed on him; a disquieting, motionless glare.

"Why have you changed?" he asked.

No response.

"Why won't you speak?"

Again, no answer.

Sitting on the couch facing Prince, with Hodgson and Waterman observing, the demon pointed to a box of cigarettes indicating it wanted one.

The doctor passed along a cigarette and lit it.

"W-won't she b-be cross?" it stuttered, taking a puff, not yet in total control of the body.

"Why?"

"She detests tobacco," it croaked. "But I shall smoke cigarettes."

"Do you enjoy smoking cigarettes?"

"I enjoy tormenting her," it snapped back. "She does not enjoy wickedness. I do. She thinks she is going to be a nun. Not as long as I'm here."

"Why?"

"I have a great objection to church and god and sermons. Who is god? Where is he?" it asked, gesturing globally. "I have better things to do with my time."

"What?"

It laughed, eyes glinting, "To smoke cigarettes."

The doctor edged forward.

"Why do you torment Miss Fowler?"

No response.

"Perhaps you don't know?"

"I know everything about her! Things she does not know and would never tell you, if she did!"

"What things?"

"I make her tell lies," it answered evasively. "I made her tell Mrs. Chambers that her husband had a brush with a whore at a brothel, and that the bitch gave birth to a monster that had to be destroyed!" It giggled. "Wasn't it fun to see claw marks on her back? Nice touch, the alcohol, don't you think? Of course, I did that, too."

"Why?"

"I hate her, that's why!"

"But why do you hate her? You are only hating yourself. She is yourself."

"No, she isn't."

"But she is."

"Nooo!" the demon erupted. "I will not allow it! She thinks she won't let me come. She's been thinking that all day. I made her stay awake last night and I will every night. I'm going to make her pay for her church and prayers. I want her dead!"

"Dead and buried?"

"Yes."

"Where would you be?"

"She is no more part of me than the clothes on my back."

"But you share the same body, isn't that right? So, where will you be when she is dead and buried?"

It sat silently, glowering at him, contemplating the paradox he'd presented. Could it as 'spirit' leave the body? Where would it go? To what existence would it be returning?

Finally, it crushed out the cigarette and leaned forward.

"Fich deine Seele, Dummkopf!" it drawled.

Prince studied its expression. Cunning. Arrogant. Deadly.

"Sprichet du flieBend deutsch Konnen wir uns unterhalter?" he ventured.

The demon threw its head back and laughed, then fixed its eyes upon him with disdain.

"Et loqui linguis, stultus natus," it answered in Latin.

"Sprechen Sie german, bitte!" he insisted.

"Le monsieur," the demon cooed in a young girl's voice, flicking its tongue, pulling open Clara's blouse, holding a bare breast out to him. *"Soucierait-il de se faire sucer la bite?"*

"You play these games because you can't answer my question."

"What question is that, *mon Cher*?"

"Where will you be when Clara is dead?"

"In Hell," it spat back, expression turned deadly. "All for the joy of seeing sweet, little Clara shut up in a wooden box with worms eating her flesh!"

The doctor contemplated the implications of the remark. Did it truly believe it could go on living with Clara dead?

"You say that you have always been 'inside' Miss Fowler," he challenged, "prove it."

"And why would I want to do that, Herr Doktor?"

"You claim you are the devil. If you are a demon, let me hypnotize you so you can prove you are what you claim to be."

The demon's lips curled into a sardonic smile.

"More of your psychology, eh, Prince?"

"Then, we shall proceed."

"As you wish," it hissed, craftily.

With that, he hypnotized the demon. Satisfied a deep trance had been achieved, the retrogression began.

"Relax and be calm. I want you to go back in time. Do you understand?"

"Yes."

"I want you to go back to when Clara Fowler was a child. How old is Clara?"

"Seven."

"What do you see?"

No response.

"Where is she?"

"In that shit town Fall River. It is unpleasant. Brats. Little moppets playing. Shut up in a schoolroom."

"Are you in the school room with her?"

"I am always with her. I have told you that over and over!"

The doctor's glance flitted to Hodgson and Waterman, their eyes fixed upon him, as he edged forward in his chair.

"I want you to go back still farther to when Clara was an infant." He checked for understanding, then asked, "What did her cradle look like?"

"It is blue. It has sixteen wooden bars, blue also. Eight on a side."

"What else do you see?"

"Her blanket is white and made of scratchy wool. It has satin around the edges with birds or some such nonsense, sewn upon it."

"Do you remember learning to walk?"

"I remember thinking what a perfect idiot little Clara was, falling on her face like one of those wooden dolls." She scoffed. "Anyone can learn to walk! The little monster fell and struck her head on a table. She had the gash sewn at the hospital."

"How many sutures did she receive?"

"Twelve."

Prince drew a gulp of air into his lungs, anticipation mounting within him. Something was calling him like a lost crying wind. Ambition? Destiny? He couldn't tell, but amazed at the effectiveness of the retrogression, he paused, dredging arguments pro and con, before deciding to probe yet deeper to a time before Clara's birth, to the place from out of which the demon first emerged.

"I want you to go back, still farther. Back to the time before Miss Fowler was born. Do you understand?"

It nodded.

"Your mind is floating, sailing back through the years as you begin to remember—"

He watched the demon, twisting in its chair, its mask of imperviousness removed, eyes clamped shut in concentration.

"What do you see?"

"Light. I see light. Fading," it rasped. "Spinning into darkness."

"And farther back," he commanded. "You are moving swiftly through time to a place where Miss Fowler is yet unborn. Beyond her birth and time, as she knows it!"

The demon shivered, jolting the room with the lash of its voice.

"Cold—nothing. Unending darkness!"

"What else do you see?" Prince exhorted. "Concentrate! What do you see?"

Its eyes rolled upward as it wrenched a shriek of terror.

"Ohhh!" it screeched in a prolonged howl. "We live and die," it sputtered. "Death—rotting—stink!" It wet its parched lips. "Everyone has a home," it cried out, marooned and forsaken. "Terrible cold," it shuddered pleadingly. "It is too painful!"

"Who are you?"

The demon sat silent, body quaking in terror as Prince sprung up at it, looking deep into its bulging eyes, maddened with fear.

"Who are you?" he demanded. "Why do you torture Miss Fowler?"

The demon stared back at him, eyes flaring with venom.

"Because I am the devil," it swore, seething, "and I want her dead!"

Slowly, it staggered to its feet. Now it stood, chest heaving, gathering air and dominion as it leveled a fiery glower at Prince, then turned away, trudging toward the door.

"You cannot leave!" Prince ordered, gripping the demon by its shoulders.

It whirled around with a savage growl, then threw him to the floor, continuing its march toward the door.

"Stop her!" The doctor shouted to Hodgson and Waterman from the floor where he lay.

The two men leapt forward, tackling the demon from behind. It flung around with a blood-curdling screech, clawing at them, as they tried to wrestle it to the ground.

Prince, on his feet again, scrambled to his desk. He yanked open the drawer, pulled out a bottle of ether, soaked a cloth with it, then dashed toward the melee. He seized the demon from behind in a desperate chokehold. It made croaking, struggling noises, flailing its arms as he clapped the ether-soaked cloth over its mouth—and it was like watching a clock unwind.

"You hypocrite!" it cried out in a voice that shattered the air, body sinking slowly to the floor. "You shall pay with the thing you love most!" it vowed before losing consciousness, its hideous gaze fading by degree as Clara Fowler returned to herself.

"I think I'm dreaming," she whispered. "Am I dreaming?"

"No, my Dear," Prince answered with a bleak smile. "We are here in my office with Mr. Hodgson and Dr. Waterman. Everything is going to be all right now."

***

The next day, while consulting in his office with a patient, Prince was summoned to the phone. It was Cody. In a freak accident, Garland, his prize Quarter Horse, had been hit by a car outside his home and killed.

Devastated, the doctor returned to his patient, the demon's threat darkly resounding, "You shall pay with the thing you love most!"

FIVE

Tavern Club
Boston, Massachusetts
January 17, 1899

The private room in the Tavern Club rumbled with discussion. Morton Prince's blue-gray eyes flicked across the heavy oak table to William James, Hodgson and Waterman. He handed them a written update on the Fowler case along with his recently completed study, "The Physiology of the Demon." In a word, it was *stunning*.

To this point, the demon's effectiveness in taking over Clara Fowler's body was sporadic, but periods of "lost time" had lengthened from minutes to hours. The explanation was given to Prince by the demon, itself. Since it was "always present" and privy to her "every thought," it discovered she was most vulnerable when physically and mentally exhausted. Its goal now was to "kill" Clara and take over her body permanently.

Prince deposited his cigar into an ashtray on the table beside him.

"Gentlemen, the cold-blooded delight the second consciousness takes in tormenting Miss Fowler is alarming. Hell bent on the annihilation of the primary 'self,' its strategy is to weaken her by every means possible. Its tactics are mind-bending," he added, probing the faces of the three scientists. "By day, it takes her on forced marches, awakening her miles from home. Humiliated and defeated, Clara has no choice but to make her way back, tramping through the streets of Boston, to the point of physical collapse. At night, bizarre dreams plague her. In one, she's dragged by a mob into a cathedral where, pinned to an altar, she is raped by men with the upper torsos of pigs and jackals. In another, she is walking through dimly-lit streets in a procession of black-robed figures, some with familiar faces, others with deformities that change from moment to moment. Dreading sleep, she lies awake in bed beset by visions of red-eyed gremlins who sit on her bedstead. Though she has no direct contact with the demon, she complains of an 'incomprehensible freakishness' inside her. Last week, I received this letter, dated January 10th," he said, flipping through the report. "Dr. Waterman, would you read it aloud, please?"

"Yes, of course," Waterman answered and began.

> 'Dr. Prince—I am afraid of everything now—of myself most of all! It is as if Satan himself is mocking me, playing with me as a cat with a mouse. 'Absurd', you will say, yet it is horrible beyond words to live in such fear. Do you understand? Can anyone understand without having experienced it? I have lost the past twenty-four hours as if it was twenty-four seconds!
> Sincerely Yours,
> Clara Fowler.'

"But it doesn't end there," Waterman warned, quiet and stolid-eyed. "The patient's *neurasthenic* condition persists—weight loss, headaches, malnutrition—along with a new disorder, *self-mutilation*, the act of deliberately inflicting pain and damage to one's own body." He pushed his glasses up on his nose digging deeper into the report. "Here is a letter, demon to Miss Fowler, dated January 4th:

> 'You dear, sweet, good little girl! Never heard of Forest before, did you? No wonder Prince is utterly disgusted with you, can't even confess straight! I'm going to tell him everything, then we'll see what he thinks of you. Damn you, lying little harlot, from here to eternity!
> Your Loving Guardian,
> X'

"Letters like this, laden with innuendo about Dr. Prince, and lately Richard Forest, trigger the patient's deepest anxiety. During consultations, she describes terror so intense it leaves her shivering with fright. Christmas day, for example, was a total blank. On December 26th, while attending what she thought was Christmas mass, Clara awakened to the sound of the choir singing on the right side of the church after having been seated on the left with no idea how she got there. As she later discovered, the demon had overtaken her while in church listening to the choir on Christmas day and awakened her during another mass twenty-four hours later! What transpired during that period of "lost time" was a mystery with one clue left behind. When she returned home and undressed that night, she found her undergarments soaked in blood and semen, the image of Richard Forest flashing before her eyes."

"Her ex-husband?" Hodgson asked, incredulously. "Does a connection still exist between them?"

"Too early to tell," Prince interjected. "As we know from Putnam's investigation, Miss Fowler eloped to San Antonio with Forest at fifteen. The marriage was short-lived. She returned to Fall River, without him, two weeks later."

"That could be significant," James speculated, "but given her 'saintly' disposition, is a sexual relationship even possible?"

"Their history together is sketchy, even today. If a carnal relationship exists between them, she seems unaware of it and is loath to discuss Forest, even while hypnotized."

"Another dark alley to walk down," James lamented, stabbing an index finger into Prince's study, 'The Physiology of the Demon', "but what interests me is this."

He struck a match and lit his Meerschaum pipe.

"See here," he noted, tracing his finger down the page, "it's quite astounding! *Personality*, the demon is a distinct consciousness different from Miss Fowler. *Permanent Existence*, it claims it has always existed and knows what the patient thinks, hears, and says since birth. *Immune to Pain*, the demon has a peculiar form of *systematized anesthesia*," he continued. "You may burn, prick, or jolt it with faradic shocks and it does not feel it. *Freedom from Ill-Health*, the demon does not know the meaning of bodily discomfort or disease. It is always well. *No Need of Sleep*, the demon is always awake and knows the patient's dreams to the minutest detail. *Automatisms*, Miss Fowler will talk, her face sad and weary, when suddenly the gleeful expression of the demon flashes over it as if its joy at her misery is too intense to hide. Then, out of the depths emerges a raging bass voice accompanied by a hideous expression not easy to describe or look upon." Professor James studied the report for a while, then asked, "These conclusions were drawn from empirical study?"

"Absolutely," Prince responded. "The demon boasts about its power and is eager to show it."

"Formidable advantages in the battle for predominance," James reflected with a calculating look. "Let me ask you, Morton, is its intention to kill Clara Fowler?"

"Not likely," he replied, taking a puff from his cigar. "Since the "demon" is obviously a delusion, it would die with her. If it's 'spirit,' as it claims," he joked, turning to the others, "I suppose it will lose its lodging and go straight to Hell!"

The doctor's eyes swept the faces of the others, laughing; except Hodgson.

"But I have a preliminary theory. The idea came to me while reading Dr. Albert Wilson's account of Edmund Gurney, a man who, like Jekyll and Hyde, was divided into two personalities. One, a well-mannered shopkeeper. The other, a psychopathic criminal. In the Gurney case, as in most others, there is the induction of trauma into the patient's life. A *psychical catastrophe* that triggered a state of hysteria during which the primary self disintegrated into two or more personalities." Prince leaned forward over the table toward them. "Think of the human mind as a mirror comprising eugenic traits, intelligence, and life experiences fused into one all-encompassing entity." He cast a glance at Waterman, "When you look into a mirror, George, what do you see?"

"Why, myself, of course."

"Exactly! Dr. Waterman sees himself. How he appears. What he thinks, sees, and feels. Namely, 'self.' But if we see only our primary identity, what happens to our baser instincts that lost the contest for predominance? The answer is, they lurk inchoate, beneath the surface, always there, but hidden so that what we see when we look at ourselves is a well-balanced individual. However, on rare occasions—often triggered by trauma—that mirror shatters leaving behind scattered shards that, once reassembled, form two or more fragments of the whole."

He crushed out his cigar in an ashtray, gauging their reactions.

"Now, let's examine the histology of Clara Fowler, a young college student, morbidly religious, predisposed to see the world as a battlefield where angels and devils fight for the eternal souls of humans. Well, that's a different sort of mirror. When it shattered, the 'saintly' pieces formed one entity and the 'demonic' another, each convinced it was the real Clara Fowler."

"Are you suggesting that Miss Fowler isn't real?" James demanded.

"Think of it this way," he explained. "The original Miss Fowler—like Edmund Gurney—experienced a catastrophic shock that triggered a *hysterical delusion* whereby the authentic 'self' split into two distinct entities, each an extremity of the original, neither one 'real,' neither one, a wholly integrated person."

Waterman looked up from behind his glasses, his boyish face turned crimson.

"With all due respect, to my way of thinking, Miss Fowler is a morally grounded, highly intelligent college student as real as you, Dr. Prince, Professor James, Hodgson or myself!"

"No," Prince answered, shaking his head in the negative, "that, Dr. Waterman, is what you see. In reality, the Miss Fowler we know is chronically *neurasthenic* with demonstrably limited knowledge of Clara Fowler's background. Have you ever asked her about her childhood? She knows nothing of it. Her marriage to Forest? Her mind is blank. No, no," he repeated, convinced, "what we see is a phantom, too ephemeral to fight back; too transitory to maintain her existence."

"You see the significance of what you're saying," Waterman persisted, "and its implications for Miss Fowler?"

"If my theory is correct," the doctor answered in a slow, steady voice, "we must fuse the two entities into one, eliminating both the "saint" and "demon" to re-create the integrated 'self', the real Miss Fowler."

He stared across the table, eyes pinning each of them.

"Gentlemen, today we stand on the brink of a uniquely important scientific discovery. The opportunity to study a rare form of *hysteria nervosa* that in Biblical times would certainly have been labeled demonic possession. A condition to which we can now apply modern scientific method."

"But Morton," James asked, pensive, as he drew on his pipe, "the *psychical catastrophe* that set all of this in motion, what was it?"

"That, Professor James," Prince confidently declared, "is what our experimentation will uncover."

Hodgson, quietly seething until that moment, lurched to his feet, eyes blazing with indignation.

"My God, listen to yourselves! You talk about Clara Fowler as if she's a 'thing', a subject for your 'experiments' to be burned and pricked and electrically shocked. But she isn't a 'thing.' She's an intelligent young woman with hopes and dreams, like any other person. A patient, tortured to madness, whose life hangs by a thread!"

"What do you suggest we do, Richard?" Prince asked, the tension in the room mounting. He snatched a cigar from his breast pocket. "How does one treat a condition without first understanding its etiology?"

"Exorcism," he shot back at him. "Will you not concede that conventional methods have failed to produce a positive result and that, in fact, Miss Fowler's condition has turned critical? Will you still not consider the possibility that the source of her disorder is not an anomaly of the mind, but a malevolent external force that is gaining strength within her?"

"No, I will not!" Prince blustered. "I can understand how ignorance about the psychological basis for unusual behavior can elicit absurd explanations from laypersons, but you, Richard? A highly educated man living in Boston on the cusp of the twentieth century?"

"You call it 'absurd', but Miss Fowler's symptoms speak for themselves! The startling change in voice and appearance, displays of paranormal strength, *psychokinesis*, clairvoyance!"

"Gentlemen, please—" James interjected.

"No, I want to answer him," Prince countered, shifting his glare back to Hodgson. "Let me take them one at a time. Startling change in Clara's voice? The constant screaming has thickened her vocal cords with a consequent deepening of the voice. Startling change in Clara's facial features? It's not unusual for a person's physiognomy to reflect their emotional state. Consider the change in the facial expression of an individual whose disposition turns abruptly from happiness to rage. Then imagine that change in a person whose sensitivities are ten times the norm because of *hysteria* or *schizophrenia*."

"And her paranormal strength?" Waterman asked.

"Increased adrenalin production. Think of the mother who lifts the wheel of a thousand-pound carriage to rescue her child."

"The displays of *psychokinesis*?" asked Hodgson.

"Fakery! Consider Edouard Buguet, who in his famous photo, *Fluid Effect*, faked the levitation of a woman sitting in a chair. As for clairvoyance? Yes, it was shocking to hear about the accident that killed Garland. But think of what the demon said, 'You shall pay with the thing you love most." That could be anything, the death of a loved one, a financial setback, news of a friend's illness. No, what one looks for is what one usually finds!"

"Perhaps, each of these phenomena can be explained individually," Hodson objected, "but when taken together, they point in one direction, demonic possession! Who are we to mock Miss Fowler's theological view of the world? You, Dr. Prince, call her 'truth' a disease that distorts her perception of reality, but I believe the opposite. How many scientific 'truths' have been proven ludicrous over the passage of time? The pseudoscience of *alchemy*; Becker's theory of *phlogiston*; dammit, man, the leading scientists in the Europe believed 'spontaneous generation' a scientific truth until Pasteur proved it wrong just thirty years ago." His scorching gaze brushed the faces of each of them. "I don't pretend to be Charcot, or Prince or Freud, but I make this prediction here today. What everyone believed yesterday, and we believe today, only fools will believe tomorrow!"

Prince examined Hodgson, his friend and colleague of twenty years, with incipient dismay. His hard, clinical gaze, softened.

"The sudden death of your fiancé, Miss Dunn, was a shock to us all, Richard, so I can only imagine the pain it caused you." He paused, choosing his words carefully. "What I'm trying to say, is that I understand your desire to communicate with Jesse; your need to believe in a spirit world where life—"

The color drained from Hodgson's face. His handsome features pulled taut over high cheekbones, incensed.

"Don't dare bring up Jesse's name to me again," he threatened, pointing a quaking finger at him. "I'm a man who has survived the death of the only woman I ever loved, so you may think my belief in Spiritualism disguises a compulsion to reconnect with her and, I confess, that is a hope I ponder every minute of every day. But understand this: the interest I have in Clara Fowler derives from the compassion I feel for her as a human being. You're a man obsessed with making a name for himself, Morton. Your motivation is pride. I pity you because the cure for your disease comes from within and I fear you will never find it!"

The psychical researcher turned his back to them and stormed toward the door.

"Mr. Hodgson!" Waterman called after him.

"Richard!" James commanded.

But it was Prince who jumped from his chair after him.

"Wait!" he urged. "There's something I need to say—"

Hodgson stopped at the doorway and turned.

"Yes, what is it?"

"I want to tell you," the doctor swore, clasping his shoulders, holding him at arms' length, "I am a scientist and believe in facts, not faith, but I give you my word, if I'm wrong and Miss Fowler's condition doesn't improve, we will do as you suggest. We will attempt to save her using the Roman Catholic rite of exorcism!"

III: ONSLAUGHT

"The Dark One was at my bedside when I was brought into this world, and he has not left me since."
–H. H. Holmes
America's first known serial killer

ONE

The new year brought with it the Great Blizzard of 1899, paralyzing Boston and much of the northeast, an end to the Spanish-American War as a result of the Treaty of Paris, and the beginning of the Temperance Movement begun by crusader Carrie Nation who, much to patrons' chagrin, marched into a saloon in Kiowa, Kansas destroying their liquor supply with a baseball bat. What the New Year did not bring was an improvement in Clara Fowler's condition.

Unable to carry on day-to-day activities, she was forced to drop out of school and give up her job as a stenographer. An ominous addition to the symptoms she manifested was *Angst-Neurose*, an unanchored dread of nearly everything around her. But none was as acute as her fear of thunder and lightning, a phobia that, unbeknownst to Prince, would become a prelude to heart-dropping tragedy.

While meeting with two former classmates at a Back Bay tearoom, Clara watched, breathless, as clouds gathered signaling an oncoming storm. The thought of lightning ripping through the nighttime sky and fury of thunder like canon blasts, set her teeth on edge. Throat constricting, feverish with terror, she watched the clouds blacken until, unable to suppress her fear any longer, she fled the tearoom in silent anguish.

The trolley ride to Blagdon Street was a short one, but the storm was fast-moving, carrying gusting winds and sheets of icy rain accompanied by savage thunder bursts and lightning. Scurrying blindly into the storm, she made it to the rooming house, then ran to her room, closing the door and bolting it behind her.

Safety. A building to protect her. From what? Thunder? Lightning? Since when had these fears—powerful, debilitating—affected her? She tried to remember, but the memories were ephemeral and the thunder, jolting the house to its foundation, and lightning flashing through the windows, too frightening to ignore.

Get a grip. Calm yourself. Control your thoughts. With these words rifling through her mind, she rushed to her dresser for a packet of bromide. She steadied her shaking hands, mixed the sedative with a glass of water and drank it down, hoping it would calm her. *"He maketh me to lie down in green pastures: he leadeth me beside still waters,"* she prayed, sitting at her desk, taking pen in hand to scrawl a note begging the doctor to see her the next morning. *"He restoreth my soul: he leadeth me in the path of righteousness,"* she entreated, panic rising, until the words trailed off, then stopped entirely. The room was airless. Tight. Brooding. Every clap of thunder and flash of lightning seemed to usher in visions she had, so far, encountered only in dreams. Within seconds, the temperature plunged. It was freezing! She wrapped her arms around her, watching in shuddering awe as the cramped room became a landscape from Hell; red-eyed gremlins perched on her bedstead with grins, eager and sadistic, pasted on black leathery faces; corpses, some decomposed, others' bone-white countenances pressed against the windows, wordlessly clawing, trying to break in!

Her room, like a torture chamber, had become the stuff of nightmares. *"Yea, though I walk through the valley of the shadow of death, I will fear no evil!"* she whispered but, like printed words filling blank pages on their own, images appeared, swirling around her like ghosts risen from the grave. **HER MOTHER**, apoplectic with rage, shrieking, "Get out! Get out of my sight!" Her infant sister, **BESSIE**, held out above a rocking chair by adumbral hands, purple-faced and screaming. **HER FATHER**, stomping the slat-wood floor of their house, drunk and ranting, "Have you no eyes? Can't you see? It was she what killed our babies!" **RICHARD FOREST**, his fleshy bulk atop her, hot breath cascading down like bellows as she struggled to break free. "This is not happening," she screamed. "Sweet

Jesus, tell me this is not real!" Then, like a whirlpool swirling into the ocean depths, the images began collapsing into themselves, until she stood trapped between the polar opposites that defined her existence!

Faint. No air. Lungs stinging. Eyesight blurred. She watched the transformation that left them standing stark before her. Not her father. Or mother. Or Forest. But the One, eyes rabid, grin hideous, three-fingered hand stroking the infants nestled in its arms. And across from it. Shrouded in a luminous vapor. Beautiful. Splendorous. A Vision of Jesus Christ. "My dear, Lord and Savior! Please help me!" Clara pled, arms outstretched, rushing toward Him. Eyes brimming with ardor, she fell to her knees before Him. "Your faith will save you," He promised, smiling tenderly as He looked down upon her. Then, like melting snow, the vision dissipated, leaving only the One. She could feel its menace. Smell its sulfurous vapor infusing the room. Dagger teeth bared. Red eyes flaring. Two infants held out like quarry snagged by a hunter. Charles and Bessie. Necks wrung. Dead. And she flew from it! Fast as her legs would carry her. She needed to be out of this room *now*, her brain was screaming as she threw open the door, then looked up. Can't breathe. Legs giving out from under her. Body dropping to the floor. The One glowering over her!

Lying unconscious, arms and legs splayed beyond the doorway, Mrs. Kerr found her. She rushed from the staircase to the landing, raised Clara's head, cupped in both hands. Other borders, a man and two women, hearing the commotion, drifted from their rooms.

"Don't stand there gawking!" Mrs. Kerr squalled. "Get her water! Someone, call Dr. Prince!" Then, turning toward the room one door over, she hollered, "Sylvia! Miss Griffin, come quick! You are needed!"

It was then that Clara, delirious, came around.

"I saw Him. Our Lord and Savior," she muttered. "He spoke to me!"

"It's a gift, my dear Clara. A gift from God, Himself. You see what others only feel. You've been blessed with the 'second sight'—" Then, loud and frustrated, she shouted. "Sylvia! Miss Griffin! We need Dr. Prince, now!"

But there was no response.

When the boarder, a thin, nervous-looking man, approached holding a glass of water, she rose to her feet, achingly.

"Give her water," she instructed, changing places. "She needs water to revive her," she added, bustling to Miss Griffin's door, knocking. Then, banging. Finally, opening it with her key.

What she saw left her screaming. A prolonged, piercing howl that echoed through the hallways into the abyss of endless night.

TWO

Prince Home

"Papa! Papa!" Claire Prince called, charging up the stairs to the second-floor landing. "Come downstairs! Mother needs you!"

The doctor looked up from the nest of paperwork that covered his desk as she entered the study.

"And what's this all about?" he asked with an affable grin.

"It's the man with the hat. The one who brought you the envelope. He's at the door with mama!"

The twinkle in Prince's eye vanished. He pushed away from his desk and rushed out of the room, the sound of Fanny's voice parrying with the stranger ringing in his ears as he ran down the stairs to the foyer.

"You, sir! What's the meaning of this?" He stalked toward him, handlebar mustache, black long coat, steed derby, just as Fanny had described him. "Who the blazes are you?"

Bassett raised his hands, palms up, "No need to get excited, Doc," he said with a thrust of authority that stopped Prince in his tracks. "My name is Rufus Hilliard." He reached into his jacket, took out a badge and ID. "Marshal Rufus Hilliard, Fall River police."

Fanny's blue eyes shifted to her husband. His anger turned to a look of puzzlement as he examined Bassett more closely: hardscrabble face, craggy and rutted; eyes, bloodshot.

"Very well," he said tersely, "what do you want? I read the newspapers you delivered the last time you came here unannounced and found them appalling."

"I apologize for that," he drawled. "I figured it would get you thinking."

"Thinking," Prince demanded, "about what?"

The two men traded glances.

"What I came to tell you is best said in private."

But Prince was skeptical, Bassett could tell. His arrival without forenotice, his appearance, the articles he'd delivered, created a nimbus of danger around him.

"It's about Sylvia Griffin," he said bluntly. "The young woman living at the Blagdon Street rooming house."

Prince took a moment to absorb the implications of the Marshal's remark. He nodded his ascent then touched Fanny lightly on the shoulder. She looked to him and stepped aside.

"Come with me," he muttered, leading Bassett up the staircase and into his office.

Prince motioned him to sit then dropped into the leather chair behind his desk.

"So, you have something to tell me about Miss Griffin," he began curtly.

The Marshal grimaced as if to flag an advanced warning, "She is dead."

"Dead? I don't believe it. I saw her just three days ago and she was perfectly healthy."

"It was not an illness that took her, Dr. Prince. It was suicide."

The news hit him like an ice pick to the chest.

"Are you sure? It seems out of character for a young woman so—" he searched for the word, "—gentle, full of hope. How?"

"They found her hanging from a rope tied to the water pipes above the ceiling in her room."

The doctor looked to him, disconnected, "Could it have been an accident?"

"No, it was suicide. Sylvia Griffin climbed up on a chair, put a noose around her neck and jumped. That clear. That simple. And if you're thinking she may have been strangled then hung to make it look like suicide, I was there when the detectives examined the body. Hanging by rope leaves an inverted V bruise. Bleeding sights were on the lips and inside the mouth, all indicative of death by hanging."

"By God, this is terrible," Prince said, mind adrift, until the question came to him. "Is that why you came here? To tell me Miss Griffin was dead?"

Bassett plucked a notepad from his jacket pocket, "You became acquainted with Sylvia Griffin through one of your patients," he said, flipping through the pages, "Miss Clara Fowler."

"I was acquainted with Miss Griffin in passing," he answered sternly. "As for the rest, I'm not at liberty to discuss who my patients are or are not with marshals, detectives, or anyone else."

"Doctor-patient relationship." Bassett smiled widely. "You took an oath."

"Correct."

"Still, the detectives discovered a detail during the examination of the body." He tapped out a cigarette from his pack of Old Judge. He lit it, then drew deep, exhaling a stream of smoke. "A word carved into the flesh of the victim's back; still fresh, still bleeding. The word was 'SPITE.' Does that mean anything to you, Dr. Prince?"

"An odd word, but not without meaning in the context of suicide. Anger, hatred, deliberately hurting someone for the sheer pleasure of causing mental or physical distress. In psychology, behaviors like that are signs of psychopathy. The inability to experience human emotions like remorse, or empathy, or love. But it's strange to think that any of those would apply to Miss Griffin."

"No, I suppose not. Let me elaborate. It wasn't just the word carved into her the detectives could not explain, but where it appeared—out of reach—on her lower back. Miss Griffin might have been able to touch the spot where it was carved, but to take a knife and carve it into her own flesh?" He shook his head. "No, highly unlikely, unless," he said, reasoning the mystery out aloud, "someone else entered the room after she hung herself, carved the letters, and left undetected." He shook his head again, perplexed. "But, no, that wouldn't explain it, either. The room was locked from the inside so no one without a key could get in, except Mrs. Kerr, who I think we can both agree would never commit such a heinous act. Who? How? These are the questions that need to be answered."

"But not by me, Marshal Hilliard. I think I've heard quite enough about Miss Griffin's suicide and the mystery of the word 'SPITE'." He glanced at him, half-rising from his chair. "You'll excuse me, but I have patients—"

"Yes, of course, you do," he interrupted, stubbing out his cigarette, "but that's not why I came to see you. In fact, I've been wanting to visit for some time."

Prince sat down again.

"Oh?"

"Dr. Prince, I'm a man who enjoys the hunt; to dig as deep as need be to ferret out answers. Did I tell you what the deputies at central station call me? They call me 'Bassett' after the hunting dog of the same name. No, it was Miss Fowler I came to talk to you about." He lifted his hand in the doctor's direction. "Now, I know you can't discuss details, but let me give you information to ponder before I leave. Those newspaper clippings with the headlines about the murders? Before Elizabeth Borden or Jose Corriero, I was twice called to the Fowler house to investigate reports of domestic violence. Of course, I'd been there before, but on two of those occasions what I found was the corpse of an infant, four-days-old each of them. Doc Landry, who tended to the Fowler children, concluded both died of natural causes. A coincidence to be sure, but not homicide although John Fowler, the father, was a drunk and wife-beater.

"Three months later, I discussed the Fowler tragedies with the county coroner over a drink at the Washington Club. 'Ever come across the term *petechiae* in the course of your duties, Bassett?'" he asked. "'It comprises small purple dots around the eyes caused by asphyxiation. When blood flow is cut off, pressure builds, causing the capillaries in the eyes to rupture. Those dots were present on the eyelids of those babies, along with bruises that even the local mortician could identify. Doc Landry got it wrong. The causes of death were not 'convulsions' or 'congenital disability.' In my opinion, John Fowler murdered those babies'"

"Why tell me all of this, Hilliard?" Prince asked. "Clara Fowler has seen a lot of tragedy in her life, but what does any of this have to do with her now, as she is today? Don't stir cold ashes is my motto. Perhaps it should be yours as well."

"My sobriquet is 'Bassett.' I thought I made that clear." He sniggered, lit another Old Judge, and strolled toward the window. "Much later, long after Charles and Bessie were buried, one of my deputies came upon something strange tucked away in a hollow outside town: a goat's head stuffed with pages from the Bible, a crucifix, and statue of the Virgin buried in a mound of excrement and what appeared to be human remains. It seems a Satanic cult was operating in Fall River for years, even decades, and what my deputy had stumbled onto was the place where their Black Masses were held." The Marshal turned and ambled slowly toward Prince. "So, what's terrible about that? I am not a religious man. If you believe in such nonsense, go ahead! Religion, black or white, is of no consequence to the law, except there's another aspect to the ritual. The highest offering to their Lord and Savior, Satan, is the blood of a newborn child." He crushed his cigarette out in an ashtray. "After hearing that, a powerful thought struck me. It came from my conversation with the coroner and my own suspicions about John Fowler. So, I went to the cemetery and dug up what was supposed to be Charles and Bessie Fowler's remains. They weren't there, Dr. Prince. The bodies had either never been buried or were torn from the earth, denying them their final resting place."

"Are you implying that John Fowler was responsible for all of this?"

Bassett pounded his fist onto the desktop with the power of a falling ax.

"Not implying, Dr. Prince, accusing! John Fowler and Doc Landry were members of that goddamned cult!"

"So, Fowler murdered his two children to be used as human sacrifices in Black Mass ceremonies and Landry covered up for him. Is that your theory, Bassett? Because if it is, these allegations are a law enforcement matter, not a psychological one involving my practice!"

"I've told you where the 'connection' begins, Dr. Prince, now I'm going to tell you where it led me." He pulled out the letter he had stolen from Clara's room. "It seems your patient is well acquainted with the dark side of her Catholic beliefs. 'Dr. Prince, I am afraid of everything now,'" he began reading. "'It is as if Satan, himself—'"

"Where did you get that?"

"That's my business, but I know how Clara Fowler became immersed in this monstrous world of demons and human sacrifice. It was her father, who raped her. It was her father, who beat his wife half to death. It was her father, John Fowler, who killed Clara's four-day-old brother and sister leaving her psychologically scarred for life by the horror of what she'd seen!"

"I'll take that letter," Prince demanded, pressing the silent alarm, summoning Cody. "I want you out of my house. Do you understand? Now!" he shouted, rising to his feet to confront him. "And don't dare come near my wife and daughter ever again!"

Alerted to the potential for violence, Cody burst through the door, drew a derringer from inside his belt, and leveled it at the lawman.

Bassett held up his hands to show he was unarmed then dropped them to his sides.

"You're right, Dr. Prince," he agreed, putting on his long coat, snaring his derby. "This is a law enforcement matter. But Clara Fowler was witness to two unsolved murders. She was there. She saw what happened. The county coroner is ready to testify, but that's circumstantial and would never hold up in court. But a witness to the killings, a witness like Clara, would be enough to convict John Fowler of his crimes; crimes against God, crimes against humanity!" he swore as Cody, gun pointed, ushered him toward the door. "I know there's something she's told you; information that came out during your psychotherapy sessions," Bassett screamed thrusting an accusing finger at him. "You can get her to testify. You can help bring that monster sent from Hell to the gallows!"

Prince watched Bassett leave from his office window. Convinced he was gone, he walked to his desk and did something he swore he would never do during daylight hours. He opened the bottom drawer, took out a bottle of brandy and opened it. He poured a drink for himself, took it down in a gulp and, hands trembling, poured himself another.

The Fowler case frightened him, and it was tangible fear, as if the moment he left his office, the buried corpses of half the world would be lying outside his door.

THREE

Lowell Lecture Hall
Harvard Medical School
Boston, Massachusetts

Morton Prince slipped into Lowell Hall at the tail end of Professor William James' lecture. The hall was not large, but the space it occupied was put to good use with sixty students seated in tiered rows forming a U around him.

Bassett's visit had left Prince unsure of what direction to take the Fowler case. The Marshal was intimidating, but the thought of cooperating in his investigation was anathema to Prince. Clara Fowler had enough conflict in her life. No need to open old wounds. Still, he knew Bassett would not quit easily.

He shifted a desultory glance at William James and studied him. Full beard, deep-set eyes with a loose-fitting suit draped over his gangly frame, he stood, voice bounding through the crowded lecture hall.

"In conclusion, it is impossible to dismiss the near-death experiences of patients whose heart, pulse, respiration—every trace of life—is absent and their perceptions of an after-life. Rather, let us make these experiences a lens through which to peer at the inner workings of the human consciousness, a mystery even for the most resolute materialist."

Prince looked on as James strode to the lectern ready to take questions. A practitioner of both science and philosophy, it was his uncanny ability to analyze a situation from multiple disciplines and produce practical solutions that drew Prince to him. He was at a crossroad with the Fowler case and he knew it.

"Questions?" the professor inquired.

A young man dressed in a blazer, tie, and high-collared shirt, raised his hand.

"Professor James, it's well-established that *hypoxia*, an oxygen shortage in the brain, can lead to hallucinations. Could it be that these 'near-death' experiences are nothing more than the spasms of a dying brain?"

A spate of nervous chatter rippled through the hall. The professor stroked his beard thoughtfully, then answered.

"At some level, I find that reasonable, but far from conclusive. How does *hypoxia* account for experiences occurring after, not prior to, the cessation of brain activity? It does not!" His ponderous eyes came alive. He paced the stage, excited by the challenge. "Patients, long dead, once resuscitated, reveal the conversations and even the instruments used by surgeons operating on them. Upon their 'death' the body, after the spirit has departed, becomes nothing more than the shell that once bound them to this earth. Many relate, in vivid detail, their passing into a heavenly world of intense beauty or hellish nightmares from which there is no returning. No!" he said, rejecting the possibility. "If the soul is only neuro-impulses firing in the brain, that makes it energy. But, as the German physicist von Helmholtz has proved, energy cannot be created or destroyed. It can only be transferred from one thing to another. And so, like the ghost of Hamlet's father, the discarnate glare down at us from heaven, or hell, or a dimension yet undiscovered, compelling us to ask, *exactly where does the human spirit go?* That's not superstition, young man. That is science!"

A dark-haired woman wearing a tailored morning dress and tortoise-framed glasses raised her hand.

"What people want, Professor James, is proof. Evidence that one can see, touch, feel. Without proof, belief in an afterlife is little more than a delusion."

"Miss—"

"Hawkins," she offered.

"Proof!" he touted, hoisting his hand in the air like a flag. "Evidence! It's my contention that if Jesus Christ appeared in thunder and lightning atop Trinity Church it would not affect the beliefs of anyone who witnessed the phenomenon. Those who already believe would find re-enforcement of their faith. Those who did not would convince themselves that what they saw was autosuggestion, mass hypnosis, or charlatanism." He looked to the students tiered above him, speaking with utmost seriousness. "In astronomy, there is a technique known as 'averted vision.' The idea that, sometimes, one can see the essence of something more clearly if they're not looking at it directly. It's as if what they are after is sitting on the periphery rather than at the center of one's gaze. The mystery of faith is like that, Miss Hawkins. It lies not in miracles or science, but in the individual's will to see the truth that is obscured from him. Any more questions?" His eyes swept the faces riveted upon him. "Very well," he said, seeing there were none, "I shall leave you with the words of William Shakespeare. 'There are more things in Heaven and earth, Horatio, than are dreamt of in your philosophy.'"

A wave of applause echoed through the hall. James gathered his notes from the lectern where, turning to leave, he spotted Prince.

"Morton," he joked, delighted, "I didn't see your name on the class roster!"

They shook hands warmly.

"No, but I've never stopped learning from the erudite Professor James."

He stared into Prince's eyes sharp as pins; noticed the pang of concern in his voice.

"To what do I owe the pleasure?"

"The Fowler case," he answered, "a complication that's developed since our last meeting."

"Well, we'd better hasten to my office to discuss it, hadn't we?" James suggested, leading him out of Lowell Hall onto Boylston Street where pedestrians bustled, bicyclists sped, and newly introduced Autocars wended their way along cobblestone streets.

On the way, Prince told him the news of Sylvia Griffin's suicide, Bassett's visit, and the alleged atrocities John Fowler had committed from the strangulation of Charles and Bessie to the sacrificial offering of the infants' bodies.

They entered James' office.

"Please have a seat," he said, motioning toward a sofa.

The professor strode across the room to a world globe that opened up to a cache of liquor. Prince took in the décor: dark wood furnishings, Victorian fireplace, walls adorned with portraits of Charles Elliot, Dean of Harvard Medical School; his brother, author Henry James; his mother, Mary Robertson Walsh; bookshelves stacked with the latest volumes relating to science, philosophy, and religion.

"Care for a drink, Morton? A touch of brandy," he suggested, then seeing the doctor's somber expression, "or, perhaps, a glass of whiskey is more in order."

Prince drew a deep breath, shut his eyes and nodded, "Whiskey," he agreed with an edgy smile.

James poured a glass for the doctor and himself.

"I'm guessing Marshal Hilliard suspects Clara witnessed the murders at the Fowler house," he ventured, handing him his drink.

"Yes," he said, draining the glass. "He wanted me to persuade Miss Fowler to bear witness against her father." He chortled. "That was before I threw him out of my office!"

James took down the last of his whiskey. He stepped toward the fireplace, ignited a spill, and stoked it.

"You were right in leaving him to his own devices. Who in his right mind would have a young woman in her condition testify in a court of law? Besides, his investigation has little to do with Clara and nothing to do with you."

"Bassett is a madman. He looks like he's lived on a diet of alcohol and opium since the Borden murders. He talks incessantly about those and the Corriero killing like they happened yesterday. To be honest, it's unclear whether he's still employed by the Fall River police."

The professor caught a pulse of fear in his friend's voice; watched his index finger twitching as he took a seat across from him.

"He tried to bully you, I take it?" he asked, then smiled. "He obviously has a lot to learn about the indomitable Morton Prince."

"Psychotics trouble me, Will," the doctor brooded. "It bothers me that he barged into my home uninvited. And the articles he left with Fanny about the Borden and Corriero murders? Grisly. Sick. It was nothing I wanted to see and tells me all I need to know about Rufus Bassett Hilliard."

James lit a pipe.

"Have you considered contacting the police? Chief Homer is a family friend."

"No, I've dealt with personalities like this before. It would only strengthen his conviction."

The doctor's gaze probed the crackling flames of the fire in front of him. "What do you know about the Black Mass?" he finally asked.

"I've never attended one, if that's what you're asking,"

"But the research you did for *Varieties of Religious Experiences*, wasn't that part of it?"

"To be honest, Morton, I've tried to avoid the subject. While I want my writing to be inclusive, it's not my aim to fan the flames of depravity." He looked to Prince, who seemed unwilling to accept his response. "So, yes," he sighed, "I know something of its history, but I warn you, it's horrific."

"Things like that really go on!"

"To this day. In Fall River and right here in Boston. The Black Mass takes the Catholic Mass and inverts it, intentionally mocking the ceremony. The celebrant wears black vestments embroidered with an inverted cross. Black candles are substituted for white ones. In the recitation of prayers, the Latin is directed at Satan instead of God.

Participants use sacred objects and desecrate them, stomping or spitting on the cross, stabbing the consecrated host with knives, performing obscene acts with it, which is why tabernacles in Catholic churches have locks protecting the Eucharist today."

"Bassett claims the infants were used in a Black Mass by a Satanic cult in Fall River, is that possible?"

"More than possible. The ritual goes back to a time shortly after the crucifixion of Christ. The Council of Toledo banned it in 694 under punishment of death," he said, reciting dates from memory. "In 1307, the Knights of Templar were disbanded for conducting blasphemous rites in which Christ was renounced, Satan exalted, and idols made of stuffed human heads worshiped. One hundred years later, Gilles de Rais, a French baron, was arrested for conducting Black Masses to gain riches and power. He was later charged with kidnapping, torturing, and dismembering more than one hundred children. But the most notorious account comes in the late 17th century when the Marquise de Montespan, mistress of King Louis XIV, sought the services of a defrocked priest, Abbe Guiborg, because she found the King courting another woman. Using the Marquise as a naked altar, Guiborg said Black Masses over her while invoking Satan and three of his demons. While in their presence, the throats of infants were slit, their blood poured into chalices and mixed with flour to make a host. Guiborg consecrated the host over the Marquise genitals and inserted pieces into her vagina. The ritual was followed by an orgy where she was raped and sodomized for hours at a time. The monster produced was said to be half-human and half-beast. It died upon birth along with the King's new lover, who threw herself off a cliff into the sea. When the scandal broke, the King arrested 246 men and women, many of France's highest nobles. Confessions were made under torture. Afterward, the streets ran red with the blood of one-hundred-thirty-six people who were disemboweled then burned alive in the public square."

"My God!" Prince gasped.

"So, to answer your question, yes, they go on, perhaps never more than today with the rise of Spiritualists where communication with discarnate souls attracts the curious as well as the damned."

"And where do you suppose Miss Fowler fits into all of this? Unlike Hodgson, who sees spirits around every corner, I believe we have encountered something unprecedented, but entirely natural, despite its symptoms."

"Certainly, her childhood experiences provide a proclivity toward the demonic. Still, I favor your theory rooted in something akin to *hysterical conversion reaction* or, as you call it, *dissociation*."

"But the catastrophic event that caused the fracturing of her personality into the "saint" and "demon." What was it? I've tried every way I know to bring it out into the open. Now, I'm convinced Miss Fowler knows nothing about it."

"And the demon?"

Prince shook his head, confused, "What?"

"The demon knows Miss Fowler's every thought and action, even her dreams, since childhood. Perhaps we're seeking answers from the wrong entity. Look here," James said, pulling a notebook from his jacket pocket. "'There are messages in its letters to Clara like a voice calling out to her from the distant past. The demon is trying to tell her something, some hidden secret, and in doing so is calling out to us along with her.'"

He flipped open the notebook and began reading.

"Letter, September 14, 1898, demon to Miss Fowler:

> *'Hypocrite! Whore! How I hate you! The pains of*
> *Hell shall come down upon thee. You shall find no help,*
> *no comfort in heaven or earth from my wrath—not till*
> *student Clara is dead and puts a bullet through her head!*
> *Devil! Devil! Devil!'*

"Why would the demon call Miss Fowler a 'hypocrite'? Why a 'whore'? Even the perspective from which it's written suggests punishment, not for being a 'saint,' but the reverse! Here is an excerpt from your consultation with Miss Fowler while in her demonic state, taken from your notes, October 7, 1898:

'Prince: Why do you torment Miss Fowler?
No response.
Prince: *Perhaps you don't know?*
Demon: *I know everything about her! Things she does*
not know and would never tell you, if she did!'

"What 'things?' What does Miss Fowler 'not know' and 'would never tell you, if she did?' Now, see how the focus narrows," the professor noted, "as the mysterious Richard Forest re-enters her life.

"Notes, Dr. George Waterman, addressing Fowler team RE: December 26, 1898, incident:

> *'Letters like this (demon to Miss Fowler) laden with*
> *innuendo about Dr. Prince, and lately Richard Forest,*
> *trigger the patient's deepest anxiety—when she returned*
> *home (after experiencing 'missing time') and undressed that*
> *night, she found her undergarments soaked in blood and*
> *semen, the image of Richard Forest flashing before her eyes.'*

"Again, Richard Forest rises from the depths of Clara's past—not only in letters from the demon—but in actual experiences, perhaps even sexual encounters. Why? What is the relationship between Forest and Miss Fowler, past and present? If these references whet one's appetite for a more conclusive connection, it comes in the form of a letter, again, from the demon, who threatens to divulge Clara's 'secret' to you.

"Letter, demon to Miss Fowler, January 4, 1899:

> *'You dear, sweet, good little girl! Never heard of Forest*
> *before, did you? No wonder Prince is utterly disgusted with*
> *you, can't even confess straight!*
>
> *I'm going to tell him everything, then we'll see what he*
> *thinks of you. Damn you, lying little harlot, from here to*
> *eternity!*
>
> *Your loving Guardian,*
> *X'*

"The key to Miss Fowler's treatment, I believe, lies in the relationship between Forest and Clara. What happened between them? What role might it have played in bringing about her condition? Therein lies the answer to the deep-seated terror that plunged the real Miss Fowler into the abyss of her unconscious, exactly as you theorized."

He handed Prince his notes. More than familiar with the content, he examined them perfunctorily and handed them back. He thought for a moment, then smiled at James, feeling in that instant like he was riding the spine of medical history.

"Thank you, Will," he said, rising from the sofa, shaking his hand heartily. "Odd, is it?" he reflected before turning to leave. "That the key to Miss Fowler's cure would come from the demon that possesses her."

Professor James watched him walk to the door and open it.

"He won't stop, you know," James declared in a hard-edged voice.

"Beg pardon?"

"Bassett. He won't stop until he gets what he wants."

"I know," Prince said, then walked out the door.

FOUR

Leonora Piper's home
243 Park Avenue
Arlington, Massachusetts

A covey of Boston elite stood at the door to Leonora Piper's home where she lived with her husband William, and two daughters, Alta, thirteen, and Minerva, fourteen. The sitters for the evening's séance included British Physicist, Sir Oliver Lodge; Alice James, a believer trying to contact her deceased son; Caroline Endicott, wife of industrialist Henry, an agnostic attending her first séance; Dr. George Waterman, Prince's protégé; and Richard Hodgson, representing the Society of Psychical Research.

Mr. Piper led them into the living room where the medium conducted her sessions.

"Leonora will be out momentarily," he told them.

Hodgson watched Alice James and the others drift toward some family portraits hung on the wall, then looked around the familiar setting. The room was unremarkable: Chesterfield sofa, carved wood armchairs, dark floral rug, and a fireplace. What was remarkable to Hodgson was the complete absence of Spiritualist props, no cabinets, crystal ball or circle of chairs, just a modest oak table with three candles at its center, a pillow, a stack of writing paper, and 5 pencils.

"Do you know Mr. Hodgson?" Alice James asked Sir Oliver, broaching the silence.

"Yes, I'm here as Richard's guest—from Great Britain," he answered succinctly.

Caroline Endicott, speaking to Alice James, said, "What is that you have with you?"

"It's my son, Herman's, blanket. Mrs. Piper suggested I bring an intimate possession to the séance."

"Are you a believer?" Sir Oliver asked Dr. Waterman brusquely.

"Like you, I'm here as an observer. I've never been to a séance."

"Just so," interrupted Hodgson, patting him on the back as he approached. "I've attended dozens, examined Mrs. Piper, head to toe, for any sign of chicanery and I can tell you her psychic abilities are genuine."

Waterman pushed his glasses up on his nose.

"Well, I suppose we should sit," he suggested.

And they did. Each positioned around the table. The chair with the pillow in front of it left glaringly empty.

"You say you've done this before?" Caroline Endicott inquired.

"Many times," Hodgson answered.

"How does it work exactly?" Sir Oliver asked. "I'm new to all of this."

"It's simple. Mrs. Piper sits, lays her head down on that pillow," he explained, pointing, "and meditates, elevating her mind to a higher plane where she communicates with the spirit world. Once there, she petitions her 'spirit guide' to channel a particular soul from amongst the others. The 'spirit guide,' usually a man named George Pelham, uses Mrs. Piper's eyes, ears, and vocal cords to describe what he is seeing and hearing in the life beyond."

Alice James turned toward the entrance, followed by Mrs. Endicott and the others as Mrs. Piper entered. They stood to greet her.

Described as a "reluctant" talent in Spiritualist circles, Leonora was tall and thin with wan, gentle eyes, and raven-black hair pulled back tight in a bun. She wore a plain ivory-colored dress, long and cut tight at the waist, looking staid and dignified.

"So good to see you, Richard," she said to Hodgson, working her way around the table. Then, she sat, hands folded in front of her, and began.

"For those attending for the first time, I must warn you. There will be no manifestation of spirits, no chairs levitating, or mysterious raps coming from the walls. What you will see is me go into a trance after which one of my 'spirit guides' will take over. There may or may not be messages given."

With that, the lights were put out and candles lit. They held hands, eyes shut in the near-dark.

"Dear spirit friends," she supplicated, "please draw near me. Give me a glimpse into eternity while we open our souls to the departed. We cherish God's light within and reject the devil's darkness without. Come forward bounteous spirits. What do you have to tell us?"

She took the baby blanket Alice James had given her, brought it to her cheek, then rested her head on the pillow in front of her.

"What's happening?" Mrs. Endicott whispered to Hodgson.

"She's putting herself in a trance," he answered, eyes locked on Mrs. Piper. "Once in that state, she can be cut, burned, even made to inhale ammonia, and it will not affect her."

Piper's body began to quake, unnoticeably at first, then beyond denial. The legs of her chair began to rattle on the hardwood floor.

"The voice you will hear is not her own, but that of her 'spirit guide,'" Hodgson confided in hushed tones. "Her pulse rate will lower, her respiratory functions, tactile sensibilities, and motor innervations will be suspended."

The sitters watched eyes fastened on the medium. She slowly lifted her head from the pillow. The skin on her face contracted. Her eyeballs rolled back into their sockets as she tried to discern a single voice from the myriad voices that cried out to her. Then, with a stab of discovery, she said, "Pelham!"

"What's happening now?" Mrs. Endicott asked, excitedly.

"Imagine static coming from the worn cylinder of a gramophone. Mrs. Piper is channeling powers, trying to receive signals in this world from discarnate spirits subsisting in the next."

Piper's body turned rigid. She began trembling with a fury that rocked the table. Her eyes squinted as if staring into some dark corner of eternity. She shuddered with one last tremor, then a grunt, as if Pelham had finally reached his destination.

Piper's spirit guide introduced himself, the medium's facial expression, mannerisms, and voice now unmistakably a man.

With eyes closed, Pelham took the baby blanket in his hands, kneading his fingers through it, then reached for a pencil and wrote the name "**HERRAN**'.

Hodgson snatched the paper and handed it to Alice James.

"Herman, yes, yes—"

"I see a woman holding an infant in her arms," the spirit guide professed, face taut, eyelids fluttering, "she says her name is Mary."

"Yes," Mrs. James said, excitedly, looking to the others, "that's my husband's mother who passed away three years ago! But the baby," she asked, worriedly, "is he better now? Is he still so terribly ill?"

A jittery silence followed. All that could be heard was the beating of Alice James' heart, until finally Pelham wrote the word "**GUILT**' and the world seemed to stop moving.

"Yes, guilt that haunts me! I should never have come home so soon after recovering from the fever," she confessed, weeping. "The doctors told me not to, but I did anyway. It's my fault, Herman, that you took ill and died!"

"No, it was not you," the spirit guide said, speaking in a woman's voice, firm and clear. "It was god who called him home."

"Mary, is that you?"

"Your child is at peace. Healthy and happy here until you join us."

"It is!" she marveled. "It is you!"

"You mustn't feel guilt. There is no guilt here," the voice of Mary Robinson Walsh revealed, trailing off as it departed, "only peace."

Pelham returned the blanket to Alice James, who clutched it to her breast, crying for joy.

"Your baby is safe now, Mrs. James. No pain. No illness," Waterman said, gently touching her shoulder.

"Yes," Caroline Endicott comforted. "Herman is home now. He wishes you peace and happiness."

The table was suddenly alive with joy. Alice clung to her baby's blanket. Then noticed, "Pelham is still here! He's making contact!"

All eyes darted to the spirit guide, his features contorted, struggling to channel a solitary soul from the sea of voices that engulfed him.

"Something's wrong," Hodgson muttered. "It shouldn't be like this!"

Pelham writhed in his chair, weird and chilling. The sinews of his neck pulled taut like cables.

"He has gone too far," Hodgson spouted, rising from his chair. "Mrs. Piper's body. I don't think she can take much more!"

Heart throbbing with nightmarish resonance, Pelham looked to Hodgson with absent, haunted eyes. His lips moved wordlessly as if trying to warn him. But it was too late. A single soul had announced its presence.

The spirit guide's voice and mannerisms changed to those of Sylvia Griffin.

"Where am I?" she asked.

"You are in Boston."

"Mr. Hodgson, is that you?"

"Yes, it is me, Miss Griffin."

"My throat," she complained, Pelham lifting his hands to his neck, "something about my throat. I think I am dead," she said, vaguely. "Am I dead?"

A baleful silence followed.

"Yes, you killed yourself by hanging," Waterman answered, blue eyes wide behind his glasses. "Why did you do it?"

The spirit guide became agitated.

"Did it have to do with Miss Fowler?" Hodgson persisted, then stopped abruptly.

He and the others watched, spellbound, as Pelham, staring ahead blankly, put his right hand over his shoulder, stretching his arm beyond anything that seemed humanly possible. Down and down still farther, until his hand reached the base of his spine, where he began tracing letters with his finger as if carving them into his flesh. Then, with a contemptuous grin, he scrutinized each of them, feature by feature, as if to affirm the contortions Sylvia Griffin had gone through moments before hanging herself.

A sense of foreboding swept like a chill through the hearts of the sitters.

"What in god's name is happening?" Alice James gasped, eyes wide and harrowed.

"Yes, exactly what, Hodgson?" Sir Oliver demanded.

The psychic researcher spun around to face him.

"I don't know!" he screamed, the blood draining from his face.

Waterman leaned his body forward on the table, about to say something, but fell back in his chair, open-mouthed. Pelham had taken two pencils, one in each hand, and was writing furiously on two separate sheets of paper as Sylvia Griffin's voice spoke through him.

"I wanted to be a nun in a convent and devote my life to Jesus," she lamented. "That is all I ever wanted."

Her words faded into the sullen air, then hung there, dark and chilling. But her writing continued. The sitters watching, breathless.

"What did she write?" Waterman implored.

Hodgson snatched the sheets from the table and examined them.

"She wrote the word 'PUNISH'," he read, eyes devouring the first sheet, "and two words and a number on the second: 'BURN', 'NUNS', '870'," he told them.

"What does that mean?" Waterman asked.

"Don't you see, it's gibberish!" barked Sir Oliver. "All of it nonsense!"

The boneyard quiet was pierced by Sylvia Griffin's screams.

"Burn! Burning with the others!" she screeched, as if consumed by flames, while both hands scribbled madly.

'CUT', 'SCOTLAND', she scrawled with one hand; 'LIPS', 'BLEED', 'FIRE' with the other.

Hodgson's head jerked up. Pelham went pale with horror as Sylvia Griffin unleashed a scream straight from hell.

"Dark. It's dark here," she muttered, voice receding. "Cold. Insane. Here with things that were never human!"

The sitters watched, a crawling terror mounting within them as Sylvia Griffin's spirit withdrew, leaving Putnam behind, facial musculature twitching spasmodically, before Leonora Piper collapsed on the table.

Alice James dashed to her; Caroline Endicott one step behind.

"She's breathing," Mrs. James reported, putting her palm to the medium's heart. "Her pulse is weak," she said, feeling for it, "but getting stronger!"

Hodgson, standing by the fireplace with Sir Oliver, held the sheets of paper at eye level, studying them, mystified.

"I know what it means," Waterman said in a voice devoid of emotion.

"What?" Sir Oliver pounced. "What's that you said?"

The young professor looked up at the two men, the fire's flames reflecting off the lens of his glasses.

"I came across the story in my research for Dr. Prince. The number '870' and the words 'convent', 'nun', 'burning' and 'Scotland'—those references point to just one event. In 870 when an army of Viking raiders closed in on a Benedictine nunnery in Scotland the mother superior, Sister Aebee, told the nuns to disfigure themselves to keep the Vikings from raping them. Then she cut off her nose and lips, her fellow sisters following suit. When the Vikings arrived, they recoiled in horror at the sight of them and Sister Aebee's scheme seemed to have worked, until the Vikings carved a word into their backs, put them in cages, and burned them alive."

Caroline Endicott flew into Alice James' open embrace and buried her face in her bosom.

"This has all been too much for me, much too much for a woman of my sensibilities!"

"I know, Caroline, I know," Alice assuaged, watching over her shoulder as William, Leonora's husband, entered the room and, seeing his wife's condition, rushed to her.

"I've never seen this happen before. Nothing like it in the dozens of sittings Leonora has held here!"

Mr. Piper, bald, tall, wiry, helped his wife to her feet, clapped an arm around her, and began walking toward the foyer.

"I think it is time for you to leave," he said bluntly.

"Yes, of course," Hodgson began, "I cannot tell you how sorry I am," then stopped at seeing Piper's withering stare.

The ladies composed themselves as best they could and started for the door. The three men turned to take a last glimpse at the chair from which Leonora Piper had channeled her spirit guide, Pelham, moments before. They started to leave when, walking toward the foyer, Sir Oliver stopped and pivoted to Waterman.

"The word?" he said.

"Beg pardon?"

"You said the Vikings carved a word into the nuns' backs before burning them. What was it?"

"It was 'SPITE', Sir Oliver. The Vikings tortured and murdered those women for spite."

Hodgson, overhearing, said, "Isn't that the word that—"

"Yes," Waterman answered before leaving the Piper residence, along with the others.

FIVE

Prince's Office
September 4, 1899
2:15 p.m.

Dr. Prince hunched over his desk reading the latest letters forwarded to him by Clara Fowler to prepare for their afternoon appointment. He dropped back in his chair, thinking. His discussion with William James left him heartened but no less fearful about his patient's wellbeing. Prior to that, he felt rudderless; hellbent on achieving his goal, but unable to get there. It had been more than a year since Dr. Putnam turned over the case and while he and his team had gained a deeper understanding of her condition, they had accomplished almost nothing in the way of a therapeutic breakthrough.

If his theory of *dissociation* was correct, it was vital that the "psychical catastrophe" that shattered Miss Fowler's identity be uncovered. Now, thanks to James, he believed he had found the key to unlocking her unconscious memories. Her relationship with the ubiquitous Richard Forest.

The doctor perused a March 30th letter, demon to him. Its animus toward Clara Fowler was heart-stopping.

'My dear Dr. Prince—you are absurd and idiotic to waste your time on such a hypocrite and liar as our friend {Clara}. I don't like it and will not allow it.

Do you understand? Our friend is going to weep salt tears when she finds out the things I have planned for her. Won't it be jolly? And serve her right, too, for she thinks altogether too much of you and too little of my long-suffering Forest {Richard Forest}.

She needs discipline and my tender care. I know her a great deal better than you and I know she is wicked. Believe what I tell you!'

As Professor James deduced, the name Forest was never far from the demon's mind. What did it mean? Was the demon, as James theorized, trying to tell Clara some "dark secret" about her past? Whatever the motive, their effect was toxic.

Letter, Clara Fowler to Prince, April 2nd:

'Dear Dr. Prince,

I am so anxious to see you—and want you to please, please hypnotize me again. You know it is the only thing that can help me, and I am sure it is the only way, save fasting and vigil, to cast out this demon which rules me at its will. The bromide you gave me does not help, and I am beside myself. I try to remember, really I do, but my life is slipping away, and I am so nervous and tired. I want to sleep but cannot because I am in such terror of an attack.

I am stuttering awfully. It is so dreadful—all of it. If you are in the office tomorrow, I beg you see me!

Clara Fowler'

If Prince didn't know time was running out for his patient's physical and psychological survival before, he had no choice but to confront that reality now with the demon's ascent to unfettered control.

Letter, Demon to Prince, April 3rd:

> *'My dear Dr. Prince—rejoice with me and be exceedingly glad for I am on top of the heap at last! Never again shall I be squeezed {out of existence}. Ah, how good it is to do as I please while killing —ever so nicely—the saintly Miss Clara! And you, beast of a man —refused it to me. Hereafter, you shall be dead to us all!*
> *From Hell,*
> *X'*

Convinced the key to unlocking his patient's unconscious memories lay in understanding her relationship with Forest, the question remained, how to get there? The demon, who knew everything about Clara's past, was unwilling to cooperate. Antithetically, Clara, who wanted desperately to help, knew almost nothing about her involvement with Forest!

Still, there could be another path forward. During a recent consultation, Miss Fowler described being "stricken with terror" at the onset of a violent storm that passed through the city. An acute phobia acquired "five or six years" ago. Prior to that, she confided, thunderstorms were of little concern to her. So, what changed? If Prince had to pin down a timeframe, it began during the summer of 1893 while employed at Fall River Hospital. Could Clara's phobia and amnesia regarding her past be connected?

A knock sounded at the door.

"Come in," Prince said, pushing the letters aside.

Miss Fowler entered.

"Please," he said, gesturing toward the settee, "make yourself comfortable."

His careful gaze held steady as he took a seat across from her: frightfully thin, face drawn and anemic. A ghost of the woman he first began treating.

"During our February 26th consultation, you described being 'stricken with terror' at the coming of a thunderstorm. I believe it would be helpful to take you back to that day through hypnosis."

"Yes, please do, Dr. Prince," she pleaded. "Anything to rid myself of this 'thing' inside me!"

The doctor began the hypnotic process. Moments later, she was in a deep trance.

"Three weeks ago, you said you became terrified at the coming of a thunderstorm, do you remember?"

"Yes."

"What happened after experiencing that 'terror'?"

"I ran from the tearoom and took a streetcar home."

"And then?"

"It was raining—thunder, lightning. I ran to my room and bolted the door!"

"Were you ever afraid of thunder and lightning before?"

"Yes," she answered, "for some time now."

"Can you remember the first occasion you became afraid?"

"No," she said flatly.

Prince twirled the corner of his mustache between his thumb and forefinger contemplating his next move.

"It was five or six years ago while employed at Fall River Hospital," he said, looking down at his notes.

"I don't remember—"

"You were working as a student-nurse," he prompted.

She shook her head as if trying to break loose some far-removed memory from her past.

"Great explosions of thunder!" she cried out abruptly. "A patient running down the corridor toward me."

"Yes, go on."

Her eyes flashed open as a vision of the events that night erupted, volcanic, from her subconscious.

"Thunder crashing. Lightning, like flashes of daylight, ripping open the sky!" She shivered. "The man grabs me by the shoulders screaming! I look into his eyes. He is raving. The orderlies take him away!"

"Where are you now?"

"Still in the hospital."

The doctor's stare turned intense.

"What day is it?"

"Thursday, June 7, 1893."

"Try to remember," Prince prodded, "did anything else happen that night to frighten you?"

"Forest!" she sputtered. Then, straining to remember, "Something to do with Forest."

"Fix your mind back to that night," he urged, "June 7, 1893. There is thunder and lightning. The orderlies have taken the patient away. What are you doing now?"

She squirmed in her seat; shook her head violently.

"I don't know!" she screamed, clapping her hands over her ears. "I cannot tell you!"

The doctor tried to bring her back to that moment in time, but it was no use.

Miss Fowler either could not, or would not, remember.

SIX

Harvard Bridge
10:35 p.m.

Clara's thoughts found grip on the fog-silted night. She looked to the cluster of students who made their way from the Boston side of the Harvard Bridge to Cambridge, gray figures passing in the night. She leaned her body against the guardrail midway across the mud-brown darkness of the Charles River and stared dazedly at the fast-flowing water, her face blank, her mind numb with confusion. Only her breath had life. It came shallow and labored, then vanished in the hungry air.

Desperate. Lonely. Cursed. Her life had been absorbed by a nameless, shapeless presence. Who was she? What had she become? Even moments she called her own were plagued by shame and the corrosive dread that she would succumb to it again. She had dropped out of school and lost her job. Bills were piling. What money she had was destroyed by the demon upon receipt. Mrs. Kerr, frightened of her now, demanded she move. Even Dr. Prince's optimism at finding a cure had ebbed into a mire of hopelessness.

She shifted her eyes to the moon. Clouds scudded past, magnifying its beaming light with images of Christ nailed to the cross; the Virgin sobbing, blood-tears streaming down the sides of her face; her mother, Mary, "Jump," she hissed, eyes lit with fever, "do it for me!" Her father, John, leaning on a dirt-covered spade, spurring her on, "Yes, jump; penance for the evil you done!"

Clara climbed up on the steel-slat railing, swung a leg over it.

"We know what you are," Sylvia Griffin accused, neck wrung, head lolled to one side; Mrs. Kerr looked Clara up and down with disgust, "Girls like you do not deserve to live," she snarled; then the lilting trill of Charles, her brother, "We love you, Clara," he swore, "and want you with us," "want you with us," Bessie's voice echoed, floating amid the undulating clouds.

Clara whipped her body over the railing into the slashing wind. She stood wavering precariously at the bridge's fringe.

"Jump!" her father shouted, face twisted with fury.

"Jump," Sylvia Griffin advised, "you know, you are better off dead."

"Jump!" her mother screeched, rising from her deathbed.

"Jump," Charles and Bessie wheedled, voices in perfect unison.

"Yes, do it!" shouted Mrs. Kerr, face turned crimson. "Die, you bitch!"

Clara's eyes dropped to the river's raging current. Her hands clutched the rail from behind, fingers absorbing the tingling cold of metal on flesh.

"The time is right for you to join us," the One counseled, jackal teeth bared, face molded into a seductive smile. "Die and you shall live with me forever. No more sickness. No more disease."

Clara's eyes grew large. She shifted her weight forward onto her toes, bent her knees, and thrust her body outward toward the sky and river.

"No! Don't do it!" she heard a man's voice lash out into the night, her body jerked back forcibly by the thick-muscled arm coiled around her waist.

Heart in throat, her eyes fluttered awareness. Perhaps she'd passed out, her mind darted, or dropped like a marionette whose wires had been severed from the demon's clutches. She did not know, cognizant of just one reality, the face of the man staring down at her, rubbing her cheeks and eyes and temples, trying to revive her.

"Who are you?" she breathed, grasping that she lay sprawled on the bridge's walkway.

"A friend," he answered, lifting her to her feet.

With arm clasped around her, he hailed a cab and ordered it to the home of the only man he knew could help her.

They exited the cab at 458 Beacon Street. He helped Clara up the stone stairs of the red-brick row house and rang the doorbell. Dr. Prince answered aghast at the sight of them.

"Bassett!" he huffed.

"She had nowhere else to go," Bassett explained, steed derby held at his side, "and I couldn't take her to my hotel."

"Certainly not!" he said indignantly, taking Miss Fowler into a protective embrace. "What in blazes is going on here?"

The Marshal looked him straight in the eye.

"I found her on Harvard Bridge. She tried to jump and would have had I not stopped her."

Prince's expression softened. He glanced into Clara's vacant eyes then back to the Marshal.

"I suppose I should thank you," he said.

"No thanks needed," he replied, clapping his derby on his head. "You see, I care about Miss Fowler, too."

Prince shut the door. Fanny came running down the stairs, then stopped, startled to find Miss Fowler standing in the foyer.

"Is there anything I can get you?" Prince asked Clara. "Perhaps, you'd like to go to bed, or talk for a while?"

She did not answer, but stood, feet riveted to the floor, dead eyes staring straight ahead.

"Miss Fowler?" His soft voice turned emphatic. "Miss Fowler!"

The doctor assessed her, then watched as an amazing transformation began. Upon arrival, Clara was nervous, depressed, viscerally exhausted. But suddenly, like an electric light switching 'on', her face brightened, her eyes beamed life. She appeared an entirely different person.

"Morton," Fanny asked, "should I prepare a bed for Miss Fowler?"

But Prince did not answer, spellbound. He took a cautious step toward Miss Fowler, studying her face, eyes, posture.

Her spine stiffened as he approached. Her eyebrows raised superciliously.

"Who are you?" she demanded.

"I'm Dr. Prince, your physician."

"You know you're not."

"If not Dr. Prince, who am I?"

"You ought to know who you are!"

"Who?"

"Richard, of course."

"No," he insisted, "I'm Dr. Prince."

"Richard Forest," she chided, "I will not participate in this nonsense any longer! Why did you come here?"

"I came to see you," Prince responded, deciding to play the part of Richard Forest. "Why is that a problem?"

She shook her head, laughing, "Well, you risk breaking your neck for one thing!"

"How would I break my neck?" he asked.

"By coming through the hospital window!" She scoffed, then laughed again. "Oh, Richard, you are perfectly mad!"

His eyes narrowed. "In what place are we right now?"

"Fall River hospital."

"And today's date?"

"June 7, 1893, of course!" She sighed heavily. "I think I've had quite enough of your tomfoolery!"

The doctor tried to prolong the conversation but the woman, bright, lively, quick at badinage, refused.

"Shall I take her upstairs to the guest room, Morton?" Fanny asked.

"Yes," he muttered absently, watching Miss Fowler strut toward the staircase, "there will be plenty of time to pursue what's happened here tonight."

But exactly what had happened? Another twist in Clara's labyrinthian medical history? The demon's handiwork?

Soon, the mystery would deepen.

IV: ABYSS

"Do not pray for the damned, for prayer is a torture in Hell...It is a redoubling of pain... I am speaking to you as a damned soul, do you hear? Do you understand?"
–Charles Arnold van Gennep
Archives de Psychologie

ONE

Prince's Office
2:15 p.m.

Life was moving fast during Boston's *"belle epoch,"* Morton Prince was thinking as he gazed from his window. Theodore Roosevelt, governor of New York, was rapidly emerging as leader of the Republican Party; Sigmund Freud was basking in the success of his newly published treatise, *The Interpretation of Dreams*; Nicola Tesla rocked the scientific world proving his theory of terrestrial waves by lighting 200 light bulbs without wires from a distance of 25 miles. It was no wonder that, during moments of silent reflection, Prince felt life was passing him by—with one exception.

He strode to his desk and lit a cigar, awaiting his team's arrival. After months of failure, he may have finally found a breakthrough both in Clara's recovery and his own legacy. The past two years left him with a mountain of information, but like tiles in a mosaic the pieces required the proper arrangement to see the picture that was emerging.

Sylvia Griffin had committed suicide, shocking; Bassett had saved Clara's life, astounding; and now this, the discovery of—what to call it?—another shard in the shattered mirror that was Miss Fowler's identity. A 'shard' was one way to see it, he speculated. But, if the newcomer proved to be a full-blown personality, there was the possibility that it supported his theory of *dissociation*. Could it be that as in a Rip Van Winkle fairy tale the real Miss Fowler had returned after a years' long sleep to reclaim her identity?

He dropped back in his chair, mind adrift. There was precedent for it. Similar cases where an individual, subsumed into their own consciousness after a severe trauma, emerged months, even years, later to supplant the imposter. The case of the Reverend Ansel Bourne came to mind. Bourne woke one morning living under the name John Brown in Jerusalem, Pennsylvania running a shop he had opened. Upon coming to himself, he didn't know where he was or how he got there. It was later discovered that after surviving a railway accident, he underwent an abrupt change of identity, wandering from his home in Rhode Island to Pennsylvania, where he lived and worked for two years. After returning to himself, the Reverend's mind was a total blank for that period, believing he was still in Rhode Island and seconds, not years, had elapsed!

Prince tried to recreate the circumstances of the "woman's" arrival. Clearly, she believed he was Richard Forest, they were meeting in Fall River, and it was June, 1893. Hence, Miss Fowler's situation was not unlike Bourne's in that after a severe shock, both awakened in a location foreign to them with no memory for the time that had passed.

But could a simple thunderstorm be the "catastrophic trauma" that triggered Miss Fowler's disorder? It seemed unlikely and, while their previous session substantiated one truth, it suggested something more. First, the stormy night the newcomer perceived as current was also the date Clara's phobia for thunderstorms began. Second, when pressed about what happened that night, Clara did not say "nothing," but said instead, "I cannot tell you", suggesting that something beyond the storm had, indeed, occurred.

Today, Prince vowed, he would uncover the "dark secret" that sent the genuine Miss Fowler hurdling to the farthest reaches of her unconscious, where she remained buried for seven long years!

At 3:00 p.m., the doctor's colleagues—James, Hodgson, Waterman—entered his office. They greeted one another, then fell into their customary positions to the back of the room where they took notes documenting critical consultations.

"I agree we may be on the cusp of something massively important," William James said, advancing his argument with Waterman, "but don't see how today's session will differ from the last. Is it that Miss Fowler cannot remember or simply does not know what happened on the night of June 7th?"

"The issue is memory, not facts," Prince interrupted, joining the group. "Miss Fowler knows whatever trauma occurred that night at Fall River Hospital, but not as Clara, whose memory begins where the "woman's" left off."

James and Hodgson looked at him, bewildered.

"I realize this may sound convoluted, but I believe June 7th represents the "birth" of Clara, the "saint," and the death of the real Miss Fowler. If my theory is correct, Miss Fowler, as Clara, knows nothing of the event that created her, but the "woman," he said, stabbing a finger in the air, "the "woman" knows not only what happened that night, but how both the "saint" and "demon" came into existence."

"But how?" Hodgson interjected. "How will you unlock those memories?"

"Memories are not the problem, Richard. The problem is I have been addressing the right questions to the wrong person. Beyond that, I shall use *visual recognition*. Dr. Waterman," he said, turning to his protégé, "explain the method to them."

Waterman drew up proudly.

"To facilitate the practice of *hypnotic retrogression*, Dr. Prince will utilize *visual recognition*, a technique used by Dr. Boris Sidis in his treatment of Thomas H, a patient who, literally, lost a lifetime of knowledge after suffering a head injury. He could not speak or understand English. People he had known during his lifetime from parents to his wife and children were total strangers to him. In short, his memory had been reduced to an infant's, but his mind was that of an adult in its capacity to think, reason, and form judgements."

"*Visual recognition*?" Hodgson objected. "I never heard of it!"

Prince gave Waterman a nod of approval, then took over.

"What Sidis discovered was that Thomas H's memories were not obliterated but displaced and could be recovered. When "fixing his mind" on a crystal globe while hypnotized and instructing him to visualize certain scenes from his life, the names of individuals, places, conversations, whole passages from books, totally lapsed from his memory, flashed lightning-like into his mind."

"You'll try *visual recognition*, not on Clara, but the "woman," correct?" James asked.

"Yes," Prince answered, "that is my strategy, precisely." Then, turning toward the door, "She's here."

Miss Fowler entered the study. Prince led her to the couch, where she sat on the settee. He took a seat across from her. From the start, the doctor understood this was not Clara, nor the "demon," but the new entity, haughty, self-confident and assertive, still insisting it was Richard Forest she had seen the night before.

Moments later, he put her into a trance, using a crystal globe to facilitate the retrogression. Before him, sat the "woman."

"I want you to go back to last night when you entered my home. Do you understand?"

She nodded.

"Where are you?"

"I am in the nurses' sitting room."

"At the hospital in Fall River?"

"Yes."

"What day is it?"

"It is Thursday, June 7th."

"What year?"

"1893, of course!"

"Is that the night you saw Richard Forest?"

"Yes." She laughed. "Atop a ladder staring at me from outside the window!"

"What happened after you saw Forest's face in the window?"

"I don't remember."

"Did you see Forest after that?"

"No," she answered resolutely. "I stayed on duty the rest of the night."

"Now I want you to relax and fix your mind on the crystal globe to witness whether you saw him again."

She gazed into the globe.

"I have got it, Dr. Prince! It is curious. I see there are two. But I don't understand. No, it's impossible! It's not true—it cannot be. No! No! No! None of this is happening! None of it is true!"

"Look into the globe," Prince insisted. "Did you see Forest again that night?"

She jerked her head away, clapping her palms onto her temples.

"It's not true! This did not happen. Nothing I see is true. Nothing I hear is true. It cannot be!"

"Calm yourself, Miss Fowler. Fix your mind on the crystal globe and tell me what you see."

"I can see two," she uttered, eyes narrowing to slits as she peered into the globe. "We meet and he takes me outside. We walk—" she said, then stopped. "No! I don't see it. I do not hear it. I would tell you if what I see is true. It's impossible!"

"What do you see?"

"I see myself," she whispered tremulously.

"With whom?"

"Forest!" she screamed. "But not like himself. All is dark except for flashes of lightning." She became distracted and answered dreamily. "But it can't be Forest. His face is drawn. He is excited." Then, as the vision came into focus, "He is angry—not like himself at all—his face twisted with rage. His eyes are on fire. It's dark and lightning flashes illuminate his face. I am terrified!"

"Where are you?" Prince exhorted.

"In the woods outside the hospital. I'm sure it's not true. The vision is fading. It's all horrid. I don't like visions like this. It never happened!" Then, drawn back to the globe like steel to a magnet, she gazed into it again. "I see trees lashing in the wind. He is perfectly mad; not like I have ever seen him before. He rips open my dress," she said, voice quavering, "and throws me to the ground! I see him climbing on top of me. I scream. I am being raped! Richard Forest is raping me!" she cried out, burying her face in her hands.

The doctor took her out of trance. As in the past, she had no memory of what transpired. Stunned, neither Hodgson nor James, Waterman or Prince, inquired beyond what they had already seen.

TWO

Tavern Club

Myriad thoughts streamed through Prince's mind after the breakthrough session with Miss Fowler. None involved dinner and an art competition. Still, Fanny was right suggesting he take a break from the case, he thought, sitting at a table in the Tavern Club, post-dinner. Since giving up his professorship at Tufts Medical School, the Fowler case had become an obsession, compromising his medical practice and health. There was an unaccountable trembling in his fingers; a twitching in his bones that had become his companion since taking Clara Fowler on as a patient. When he slept, he was haunted by nightmares, always forgotten.

"Morton," Fanny said, jarring him from his reverie. "I think you may have won the competition! I've looked at the others and I'm certain yours is best."

"Not bad for a psychotherapist who never put a brush to canvas," he answered, vaguely.

"I agree with Fanny!" Howard Weller, the architect, declared hoisting a glass in the air. "Here's to Dr. Morton Prince and his career as an artist!"

The others at the table followed suit. Prince raised his glass in the air with a tenuous smile.

The contest was open to club members and local artists. Thinking painting would offer her husband respite from his work, Fanny recommended he enter a portrait. He did, and characteristically, it became a personal challenge. Though he'd never painted before, the doctor rolled up his sleeves and, with microscopic precision, turned out a self-portrait as good as any.

"Our winner, chosen by the judges, for best painting," Edward Meyer, the club president announced, "goes to our very own Dr. Morton Prince for his self- portrait 'Reflection'!" His eyes shifted to Prince's table. "Dr. Prince, would you like to say a few words?"

Shocked and flustered, he waved a hand in the air as friends and colleagues applauded.

"Go up and accept your award, Morton!" Fanny prodded.

The doctor shambled to the podium. Meyer handed him a plaque that read, 'To Dr. Morton Prince, First Place Art Competition, April 4, 1900', shook his hand, and turned the microphone over.

DREAMS, he was thinking as he looked out at the wave of guests and club members, nightmares running darkly through his bloodstream.

"As most of you know, I do not pretend to be an artist, so I am honored to accept this plaque as, what I would call, a diligent amateur."

He mopped a skein of sweat from his forehead with a handkerchief. He closed his eyes and dragged air in and out of his lungs.

HAUNTING, chilling dreams that never left him.

"I am terribly sorry, but I'm suddenly at a loss for words—"

There was inside him like a flaw in a jewel, not visible on the surface, a nagging prescience of disaster; predatory, stalking.

"I want to thank—"

His brain swam sickeningly.

"I would like to—"

PREMONITION of collapse. His legs. Weak at the knees. Then, darkness!

The glittering light from the chandelier above him twinkled, surreal. He was walking;, he knew. But how? He could not feel his legs under him, but sensed the others' presence holding him up, dragging him forward.

It had to be a dream, he was thinking, when suddenly, like a shade drawn to block the rays of a full moon, all went black again. Darkness. Nothing.

"Where am I?" he asked, adjusting his eyes to the light.

A face stared down at him. It was William James.

"Will?"

"Yes," he answered.

"Where am I?"

"Mass General. I brought you here after you passed out."

"At the club?"

"Yes, but you're all right now. It was exhaustion, Morton."

"Fanny? Claire?"

"They are outside in the waiting room."

Prince looked around the room, face taking on color, pulse strong again.

"How long have I been here?"

"An hour. Two at most. Do you want to sit up?"

"Yes, thank you," he murmured.

James pulled a chair to the bed, sat down, settled his long frame in it.

"You know, you can't go on like this, Morton. True, you are athletic: horse-riding, golf, tennis. But that's not the point. Something is wrong. Something more. I can see it in your eyes. I'd like you to tell me about it."

The doctor put his head down, pinched the corners of his eyes with thumb and finger.

"You are my friend, is that right?"

"You have no better," James swore.

"I cannot bring myself to sleep," he admitted, "and when I do, I'm haunted by dreams, horrible nightmares. Behind me, I can sense vague tracks; menacing eyes, fixed on some easy prey within me."

"How long have you been like this?"

"Months, maybe longer."

"You've tried sedatives—"

"They don't help."

James appraised his friend of thirty years.

"These dreams—do they have something to do with the Fowler case?"

"I don't know," he answered, shaking his head slowly. "But one dream I remember. In it, I watched two boys, perhaps eight and ten, busy doing some kind of work. They were on their knees on either side of a boy, about three years of age, who was lying flat on the ground with two slats of wood under him, one horizontal, the other vertical, in the shape of a T. The boy's arms were extended outward, his feet held together, one over the other. It was comforting to see the older boys, absorbed as they were, working so diligently. And in my dream, I smiled. But, then, I looked closer and realized they had made a cross out of wood and were nailing the boy to it. They were crucifying him, Will. They crucified that three-year-old boy!"

William James felt something cold land on his heart. He mulled over what he'd heard, then nodded knowingly.

"I've seen situations like this before, Morton. Cases where an individual becomes so immersed in another's delusion that he, himself, believes it. In my research, I came across an African tribe where a witch doctor put a hex on a fellow tribesman. Lo and behold, seven days later, the man died. As you know better than I, it wasn't the curse that killed him. It was his belief in the potency of it; a kind of *auto-suggestion* that convinced him the witch doctor had the power to influence, not only his mind, but his physical wellbeing." James held him at arm's length. "You're a strong man, Morton. Not the kind to let emotions interfere with progress. It's my belief your inquiry into the Fowler case will change the science of psychology forever and I have faith you will see it through to the end." His gaze probed unwaveringly into Prince's. He smiled. "Now, don't you think it's time we brought Fanny and Claire in to see you? They've been beside themselves with worry."

Prince watched James walk out of the room to fetch them. He laid his head down on his pillow, thinking about Leonora Piper's warning and the prospect of infection. That is, the physician or exorcist coming to the aid of the victim, themselves, becoming possessed. He remembered the account he heard about the possession of the nuns at the Ursuline convent. Of the four priests sent to stem the epidemic, three not only became possessed but died soon after while the fourth went insane and spent the rest of his life in a lunatic asylum.

That's when it struck him. A feeling of dread that ran like particles of ice through his bloodstream. Was he leading Miss Fowler to cure, or was the Demon leading him to madness?

THREE

Parker House Hotel
Boston, Massachusetts
June 28, 1900
7:00 p.m.

Rufus "Bassett" Hilliard crushed an Old Judge cigarette with the heel of his boot, then slipped quietly into the School Street entrance of the Parker House. His eyes flew up from the rim of his derby to the lobby's vaulting ceiling, studded with crystal chandeliers, leveling to the bronze-framed windows and red Aubusson carpet that swept from the hotel entrance to the registration desk.

Tonight was the Boston Symphony Orchestra's last performance at the Music Hall and the hotel was bristling with excitement. The orchestra, conducted by Wilhelm Gericke, would perform Beethoven's Choral Choir # 9 and everyone from the Princes to the Dwights, to the James and Lowells, were celebrating at a dinner party held in honor of the occasion.

The Marshal took a seat and waited. The dinner crowd would disperse into the lobby any minute on their way to the concert. He could not have asked for better cover.

For weeks he had been tailing Clara Fowler to the Parker House, suite 303, where her blazing sexual liaisons with Forest were observed through a bay window and concealed dictograph. What went on in that room was perverse even by his standards, grizzled, and corrupted since his plunge into the maelstrom of the Borden and Corriero murders.

Through research into public records, interviews with business associates, and clandestine study of Clara's consultations with Prince, Bassett had developed a profile of the enigmatic Richard Forest. Even now, while waiting to search his hotel room, he could tap into his eidetic memory to visualize what he had written.

SURVEILLANCE REPORT
Marshal Rufus Hilliard
Subject: Richard Forest
Age: 52
Occupation: Contractor
Employer: Prichett Coal Company
Beverly, Massachusetts

FOREST-FOWLER RELATIONSHIP
February, 1887—Forest hires John
Fowler, brick layer/mason, becomes a
close family friend based on interest
in 14-year-old Clara.
March, 1899—Clara tells Forest her
father is having sexual relations with
her.
Summer, 1889—Forest discovers John
Fowler is "Satan Worshiper." Clara
confides belief that her father
murdered her brother, Charles, and
sister, Bessie, their bodies
sacrificed in a Black Mass.
September, 1889—Forest, fearful for
his and Clara's safety, proposes
marriage; they move to San Antonio,
TX.

October, 1889—six weeks post-marriage, Clara deserts Forest, returns to Massachusetts.

FOREST ASSAULT
June 7, 1893—Forest returns to Boston, tracks ex-wife to Fall River Hospital where he rapes her during a violent thunderstorm.

CLARA FOWLER MEDICAL RECORD
1893-1897—Subject forced to abandon nursing career due to "erratic health."
March, 1898—Clara suffers from insomnia, weight loss, chronic fatigue, comes under care of Dr. Morton Prince; "dissociative" tendencies noted.
April, 1898—Demonic entity emerges; Prince is horrified/intrigued.
1898-1900—Doctor treats *neurasthenic* condition; uses *hypnotic retrogression* to uncover root cause of "curious" disorder.

SEXUAL ENCOUNTERS
May 1900—Clara re-establishes sexual relations with Forest; liaison Parker House Hotel (Clara under "demonic" control?).

INVESTIGATIVE STRATEGY: around-the-clock surveillance.

Christ Almighty! What he wouldn't give for a taste of Jack Daniels now, Bassett was thinking as he peered over his newspaper, watching dinner guests crowd into the hotel lobby. He folded the paper, returned it to the chair beside him, and got to his feet. He glanced at the cluster of guests gathered at the ground floor elevators and took the interior stairway to avoid scrutiny.

He threaded his way through the knots of men in long-tail tuxedos and women in embroidered evening gowns toward the staircase, catching a glimpse of a hand waving in the air at him.

"Bassett," Prince called out to him from across the room, "might I have a word?"

Goddamn! If there was one man in all of Boston he did not want to see, it was Dr. Morton Prince!

Instinctively, Bassett whirled around toward the elevators. He burrowed himself into the crowd and elbowed his way onto the first lift whose doors opened, leaving Prince, hand still in the air, looking as puzzled as he was chagrined.

He exited the elevator, stalked down the hallway toward suite 303. He thought he'd seen Forest leave the hotel two hours earlier, but how long before he returned? His eyes ran up and down the corridor. Seeing it was clear, he dug a pick from the pocket of his long coat, raked the lock, and pushed the door open.

He entered, sniffed the air. It was infused with the scent of cologne. A lot, he noticed, haunted eyes taking in every detail of the room from the silk window hangings to full-length dress mirror, stopping cold at the Louis XVI bed, Forest's wardrobe laid out atop it. Pensive and alert, he drifted toward the bed, charcoal dinner jacket, dress shirt, vest, men's laced-up shoes set side-by-side beneath it, and still that scent of cologne. No, more than a scent, a blizzard of fragrance, near suffocating. The smell, the clothes, untouched beyond the dinner hour. It didn't add up, he thought, whipping around at the low timbre of moaning emanating from the study to the left of him.

He pushed a lock of stray hair back from his forehead, yanked his .32 Colt revolver from beneath his belt and thrust it out in front of him, creeping toward the open annex, step-by-careful-step, until he stood at its threshold. From where he stood, he could see a bookcase, rolltop desk and high-iron floor lamp. All as it should be, he speculated. But the sound. Was it moaning, or the rattle of tortured breathing? He could not discern which, but knew something parlous waited little more than a step away.

Bassett inched forward, thoughts of his obsession with the Fowler murders wrenching him into the room, eyes shifting from right to left, ceiling to floor. Then, he saw it. Startled, at first, he staggered backward, then started toward it, alarm upended by a sense of duty.

Bound hand and foot to the arms and legs of a rosewood chair, sat a man tethered by rope with a black leather hood pulled over his head, chair planted in a pool of dark red blood.

Accustomed as any lawman to such atrocities, Bassett paused a moment to regain his sensibilities. Then, careful and resolved, he began pulling the leather hood up and up still further, to discover the unthinkable. Cut through the individual layers of *epidermis,* mid-skull to bone, the skin was pulled down from the scalp in a single sheet to an area below the chin; not cutting but ripping the skin off nerve ends one-by-one in what must have been a long train of agony.

The rattling sound from his lungs stopped. The man seemed to have ceased breathing, but upon closer inspection—ear pressed against heart, fingers feeling for pulse—Bassett's eyes widened with hope at the thump of a heartbeat. He hastened to free him, cutting the knot of rope binding his upper torso with a switchblade, then pausing to note: the breathing had stopped entirely.

Workman-like, he proceeded, releasing two wrists, then two ankles— cut, cut, cut—so, who was the poor bastard, anyway? Warily, he reached his arm around the body's upper torso, inserting his hand into the back pocket of his trousers. He tugged an alligator wallet out of it to look for identification, then froze, a glacial chill slithering up his spine. It was the corpse, clutching his wrist, dead fingers digging into his flesh!

Bassett's gaze dropped to the faceless man, his eyeballs popped shiny and maddened with head craned up, the musculature of his face laid bare, desperately mouthing a single word as he clapped a small wooden icon into the Marshal's hand.

"*Forever*," he said, pleadingly.

Then like a ship's lights fading into a distant sea, the glimmer in his eyes dimmed and the grip of his hand weakened, dropping to his side.

Slowly, the fingers of Bassett's closed fist opened. He studied the bizarre carving cradled in his palm. The icon was of a demonic deity with ragged wings, clawed fingers and taloned feet; mouth bowed-up in a feral grin.

He recognized it.

Its ferocity. Its hunger. The dizzying malevolence radiating from it.

The demon Abaddon, guardian of the Fall River cult.

Reflexively, his eyes darted to the body tethered straight up in the armchair in front of him. Still holding the man's billfold in his opposite hand, he stuffed the effigy into his pocket and flipped the wallet open. In it was an identification card issued by the Pritchett Coal Company bearing the name **RICHARD E. FOREST**.

But if this was Forest, Bassett wondered, who had he seen leaving the hotel two hours earlier?

FOUR

Prince's Home

Dr. Prince stood arms akimbo, directing Cody as he setup the Projecting Kinetoscope with Waterman, James, and Hodgson seated at the conference table in his study, waiting.

"That's right," the doctor instructed, pointing, "put the screen there, toward the front of the room."

"Did you hear the sirens blaring last night?" Hodgson asked James in a conspiratorial whisper.

"I didn't need to hear them. I was at the Parker House when it happened, or so Chief Homer tells me."

"The Music Hall reception?"

"Precisely."

Waterman's blue eyes opened wide.

"From what I hear, it was a nasty one."

"Beg pardon?"

"The murder," he explained. "Dr. Prince thinks it may have been a robbery."

"No one we know, I trust?" Hodgson asked.

"The Chief tells me the victim was an out-of-towner," the professor said, lighting his Meerschaum pipe. "A business-type from Fall River."

"Fall River," Hodgson repeated, a quiver of surmise rippling through him. "I'd wager Morton is right. He should have been a detective."

"Oh, but he is—and so are we," James reflected with a wry smile. "Detectives trying to solve life's 'Great Mystery.'"

Waterman was about to say something, but stopped. The Doctor approached.

"Gentlemen," he announced while Cody brought the projector's lens to focus, "may I suggest we return to the business at hand?"

But Hodgson ignored him, talking in that same roused whisper.

"It's like an epidemic of violence. From the killing at the Parker House last night, to the Borden murders, to H. H. Holmes' serial killings in Chicago!"

"Absolutely," James agreed, drawing on his pipe, "and that's what makes the Fowler case unlike any other. It sheds light into the darkest regions of the human psyche. Do you know what Black Goyas are?" he asked. "Then, you know that was the only time in all of art history when a genius allowed himself to deal with only the dark side of human nature. In our way, that's what we're doing."

"Dark, perhaps," Prince interjected, "but I think you'd agree Mr. Hodgson's theory of 'demonic possession' has been undercut by the emergence of the "woman"." He turned to Cody. "You can go now," he said, pointedly. Then, watching him leave, turned to the others. "Assembling the facts we've so far learned about the development of the "saint" and the "woman," I've put together the following historical summary: Miss Fowler was a single consciousness up to June 7, 1893. At that time, there occurred a psychic shock, namely Forest's assault, that cleaved her mind splitting off a quasi-somnambulistic personage that we know as Clara. The "saint" kept all of Miss Fowler's memories for the subsequent six years. That is, from June 7, 1893 to April 4, 1899 when the "woman" awakened with the memory of Miss Fowler's life prior to the assault."

"But if what you're saying is true," James wondered, "what awakened her?"

"To fully understand Miss Fowler's return, we must go back to the circumstances of her disappearance, June 7, 1893. Coincidentally, Miss Fowler's brother, Charles, died or was murdered, June 7, 1882," the doctor explained, pacing the floor in front of them. "One can only imagine what June 7th and the horrific events surrounding it meant to her. The impact of the rape, coupled with the anniversary of Charles' death, must have been devastating. So overwhelming that, rather than face the reality of Forest's barbarous act, she chose to submerge herself into the depths of her unconscious mind leaving behind a phantom self, the 'saint,' insulated from reality by religious fervor, comforted by the Virgin Mary, protected from the memory of that terrible night by her Savior, Jesus Christ."

"But the awakening of the 'woman,' Morton?" James insisted.

"Isn't it obvious? We *retrogressed* Clara back to the moment of her creation—Forest's assault—forcing her to confront the reality of her fractured existence, thus freeing the real Miss Fowler from the shackles of her self-imposed imprisonment. Then, there was this," he divulged, nabbing a sheet of writing paper from the tabletop, "a note written by the "demon" to Richard Forest the morning of the "woman's" awakening."

He began reading.

> "*Take me away at once! Prince is using his ether to make me dead. Meet me at Parker {House} and I will do anything you want, if only you'll stop him. Don't ask me more. There is a reason we must meet that I cannot tell you now. Only we must stop him!*'

"It was with the discovery of this letter," Prince theorized, "that Clara's most dreaded fears were confirmed. The demon was, indeed, engaged in a torrid affair with Richard Forest. More, she had uncovered the cause of the bruises and lacerations so often endured but never explained. The demon was subjecting her body to Forest's sadomasochistic perversions, physically torturing her to weaken it and maintain control. It was a realization that sent her reeling into the depths of despair." He leaned forward onto the conference table, his eyes scouring each of their faces. "In the end, it was the discovery of the letter that thrust Clara back to the night of June 7, 1893 and awakened the "woman"."

"Still, there's a piece missing," Hodgson objected. "Your theory doesn't account for the "demon" or the fact that it claims to have existed long before Forest's assault."

"Not unlike the psychotic who believes he is Caesar or Napoleon, I attribute it to demonic 'self-identification.' With the shattering of Miss Fowler's mind, two entities were born. The "saint" and the "demon". If the psychotic looks into a mirror and sees Napoleon, he will be adamant in his belief that Marie Louise was his wife, that he took power in the Coup of 18 Brumaire and was defeated by Wellington at Waterloo. So, too, when the demon looks into a mirror, it sees evil incarnate, a spirit possessing Miss Fowler's body, independent of time or physicality."

The doctor flicked on the projector. A grainy, black and white still-frame of Clara Fowler beamed onto the screen.

"Gentlemen, I give you the first of the three Miss Fowler's, Clara, the young Radcliffe student who has attached herself to our minds and hearts. Notice the facial expression," he said, seizing a wooden pointer from the tabletop, "pale and emaciated, *oculi* jutted out, cheekbones protruding beneath diaphanous skin. *Neurasthenic* in the extreme, she suffers from a lack of appetite, chronic insomnia, and weight loss, enduring debilitating blackouts increasing in frequency and duration. During these *fugues*, a second entity emerges, seizing control, rendering her a 'non-person,' devoid of thoughts, judgements, or willpower.

"During the past months," Prince continued, "we came to know Clara's joys and sorrows. Her exaltation in moments of religious ecstasy. Her bouts of despair spurred by the demon's hatred of her. But one complication emerges we have no choice but to acknowledge. The Clara Fowler we know is not real. The fondness we have for her, the emotions we feel, are our own projections onto a blank slate. The Miss Fowler we know is a splintered fragment of a genuine person, incapable of sustaining her existence."

Prince switched on the Kinetoscope's 'projecting' feature. The fractured frames of a consultation between he and Miss Fowler in her demonic state flickered onto the screen.

"Now, let us evaluate the second of the three Miss Fowlers filmed during a session two weeks ago."

An image of the doctor sitting in a chair across from the demon, leering, shuttered across the screen.

"You seem a trifle out of sorts today," the demon observed, sly and mocking. "Was it something I said?"

"Why do you ask?"

"It was that incident with your daughter at the party, wasn't it?" The demon nodded, convinced. "Claire! Oh, how that little girl loves to laugh! 'Ha-ha-ha, ho-ho-ho,'" the baritone voice of George W. Johnson crooned, "'and I could not stop laughing!'"

Prince tried to think without emotion, but the remark struck a chord.

"You like to sing," he diverted, jotting an entry into his notebook.

"What I like is your daughter," it growled, eyes boring into the doctor's.

Prince's mind hurtled back to Clare's bedroom, ears ringing with the sound of laughter blaring from the gramophone's horn speaker. He edged forward in his chair.

"Who are you?" he asked very clear, the words knifing.

"You know who I am."

"What is your name?"

"I love you, Papa," it trilled in a little girl's voice. "Do what he says or he's going to hurt me."

Prince went pale.

The demon fell back into the settee's cushion, appraising him.

"You like my imitations," it simpered, curving its mouth into a friendly smile. "I do them rather well, don't you think?"

"You destroyed Miss Fowler's Bible," Prince countered. "Why?"

"Changing the subject," the demon observed. "A talent of yours, *Mein Doktor*. But I prefer talking about your daughter. You kiss her each night before she goes to sleep. How lovely!"

"Miss Fowler tells me she found pages torn to pieces when she awoke yesterday morning."

"I do not want to talk about the Book!" it erupted, eyes blinking fiercely.

Prince took a King James Bible from his desktop.

"Does this bother you?"

The demon squirmed.

"I shall certainly kill her," it vowed, teeth bared. "I promise she will die for hours."

"But it's only a book. See here, it has pages with words printed on them like any other, though many believe them to be sacred; thousands and thousands of words."

"Take it away!" the demon demanded in a thunderous voice. "I swear I'll kill her. Skin her alive and cut her to pieces! Ask Bassett if you don't believe me!"

"You can't harm anyone," Prince challenged, sensing an advantage, "because you are a fraud. A delusion masquerading as the devil," he shouted, rising to his feet, brandishing the Bible in front of him. "By the power of this book, you shall be cast out of Miss Fowler's body, back to the molten lakes of Hell, never to plague her again!"

The demon wrapped its arms around itself, writhing in pain. Its fiery eyes locked on a painting that began rattling against the wall. Then, to a lamp that flew from a table crashing to the floor.

"Pain!" it bellowed, eyes lifting to the chandelier above, its teardrop crystals vibrating in tingling dissonance, until the entire fixture rocked and swayed as if caught in the tumult of an earthquake.

"Take it away!" the demon howled in agony. Then, repeated the words, "Take it away—*Take it away!*" until its screeching trailed away to nothing and its expression, fierce and malevolent, faded like the dying sun of a distant planet.

Moments later, Clara, the "saint," awakened.

Dr. Prince flicked off the projector. The images on the screen wound down, then cut out completely.

Hodgson turned to Waterman and James, astonished, then looked to Prince arranging his notes. His face, fair and handsome, flared with exasperation.

"Dr. Prince," he demanded, "can you not see that far from undercutting a Spiritualist interpretation of the Fowler case, this encounter supports it? The demon's reaction is exactly what one would expect when confronted with a Bible. Fear! Rage! Threats of reprisal!"

Notes in order, Prince looked at him with eyes, clear and cool.

"Understood," he said.

The psychic researcher sat silent for a moment, then whirled around to James, nonplussed.

"Are you suggesting that you agree with Hodgson?" James asked.

The doctor looked up from his notes.

"Let me be clear, of the cases of demonic possession I've studied, 90% were because of fraud, delusion, or misinterpretation of symptoms of psychosis. Taken all together, I did not find the slimmest reed of evidence to support a Spiritualist explanation. Nevertheless Richard —and you, Professor James—the Spiritualist interpretation of Miss Fowler's disorder is part of the therapeutic solution I'm proposing."

Hodgson's mind seemed tied in an inextricable knot. He settled back into his chair, the crimson hue that reddened his face dissolving into skepticism.

"May I continue?" the doctor asked.

Hodgson nodded slowly.

"So far, we have discussed two of the three Miss Fowlers, the "saint" and the "demon." Now, I'd like to direct your attention to the "woman," her return brought about by our efforts to uncover the 'root cause' of Miss Fowler's condition. But, to what end? Unlike the "saint", who is ephemeral, and the "demon" who is aberrant, the "woman" is physically and emotionally stable. Unlike Clara, she possesses Miss Fowler's childhood memories up to June 7, 1893, the night of the attack, and none immediately following it, until April 28th when she awakened. What does it all mean? To me, it means the "woman" is likely the real Miss Fowler. That is, the original Miss Fowler awakened to a conscious existence. If my theory is correct, both the "saint" and the "demon" must be destroyed and all our efforts devoted to sustaining the existence of the "woman"."

James lifted a hand to his chin, stroked his beard slowly.

"You say Clara is a phantom entity—"

"Yes."

"—who must be suppressed whenever she appears and the "woman" sustained?"

"Yes."

"But the "demon"?" James asked. "How do you propose to 'kill' it?"

Hodgson who sat, head cradled in his hands, lifted his eyes and spoke up wearily.

"It's the Bible."

"Bible?"

"Dr. Prince will use Miss Fowler's faith as a weapon to cast out the "demon"," he explained. "If the Bible can force the "demon" into retreat, ether used to suppress the "saint", and the "woman" kept in control, she will prevail and the others—driven back into Miss Fowler's subconscious—will cease to exist. A kind of therapeutic murder. Am I wrong, Dr. Prince?"

"Not wrong, but not entirely correct. You see, there is a method far more powerful than brandishing a Bible—"

"Exorcism!" James declared. Then, turning to Prince said, "You would do that?"

"Exorcism functions in much the same way as *hypnotherapy* or *narcosynthesis*," the doctor answered. "A trauma created the "demon" and likewise can eliminate it. The age-old ritual of casting out an invading spirit follows the same pattern as *drug abreaction*. The possessed person is worked up into a state of emotional frenzy in which he expresses intense anger and fear, leading to collapse, followed by a feeling of calm and release from the demon which has been tormenting him."

"The word exorcism is derived from the Greek word *exorkizein* which means 'bind by oath'," Waterman expounded. "The evil spirit is compelled to leave by a higher authority. Namely, God or Jesus Christ. Of course, there is no devil, merely the belief in one, but if the individual believes he is possessed, he will likewise believe that the invading spirit can be cast out by it."

"So," James proclaimed, turning to Hodgson and Prince, "perhaps a *modus vivendi* can be arranged after all. The rationale doesn't matter if you both get what you want. More to the point, we're all working to cure Miss Fowler of her illness, whatever one calls it."

"I see your point, Professor," Hodgson acknowledged, "and will go along provided one exception."

"And that is?" Prince asked.

"That Miss Piper be present at every stage of the ritual—planning to execution to post-mortem."

Prince lit a cigar as Cody entered. He stood to the back of the room, newspaper in hand, trying to get the doctor's attention.

"I don't see what harm it can do," Prince began. "We agreed to explore all possibilities—"

"Dr. Prince," Cody called out in an urgent whisper. "Dr. Prince!"

"Blast, man, what is it?"

Cody tromped up to him.

"I'm sorry to interrupt, but I thought you'd want to see this," he said, handing the paper to him.

Prince didn't have to look far to find what Cody wanted him to see. The *Telegraph's* headline read, 'FALL RIVER MAN MURDERED IN HOTEL ROOM, Vicious Assault and Mutilation!'

"Dear God in Heaven!" he gasped.

"What is it, Morton," James asked, "bad news?"

"It's Forest," he said, turning the paper over to him. "Richard Forest was the victim of last night's murder!"

A deafening silence fell over the room.

James perused the story, then looked up, whispering the lines from Marlowe's *Dr. Faustus*.

"'Faustus to Mephistopheles: Where is Hell?

Mephistopheles to Faustus: Why this is Hell, nor are we out of it.'"

FIVE

Alexandra Hotel
Boston, Massachusetts

The Alexandra Hotel had been a hot spot where well-to-do businessmen, politicians, and literary luminaries like Hawthorne and Dickens stayed while in Boston. But that seemed a long time ago, Prince was thinking as he craned his head up to examine its fourteen stories. Built in Victorian Gothic style, both the hotel and its surroundings had deteriorated since the construction of the elevated train line across the street from it. Since then, they had converted the once luxurious hotel into an overnight lodging house, its sandstone façade decaying from neglect, the building beside it already demolished.

Prince entered the lobby. Cody had warned him, but even that could not prepare him for its dilapidated interior.

"I am here to see Mr. Hilliard," he announced at the Front Desk.

The clerk pretended to search the registry.

"Room 403," he replied. Then, as Prince walked toward the elevator, added, "The lift don't work."

Prince climbed the stairs wondering how a man of Bassett's stature could end up in a place like this. He stopped to catch his breath at the fourth-floor landing and looked down the corridor to room 403. This was what he wanted. The raw, unvarnished Rufus "Bassett" Hilliard, probably drunk on the other side of that door.

He knocked.

"What do you want?" a gravel voice barked.

"It's Dr. Prince, Hilliard. May I have a moment?"

An uneasy silence followed.

"It's unlocked."

What Prince saw when he opened the door set him back a step. It was the cell of a madman with newspaper clippings of Lizzy Borden, Jose Corriero, H. H. Holmes, Jack the Ripper, plastered across the walls, police reports stacked on the hardwood floor, empty bottles strewn across it like buoys bobbing on a dead sea.

Bassett snapped his head up from the desk where he sat, and if there was one comparative that flashed through Prince's mind, it was to an aging lawman of western lore—Wyatt Earp, Bat Masterson—with piercing black eyes, handlebar mustache, sharp, sculpted features, long white hair swept back and to the side.

"Want a drink?" he asked, hoisting a bottle of Jack Daniels.

"I don't think so," Prince answered, taking in his surroundings. "Bassett—"

"What?"

"Have you ever thought about cleaning up this place?"

"Yeah, it crossed my mind—once," he said, taking a swig of bourbon.

Prince's eyes fixed on the crucifixes hung on the walls; the statues of the Virgin Mary and saints.

"Never took you for a religious man," he observed.

Bassett looked up from the bottle.

"Is that what you came here for? To talk about religion?"

The doctor strode to the desk, isolated, in the center of the room.

"May I?" he asked, touching the back of a chair.

The Marshal gave a cursory nod. Prince sat.

"What is it you want, Doctor?"

"You were at the Parker House the night of the murder. Why?"

Bassett laughed a throaty hack.

"You don't think I killed Forest, do you?"

Prince assessed him.

"No, it isn't in your character. Not murder; not mutilation of the kind I read about in the papers."

"What then?"

"I need to know why you were at the hotel that night. Did it have to do with Clara Fowler?"

Bassett pushed the bottle aside, lit an Old Judge.

"Look, Doc, maybe you think I'm some kind of renegade cop, or worse. But I'm going to tell you, know why? Because you and me, we can help each other."

"Go on," Prince said.

"I want to bring John Fowler to justice for reasons, maybe, I don't fully understand. You want to mend Clara Fowler's mind after the Hell she's been through with Forest, her father, and God knows who else. Once Fowler is in my custody, I can arrange for you to meet him to uncover information about Clara's background that even she doesn't know, about Charles' and Bessie's murder, the cult, *how* she got sick, *why* she got sick. All of that I'd make available to you."

"And what do you want in return?"

"I want to know everything Clara Fowler tells you about her father—something Forest may have mentioned, a postmark from a letter, an old address, anything that might lead me to him."

"You know I can't do that."

"Sure, you can. That's why you came here. Clara Fowler is a puzzle to you, though you pretend otherwise, and with Forest murdered your only chance at finding the missing piece is her father. That's where I come in."

Bassett ground his cigarette into an ashtray.

"I went to the Parker House to confront Forest," he finally admitted. "Like you, I knew about his relationship with the girl—burning, cutting, abusing her sexually—all the while Clara laughing like the pain and humiliation he put her through brought out some perverse joy in her. But it wasn't Clara laughing. It was something foreign to her, something I've never seen, not in Borden, Corriero, or any of the others." They exchanged tense looks. "Something I never want to see again."

"But you didn't meet Forest that night, did you?"

"Not alive, Doc. No, what I saw was not a man, but a 'thing.' With Borden it was butchery. The same with the Manchester killing. But this was beyond torture. This was unholy. Face pulled off like a mask, skin ripped from every nerve end while he was still alive, languishing for hours, until I got there and watched him die."

Bassett blasted the air from his lungs like a bellows expelling infection. For the first time, Prince saw what he had never seen before, a modicum of humanity, something beyond the madness drilled into him by the atrocities he'd witnessed in Fall River so many years ago.

"If not you," Prince asked, "who killed Forest?"

"Someone very strong, physically. Perhaps more than one man. Someone he knew since there were no signs of forced entry. The Boston police believe it may have been a disgruntled employee or business associate he defrauded. From what I understand, there were plenty of both."

"The Boston police—but not you?"

Bassett slid open the desk's top drawer.

"Let me show you something," he said, removing two wood carvings, setting them side- by-side on the desktop. "I found the first of these at the Fowlers' house the morning Bessie turned up dead. This one, the second," he said, holding it in his palm, "was in Forest's hotel room the night he was murdered. It's no coincidence I found them. No coincidence they are identical. It is my opinion, no, *my belief,* that whoever murdered Bessie also killed Forest and probably Charles, too. Maybe John Fowler by himself or with an accomplice. Either way, the cult is behind this. How do I know?" He scrutinized the effigy: wings spread, penis jutted out, a sinister grin curling its thick, brutish lips. "These carvings depict the demon, Abaddon, 'Lord of the Abyss' in the Christian Bible—purveyor of torment in the world of mortals. The name derives from the Greek word *'apollyon'* meaning 'changer of shapes.' And, as we know, since my deputy discovered the hollow where their Black Masses were held, Abaddon, was the deity the Fall River cult worshiped."

"What became of it?" Prince asked. "Where are its members?"

"They disbanded the cult after Charles' and Bessie's graves were excavated and their coffins found empty, its members spread throughout New England—the world, for all I know. But you," Bassett entreated, "Clara must have said something to you about the cult? About her father?"

"Nothing you don't already know. The childhood abuse, the escape with Forest to San Antonio and subsequent assault," he rattled off, "traumas, all of them, that led to her condition."

Bassett's face lit with concern.

"How is she?"

"As Clara grows weaker, the so-called "demon" gains strength and influence. Of course, the answer lies in psychology, but some favor a Spiritualist explanation."

"Hodgson."

"Yes, and Mrs. Piper, both convinced Clara is possessed by devils."

"Is she?"

Prince appraised him for a long moment. He reached into the breast pocket of his frock coat for a cigar and lit it.

"Marshal Hilliard, let's come to an understanding. Miss Fowler suffers from a rare form of hysteria called *dissociation*. Her cure lies, not in Spiritualist mumbo jumbo, but in the logic of modern science. We are not living in medieval times. Men drive motorized cars, electric lights illuminate our streets, soon, people will be take flight in airborne machines. There is no room in the 20th century for phantasms."

The doctor felt Bassett's eyes upon him; black, rheumy eyes that seemed to see into a man's soul.

"Why did you come here today, Dr. Prince?"

He looked straight at him, then chortled self-consciously, eyes wandering around the room.

"This place where you live—newspapers, religious icons, crime scene photos. Accounts of murders, *barbaric, inhuman*. Borden, Corriero," he reflected, "H. H. Holmes, Jack the Ripper." His gaze lashed back at him. "I am not a weak man, Bassett, but I came here because I'm frightened. Afraid for my family's safety and my own mental wellbeing."

Bassett leaned forward across the desk.

"Do you believe in coincidences, Doc?"

"As much as any man, I suppose."

"I do not."

The Marshal took a blank sheet of paper, flattened it on the desktop. With a pencil, he drew three crude renderings of houses. The first, on Wilson Road, Fall River. The next, on 2nd Street, Fall River. The third, on New Boston Road, Fall River.

"I told you that in my opinion, whoever killed the Fowler infants also murdered Forest. But let me take it one step farther." He pointed to the first drawing with the tip of his pencil, "This is the Fowler house, Wilson Street, where on June 7, 1882, Charles Fowler, age four days, was strangled to death. Four years later, Bessie Fowler, age four days, met with the identical fate at the hands, I believe, of John Fowler." He drew a straight line from the first to the second house. "Here is the Borden residence, 2nd Street, where three years later and less than four miles away, Andrew and Abigail Borden were hacked to death by their daughter, Lizzy." Bassett drew a line from the Borden residence to the third house. "Here is the Manchester Farm, New Boston Road, three miles from the Borden residence and two miles from the Fowler house, where nine months after Lizzy's murders, Jose Corriero bludgeoned Bertha Manchester to death with twenty-one blows from an ax." He looked at Prince boldly. "Five horrific murders, four in less than five years, all within a four-mile radius."

"But Forest—"

"Correct," he anticipated. "Forest was killed in Boston, not Fall River, but the connection is crystal clear. Richard Forest eloped to San Antonio with Clara for fear of John Fowler and the cult's reprisal. He knew the truth about Charles' and Bessie's deaths and the cult and was a threat to both."

"Why return to Boston?"

"Years had gone by since Clara returned from San Antonio. With the cult disbanded and John Fowler vanished, Forest believed himself safe, whatever knowledge he held no longer a threat." Bassett crushed the paper in his fist and flung it across the floor. "Forest was wrong."

The doctor took a puff from his cigar, nodded gravely.

"I do not believe in devils, Hilliard. But I believe in the reality of multiple murders—'serial killings.' Isn't that what they're calling them?"

"Yes," he said, "'serial killings' by 'serial murderers'."

"Like John Fowler?"

"Perhaps," he said, cryptically.

The Marshal examined Prince's expression as if standing at a crossroad between two alternate realities, weighing one against the other. Finally, he spoke.

"I'm going to tell you something, Doc, that sometimes I can't believe myself." He reached across the desk for a sealed envelope, tore it open. Inside, encased in Parkesine, was a handwritten letter. He undid the seal, opened it. "When does a coincidence become a pattern? When does a pattern become truth? That's the way it is with police work. A series of random events—like these murders—stream like beams of sunlight through a prism, scattered, until one morning you wake up and understand there's nothing random about them. What you thought could not be connected is; and what you found after piecing them together is, in fact, a blueprint of reality, all those coincidences originating from the same source. I received this letter during the Corriero investigation," he confided, handing it to him. "Please read it—aloud."

Prince's eyes peered over the top of the page, uncertainly.

> *"You been lookn for a kiler. One what struk Ol Berta an ripd open her brans like Lizzy done to her Ma an Fathr.*
> *It ain't what you think, Old Boss. You coppers mite get the foreener but not the kiler. Whether knife to cut or axe to bash er skull in. There aint jus one of us, Basset. Good luk!*
> *Jack the Ripper'."*

"Is it genuine?" Prince asked, handing it back to him.

"If you're asking, was it written by the killer, the answer is 'yes'. If you're asking, was it 'Jack the Ripper' who wrote it, the answer is 'no'."

"Christ blast to Hell," Prince exploded, "can you not talk straight with me!"

Bassett held the letter up in front of him.

"When I first received this, it was exciting, mysterious. I understood that if a jury did not know Lizzy Borden killed her parents, I did. With Corriero it was no different, though, like Lizzy, he claimed to have no memory of the crime. But this letter suggested something different, Doc; something that stuck with me like a steel spike hammered into my brain. It suggests there was more than one killer or, at least, more than one identity.

"My first reaction was to discard it as a fake. But once the newspapers got wind of the Ripper connection, they reprinted it, front page, and all hell broke loose. The department got letters from all over the country. Some were confessions, others offered clues to accomplices, most made no sense at all. Then, midway through the Corriero investigation, I got a visit from a man named Lawrence Banks, chief analyst for the Pinkerton detective agency in Chicago. He reported directly to Robert Pinkerton, president of the company, but came to Fall River on his own to investigate a personal theory about the White Chapel murders. He had seen a reproduction of the letter in the *Globe* and wanted to check it out.

"Banks brought his laboratory paraphernalia with him along with samples of the Ripper's handwriting taken from correspondence Scotland Yard had received. He asked if he could examine this letter," he said, cinching it tight between his thumb and forefinger, "and I agreed. The handwriting was a match not only for the Ripper's, Doc, but prescriptions for drugs and bills of lading for laboratory equipment written in the hand of H. H. Holmes."

"I don't believe it!" Prince balked.

"Neither did I until Banks took what he already confirmed one step further. You see, it was a Pinkerton, Frank Geyer, who tracked Holmes down in Boston and arrested him. The initial charge was insurance fraud, but once Geyer got to interrogating him, Holmes confessed to twenty-seven serial killings, nine that could be substantiated, and scores of others once authorities searched his 'murder castle' in Chicago.

"Geyer took meticulous notes: names, dates, how he disposed of the bodies, mostly young women, who he dissected, selling their organs to medical schools, black market. But beyond the similarities in handwriting, it was the timelines that caught Banks' attention. The Ripper's killing spree ended in England at the start of 1891 while Holmes' began in America at the end of that same year. It was that 'coincidence' that led Banks to theorize Holmes and the Ripper were the same man."

He jotted the date, **August 31, 1888**, on the sheet of paper and drew a straight line connecting it to a second date, **November 9, 1888**.

"This is the timeline for the Ripper's murders in Whitechapel," he noted, putting the first of four points on the line he had drawn. "**August 31ˢᵗ, Mary Ann Nichols**," he began, "body discovered, Buck's Row, 3:40 a.m., throat slit, deep slashes down and across abdomen." He added a second dot, "**September 8ᵗʰ, Annie Chapman**, body discovered, Hanbury Street, 6:00 a.m., throat cut, abdomen splayed open, uterus removed and taken by the killer." He penciled in a third point, "**September 30ᵗʰ**, double homicide, **Elizabeth Stride** and **Catherine Eddowes**. Stride's body discovered, Dutfield's Yard, 1:00 a.m., throat cut, anatomy left intact as a pedestrian stumbled onto the murder scene forcing him to flee. Bloodlust unsated, the Ripper struck again that night killing his second victim, Catherine Eddowes, body discovered, Mitre Square, 1:35 a.m., face hacked, uterus and kidney removed, carried off by killer." Finally, he added a fourth dot, "**November 9ᵗʰ, Mary Jane Kelly**," he said, eyes locking on Prince's, "the Ripper's most gruesome murder, body discovered, Miller's Court, 10:45 a.m., neck severed to the bone, face mutilated beyond recognition, breasts cut off, uterus and kidney removed, placed under her skull, heart cut-out, taken away by the killer."

The Marshal's eyes raised from the paper to Prince.

"Five women slaughtered in six weeks. Then, nothing. The murders stop. The killer vanished, never to be captured, never to be identified. But killers like the Ripper, they are a special breed. They do not simply 'go away' and so theories emerged from the 'yellow press,' the London police, Scotland Yard. Most presumed the Ripper's situation had somehow changed in a way that prevented him from continuing his rampage.

Perhaps, he was institutionalized, murdered, or committed suicide. But Banks suspected something different. Could it be, he wondered, that the murders stopped because the Ripper had left England?"

"All suitably grotesque, Bassett," Prince cried out, snatching the bottle of Jack Daniels from the desk, pouring a drink for himself, "but what has any of this have to do with Clara Fowler?"

"I'm getting to that, Doc," he answered calmly, "and this is where Banks' theory gets interesting. You see, the Ripper's timeline was well established, but there was no timeline for Holmes' homicides, until Banks created one. See here," he said, scrawling the date **December 24, 1891** beside the Ripper timeline, connecting it with a straight line drawn to a second date, **October 14, 1894**. He put a dot on the timeline, "**Christmas Eve, 1891**, Holmes' victims 1 and 2, **Julia Connor** and her eight-year-old daughter, **Pearl**, chloroformed then bludgeoned to death, skeletons sold black market." He penciled-in a second point, "**April 18, 1892, Emeline Cigrand**, Holmes stenographer, lured to a bank vault converted into a gas chamber constructed in Holmes' 'murder castle.' Once inside, the steel door was closed, hydrofluoric acid pumped into the chamber, disintegrating Cigrand's bones while Holmes observed through a peephole." Bassett affixed a third point onto the timeline, "**July 5, 1893, Minnie and Nannie Williams**, forced into a fireproof room with gas-fueled blowtorches fixed into its walls, incinerated. "**October, 1894**, "**Ben Pitezel**, Holmes' business partner, doused with kerosene; burned to death. His son, **Howard**, age eight, strangled, body dismembered and incinerated. Pitezel's two daughters, **Alice**, age fourteen, and **Nellie**, age eleven, locked inside a storage trunk, hydrochloric acid pumped into it, death by asphyxiation, skeletons buried beneath the flooring in Holmes' basement.

"With the second timeline documented, Banks was able to show Holmes *could* have been Jack the Ripper so he investigated further and came up with three pieces of evidence that inextricably tied their identities. One, tax records proved Holmes was not in Chicago from August 31, 1888 to November 9, 1888. Two, a ship's manifest for the White Star Line's Trans-Atlantic listed H. H. Holmes as a passenger leaving Liverpool for New York immediately following the Mary Kelly murder. Finally, the coup de grace," he concluded, "census records for the year 1888 document Holmes had a residence in Whitechapel during the time of the Ripper killings."

"Marshal Hilliard," Prince blustered, "I'm sure these theories interest you, but again I must ask, what have they to do with Miss Fowler?"

"Maybe everything, Doc, and maybe nothing at all, but Holmes' third wife and murder victim, Minnie Williams, was born and raised in Boston, where he spent time prior to the start of his serial killings. Interestingly, after Holmes murdered the Pitezel family, knowing he was being pursued by Frank Geyer, he traveled to, get this, Fall River, Massachusetts. It made no sense to Banks, except when Geyer arrested Holmes he noticed a strange-looking medallion suspended by a gold chain around his neck. He showed me a photo of it and I could not believe my eyes. The medallion was stamped with the image of the demon, Abaddon, Doc, and suddenly it all made sense."

"Bassett, I admire your willingness to defend what you believe is right and just," Prince obtruded. "But, seriously, have you ever considered seeing a psychiatrist?"

"You still don't get it, do you, Doc? Well, neither did the boys at Central Station. But aside from Holmes confessing that 'voices' told him to slaughter all those poor people, while in prison, weeks before he was hung, guards, lawyers, even the minister attending him, all swore that Holmes' facial features had begun to mold into those of the devil. By May 7, 1896, the day of his execution, Holmes had changed so thoroughly in appearance that none could identify the man they hung. Later that day, they buried him beneath ten feet of concrete to seal his soul away forever."

"But the 'connection', Bassett! The 'pattern' that connects the shafts of light you spoke about? I'm willing to concede Holmes and the Ripper may be the same man and that elements of Satanism were intermingled with his psychosis, but *exactly how do they 'connect'?*"

"Don't you see? If Holmes was Jack the Ripper, it means not only seven or eight but dozens of killings, perhaps scores of them, are connected to the Fall River cult. The key to unmasking the killer, or killers, still at large since Forest's murder, is real. The possibility here," he pleaded, stretching out his open hand, "just beyond our fingertips. There is a 'pattern' to these atrocities, bigger than my laws or your psychology, and John Fowler is at the center of it!"

Prince leaned back from the desk, feeling his resistance to Bassett's arguments wilt in a vast desert of dread.

"Very well," he agreed, grim and exacting, "if it were not for my experience in abnormal psychology, I would think you insane. But that is not what I believe," he said, lifting himself up from his chair. "What I believe now is that to save Clara's life and put an end to these abominations, we must pool our knowledge, no matter how it comes to us," he pledged, extending his hand. "I shall do all that I can to help you find John Fowler."

V: CRUCIATION

"The one fact of demon possession, so unmistakable in our time, is the power these hostile beings exert among men and what they may, in far more subtle and less obvious ways, do to corrupt us."
–Prof. Richard Hodgson
Cambridge University

ONE

Prince's Office

Morton Prince sat at his desk pondering the situation at hand—his, Bassett's, Clara Fowler's. He clutched the talk/listen device connected to the Gramophone voice recorder, thoughts of Forest's murder, his cooperation with Bassett and the exorcism he was about to perform crowding his already cluttered mind.

His gaze flicked to the *Roman Ritual* laying on the desktop in front of him. He wiped a skein of perspiration from his brow with a handkerchief, then clapped his hand atop the Latin words, *"Vade Retro, Satana!"* embossed in gold on its cover. "'Satan, Begone!'" he read in a whisper, eyes locked on the Fowler file.

Yes, he would perform the Sacred Rites, having secretly studied them for months now. To be sure, he would help Hilliard ferret out John Fowler. Of course, he would persist in his efforts to cure Clara. But if he was to fulfill his innermost ambition—the completion of his paper for the Paris Conference—he would need to document every shred of evidence to support his prognosis. Hence, the Gramophone. There could be no stenographer, his *dissociation* theory deemed too important to be shared with anyone outside the coterie of researchers he had already chosen.

Now, he needed to break loose from the madness to record the breakthroughs that had transpired over the past five days: the arrival of the "woman," his verdict concerning Clara's survival, the treatment he was hellbent on pursuing.

"Notes, April 17th, 1901," he began reading. "From the data accumulated, it seems certain the "woman" is the real Miss Fowler and, therefore, must be kept alive while Clara must be made to disappear. If one considers the meaning of this decision, that a self, with all its memories, feelings and sentiments, must be eradicated, what I have proposed is nothing less than the annihilation of an individual. This is the hard logic of events."

The doctor rose, pensive, from his chair and walked to the window overlooking Beacon Street where bicyclists pedaled astride gas-engine automobiles, students scurried on their way to classes, and the sun shone bright in a pristine April sky. But for Prince, the passage from winter to spring was like stepping out of darkness into darkness. The path forward left him haunted by self-doubt. What if he was wrong? What if the shock of exorcism, far from curing Miss Fowler, served only to exacerbate her condition, to push her beyond the edge of sanity or stress her body could endure? If not before, he knew now that her life hung in the balance.

"During our March 31st session, Clara came to herself for the first time in several days. It was impossible to explain that her extinction meant the survival of her true self and I made no attempt to do so. As she sat before me, wearily confiding the latest horrors she endured, even the most callous clinician would have been moved by this pathetic figure, hopeless and dejected. While she talked my mind went back over the events of the past three years. I remembered all she had gone through—the trials, anxieties, the suffering—and the courage with which she had borne, not only the physical abuse, but the mental anguish of never knowing when the demon might take control. Though it might be that she was not the real or original self, Clara was as much an individual as anyone that ever lived."

The doctor turned eyes, haunted and seared, from the window and walked back to his desk.

"Venturing tentatively to hint at the question of self-annihilation, I asked Miss Fowler if she would be content to be cured at the sacrifice of all memory of her life to the present time, remembering everything from this moment on. As she thought about it, she fell into a state of reverie and, again, her demeanor changed. The expression of weariness vanished and in its place was one of strength and self-reliance. When she spoke, her voice, too, had changed, no longer expressing discouragement, but the manner and thought of a woman in normal relations with her environment. It was the "woman" who sat before me!"

A tap sounded at the door. The doctor looked up as Waterman entered. He motioned him toward a chair and continued recording.

"Believing this to be the real Miss Fowler, I told her that she was entitled to know everything and, in time, promised to divulge all that had happened. I explained she had undergone a shock while working at a hospital in Fall River in consequence of which she had changed and continued to lose and regain memories. I told her about Clara, but said nothing about the demon or Forest's assault. To this she agreed, content to wait for a full explanation. Finally, she rose to go, then turned as she went out the door and my blood ran cold. It was the creature staring back at me, eyes gleaming. 'She shall never be rid of me!" it swore with a force that took my breath away. *'Imoun edo prin yparxei o kosmos soul,'* it thundered in an ancient Greek dialect, 'I was here before your world existed!'"

The doctor switched the Gramophone 'off,' lifting a glance to Waterman.

"Have the others arrived?"

"They're waiting outside the consultation room. Mrs. Piper is inside talking with Miss Fowler."

Prince frowned, "Mrs. Piper? I thought she'd be waiting with Hodgson and James," he said, searching the young doctor's eyes. "Come along. Hurry!"

The two men sprinted down the hallway toward the consultation room. Abruptly, Prince stopped, Waterman along with him. Together, they stood rooted to the floor, listening to sounds, subtle, like the rustling of leaves. Was it people talking? Prince wondered. Because beneath the tumult there seemed voices. Words and phrases. Barely audible.

"Do you hear it? Voices. I'm not sure where they're coming from."

"Yes. I hear them, too."

"Are they real?" Prince asked, as much to himself as to Waterman.

"I don't understand."

The doctor bristled.

"It's a simple question. Are the voices real or auditory hallucinations, manufactured by our own minds?"

Before Waterman could answer, a muffled pounding jolted the hallway. Then another, steadily shuddering through the walls, the floor, the ceiling, throbbing like the beating of a heart, massive and diseased.

"That's no hallucination!" Waterman declared, blue eyes wide behind his horn-rimmed glasses.

"It's Mrs. Piper," Prince blurted. "I fear she's in danger!"

Breathless, they arrived at the consultation room where James stood, immured, while Hodgson frantically twisted the doorknob one way and the other.

"What the devil is going on here?" Prince demanded.

"It's locked from the inside," Hodgson replied, panicked.

Prince stepped in front of him and tried the lock himself.

Inside the room, the rapping continued. Faster. Harder. Its cadenced throb punctuated by the crashing sound of shattering glass.

"Break it down!" Prince ordered.

Hodgson stared at him questioningly.

"Christ on the cross!" he screamed. "Break down the goddamned door!"

Hodgson coiled his long frame into a crouch, thrusting the full weight of his body into the door, once and then again, until he burst into the room, Prince a half-step behind.

Their eyes scoured the room. It was in disarray. Shards of broken glass from demolished lamps and fixtures covered the floor; books blown off bookshelves scattered haphazard; a chandelier crashed, ceiling to floor, lay like the marooned wreckage of a ship run aground. Their eyes shifted to Leonora Piper, with her back to them. Then to the demon, its hand drawn to its mouth, giggling.

Prince darted a glance at Hodgson, who rushed toward her—a portrait jumped from its mounting! Then, to James—a lamp flew off an end table, slamming into a wall! Finally, to Waterman staring, astonished, at the demon, no longer laughing, its eyes, mouth, brow pulled taut and stern, staring at Piper like the master over a beaten slave.

A bloodcurdling scream shot out of the medium. Hodgson spun her around to face him, her eyes drawn up into their sockets, leaving only white of the sclera exposed.

"Leonora!" he cried out.

A stilted hesitation followed. In her eyes, visible now, he saw some massive, terrible struggle.

"It wants us dead," she murmured. "It wants us all dead and in Hell with it."

Hodgson led her to the back of the room and onto a sofa. Waterman checked her pulse and heartbeat, elevated to alarming levels.

"Enough!" Hodgson bellowed, lashing around to Prince. "Where is Father Lucien?"

"There is no need for a priest," he said, his eyes at once desperate and defiant. "This is not about demons. It never was."

"But we agreed—"

"We agreed there would be an exorcism," Prince said, cutting him short, "and so there shall be!"

"You?" he asked, astounded. "Have you lost your mind? The efficacy of an exorcism is rooted in the church's authority and the faith of the exorcist. You possess neither!"

"And the Rite is performed only after careful medical examination precludes the possibility of mental illness," Prince countered. "Make no mistake, we are dealing with a delusional system caused by trauma and trauma will cure it. The exorcism performed by me!"

"Don't do it, Morton," James cautioned, taking hold of Prince's shoulder as he turned to go. "I know what I said about the importance of the Fowler case, but this is something else," he warned, glancing at the creature, torporous now in its deadly silence, "something unnatural."

"No, you were right in what you said. This is the one chance I have to prove myself as a scientist. I shall not run from it!"

The doctor stalked toward the front of the room, heart pounding, pulse soaring. The brain was a collection of electrical circuits and chemical systems capable of producing a variety of unusual states, he reminded himself: epilepsy, brain lesions, seizures in the temporal lobe. Hadn't Tourette proved as much? Not to mention Charcot's studies on the effects of trauma in hysterics—all pointing to mental illness!

His footsteps stopped not five feet from the demon.

Its eyes flashed open.

"Well, well, look who's come to see me," it said, grinning. "The eminent Dr. Morton Prince."

Crouching on the davenport, coiled like a cobra ready to strike, its gleaming eyes followed his every move.

"What's in the bag, Prince?"

The doctor put the satchel on the floor in front of him.

"I'll tell you," he offered, lifting his gaze to the creature, "but first I need to see Clara."

Its eyes glinted craftily.

"The bitch is in Hell with Jesus Christ, Son of Shitdom, and his mother, Mary, Queen of Whores." It sniggered, remolding its expression into that of a little girl. "Papa, can I see it?" it lolled in his daughter's voice. "I want to play with Forest's body."

Prince stiffened.

"I doubt you know where Clara is," he said with studied casualness, "much less how to make her appear."

The demon cleansed its throat with a short harsh grunt, its face regressing to a ravaged skull-like contour, skin pulled tight over jutting cheekbones, mouth a parch-lipped slit.

"More of your psychology, Father Prince?" Its eyes glistened fierce and coercive. "Oh, ye of little faith. I shall give you two times what you asked for!"

Prince braced himself for a new shock. Its prescience filled the room.

"Doctor Prince, is that you?" Clara asked, the demon's scowl falling away to reveal the "saint" gazing at him wondrously. "Do you see Him?" she asked. "Don't you see Him? He's standing right beside you!" she declared, ecstatic. "It is He—our Lord and Savior, Jesus Christ. He is holding His arms out to me, Doctor. He wants me to join Him in Heaven!"

No sooner had the words left her mouth than the "saint" transformed into the "woman," spine stiffened, eyebrows raised, incensed.

"What is the meaning of this!" she spouted. "Where am I? Why am I here?" She took in her surroundings, her indignation slowly fading as she recognized Prince, the consulting room, and the fact that she had been resurrected by something beyond her understanding. "Is it possible," she asked in a voice tinged with horror, "that there is a second 'thing' inside me?"

A yelping laugh gushed up from the demon's throat.

"You see? I told you," it touted, rearing up on the settee. "Now you've seen them. The "saint" stupid as ever; and the other, the "woman", as you call her, who I have a special plan for. Now, tell me," it fulminated, eyes narrowed, glare leveled squarely at him, "what's in the bag, Prince?"

A niggling sensation skittered up Prince's spine. He was walking a tightrope, and he dared not look down. According to the Rite, the exorcist's first challenge was to uncover the demon's identity. Only after its name had been revealed could the Ritual begin.

"If you are the devil, you must know what's in the satchel," he challenged, holding the bag in front of him. "Do you?"

The demon's eyes locked onto his. Deadly. Sinister.

"Soon you will join me in Hell, Mein Doktor, where you can burn with your daughter. And that?" It scoffed, gesturing toward the satchel. "The trinkets you carry in the bag are useless against me."

"Why, useless?" Prince probed, white-knuckled fingers clenching and unclenching on the bag's leather handle. "Who are you? What is your name?"

"I am more important than you know," it bragged. "An emissary for the Evil One." It grinned mockingly. "A conscript on a mission."

"If you are an emissary, identify yourself. I'm intrigued by your presence here among mortals. Tell me your name and I'll announce it to the world."

"In your book, I suppose." It sniggered. "I know all about it."

"Are you Barbatos?" he persisted. "Malphas?" Then, more pointedly, "Are you the demon Abaddon?"

"I am the devil!" it shrieked, fingers crushing hard against its temples at the mention of the name.

"No," the doctor fired back, "you are no one. You do not exist except in Miss Fowler's mind." He lurched forward. "If you are the devil, tell me your name!"

The demon jerked its head up, the mouth and neck trembling with rage.

"Nooo!" it exploded in a protracted screech that shook the walls of the room. "You are a hypocrite and a liar!" it hissed pointing an accusing finger at him and no doubt another far more powerful entity had replaced the demon, Abaddon. "Do you know what your father says about you? 'Morton, my eccentric son.' 'Morton, the failure. An embarrassment to the family name!' You dare to ask who I am? No, no," it seethed, "WHO THE FUCK ARE YOU?"

Prince felt his chest tighten. Something in the room congealing. A pulsing, like energy seeping into the darkened chamber of his heart.

"Who are you?" asked **Elizabeth Stride**, throat slit ear-to-ear.

Mind floating. A crawling gray mist rising up from the ground.

"Who are you?" repeated **Annie Chapman**, face mutilated beyond recognition.

Muttering. Cursing. People emerging like ghosts from out of a dense fog.

"Who are you?" "Who are you?" demanded *Emeline Cigrand*, body scalded by acid; *Andrew and Abigail Borden*, skulls caved in from the blows of an ax; *Catherine Eddowes*, an open cavity where her heart used to be; *Charles and Bessie Fowler*, necks wrung, heads resting on a shoulder. "Who are you?" "Who are you?" *Ben and Howard Pitezel*; *Annie Chapman*; *Mary Kelly*; an army of lost souls; *Richard Forest*, stepping out of the ranks, "What's in the bag, Prince?" he asked, face stripped of epidermis. "You know those trinkets are useless against us."

The doctor brought his hand to his mouth, eyeballs quivering. Pain in chest. Excruciating. What if all the screams in Hell would not be as loud as you wanted to scream? He wondered, gathering his will, then opening the medical bag and grabbing a crucifix, jolted by what he saw. It was Christ, in miniature. Nails driven through hands and feet. Body writhing on the wooden cross. But Prince would not be deterred, summoning all the courage in him as he jutted the crucifix out in front of him, eyes burning with ardor!

Then, like an ebbing tide, the mist withdrew. Before him stood the One glaring down at him.

"My shining hour," it japed. "And that one," it added, motioning toward the cross, "with the crown of thorns bleeding. I would have cut him into pieces, too, if I had known he would rise from the fucking dead!" It spit a wad of mucus onto the floor. "Now put that splinter of wood back in the bag before I show you what real pain feels like."

But Prince did not yield, steeped in the conviction that the One, like all the rest, was a hallucination sprung from a cauldron of stress as he steeled himself, brandishing the crucifix like a fiery sword.

"With this cross and the words written in the name of God, Himself, I cast you out of this young woman back to the molten depths of Hell!"

"Hell?" the demon asked, eyes bulging with fury. "You have no idea!"

In an instant, Prince was transported to a basement corridor. Dense of air. Walls at odd angles. A door creaked open. He walked through it. Saw his daughter, Claire, pinioned to an operating table. Hands and ankles cuffed. Doctors looming over her. The lead surgeon looked to him and removed his surgical mask. By the glint in those deadly eyes and the heinous grin, he recognized the monster, *H. H. Holmes.*

"No! Not that! Never that!" he cried out to God and all that was holy.

Sensing his presence, a second surgeon pulled down his mask, beaming. And if not by sight by intuition, he knew. *"Jack the Ripper."* Then, a third mask dropped. It was *Jose Corriero.* And a fourth. It was *Lizzy Borden.*

"God in Heaven, don't let them do this!" he implored the Father, Son, Holy Spirit.

Holmes made an incision into the abdomen. A long, deep swipe of his scalpel.

"Put the cross down!" The demon boomed, its words crackling, thunderous, through the room.

Holmes' gloved hand reached into the cavity below Claire's ribs. Blood ran down the gutters of the surgical table. He began removing organs— liver, kidneys, lungs. "Can I see the heart?" asked Lizzy Borden, eyes bright with wonder. "I want to fondle it." He handed her the heart; a lung for the Ripper; a kidney for Corriero, whose hungry eyes glistened.

"My child is innocent!" Prince protested to God and the angels in Heaven, dropping to his knees. "She knows nothing about this!"

Slowly, Prince began a harrowing crawl toward his medical bag. He fumbled for the black book, *Vade Retro, Satana* embossed on its cover, held the crucifix up with one hand, seizing the Rites of Exorcism with the other.

"Put the cross down!" the One commanded, screeching now amid roaring flames and molten rock.

Desperately, Prince paged through the book, finally coming to the sacred prayers, about to take the biggest gamble of his life.

"I cast you out vengeful spirit, along with every specter from Hell, in the name of the Lord Jesus Christ!" he raged, rising to his feet, cross pitched out in front of him. *"For it is He who commands you. Harken, therefore, and tremble in fear, Satan!"*

Crouched, leaning forward, about to strike, the demon fell into a brooding silence, disoriented.

"Litteris Caesaris consulibus redditis segre abuis imperatratum est summa tribunorum," Prince continued, the words flung like daggers, *"ut vero ex litteris ad seratum referretur impetrari non potuit!"*

From the back of the room, Hodgson, James, and Waterman watched, mesmerized, as Leonora Piper leaped up from the settee.

"Leonora, don't!" Hodgson implored, reaching out to stop her, but it was too late.

He and the others watched, awe-struck, as she dashed to the front of the room, snaring the crucifix from Prince's hand, raising it high in the air above her.

The demon fell back. Twisting. Convulsing. Frothing at the mouth.

"Satan, you enemy of faith, you purveyor of death and disease, you robber of life," Prince railed, Leonora, reading from the book alongside him. *"You corruptor of justice, root of evil and vice, seducer of men,"* the two pressed on, shocked to find that Waterman and James had fallen in beside them. *"Fomenter of discord, author of pain and sorrow,"* they reviled. *"Begone, then, in the name of the Father and Son and Holy Spirit!"*

Mad with pain and terror, the demon tore at its eyes, foam spewing from the corners of its mouth.

"Please! Please!" it pled to the Heavens. "Put the cross down for it is a cudgel that bludgeons me!"

"In eandem sententiam loquitur Scipio," they continued, mercilessly, *"Pompeio esse auxilium, si postea velit, senatum imploraturum!"*

"Hate! Murder! I shall cut you to pieces and feast on the flesh from your bones!" it threatened, face pulsing with rage.

"Miss Fowler must hold the cross in her hands to rid herself of it!" Hodgson shouted above the bedlam, seizing the crucifix from Piper, charging head-long toward the demon.

"Yield, therefore, not to us but to the power of Jesus Christ," the chorus of voices persisted. *"For it is His power that compels you. His death and resurrection that brought light into eternal darkness!"*

Hodgson flinched in shock as he stood eyeball-to-eyeball with the creature, livid with anger, body writhing in mind-bending anguish. Then, breaking free from its grip, he thrust the cross onto its forehead. The effect was like an electric jolt, the demon snapping up from the settee, slamming him across the side of the head with a vicious backhand that sent the cross shuttling into the air as he reeled across the room.

"I have brought a New Age of decadence to the world. War! Disease! Barbarity! I am the Evil One, Lucifer," it cried out into eternity, "and this is my mission!"

Leonora raced to Hodgson, blood gushing from a gash on his forehead as he lay on the floor, dazed with shock, the demon sneering down at him, ready to pounce.

"Tremble before the right arm that broke asunder the dark prison walls and led evil filth into the Light!" Waterman and James exhorted voices knifing through the screeching dissonance.

Abruptly, Leonora scooped the cross from the floor, raising it up to the creature as it wrenched up a keening shriek of terror.

"This is for you, you son of a bitch!" she swore, shoving the cross into its mouth.

Hodgson staggered to his feet.

"Make no resistance, nor delay in departing from this, Christ's servant," he entreated, *"for it has pleased Almighty God to dwell in her!"*

"Amen," the others responded, coming to join him.

The demon rumbled a low, feral growl.

"For it is God, Himself, who commands you. God, the Holy Spirit commands you. The mystery of the cross commands you. The faith of the Holy Apostles and all the Saints command you!"

"Lord hear our prayer," Waterman, Hodgson and Leonora Piper answered.

The demon whimpered, weakened and struggling, then crumbled to the floor.

"My God in Heaven!" Hodgson heard Leonora Piper gasp.

He whirled around and saw her looking, stupefied, at the body lying protracted on the floor. Puzzled, he watched along with the others as crimson letters formed upon Clara's abdomen as she came to herself. Warily, Piper pulled the fabric of her shirt up to reveal the word 'SPITE' spelt out in bloody, red welts.

"Where am I?" Clara wondered aloud. "Dr. Prince? Mrs. Piper, is that you?"

"I want Miss Fowler taken to Mass General for observation, *now*!" Prince instructed Waterman, tramping from the room into the hallway, Hodgson in his wake.

Excited, Hodgson clutched Prince at the shoulder.

"I have never seen the likes of it!" he said, enthralled. "Nor has any other physician or psychical researcher. Morton, this is proof of demonic possession, real and tangible. Evidence of God's existence and promise of an afterlife!"

Prince turned to him, sober and spent.

"Not exactly," he confessed as James and Piper burst from the room to join them.

"I don't understand—"

"The ritual I read, the Latin? It was taken from *Caesar's Gallic Wars*, Richard, not the *Rites of Exorcism*. What we witnessed was *doctrinaire induction*. Miss Fowler knew what was expected of the so-call 'demon" and she gave it to us." Then, turning to Leonora Piper, he said, "I'm sorry if this disappoints you."

TWO

Prince's Office

Prince fell into his desk chair, temples pounding in headache. He mopped his icy forehead with a handkerchief, rummaged through the drawers for a cigarette. Finding a half-empty pack of Chesterfields, he lit one, and puffed deep while he contemplated the exorcism: the demon's violent reaction, Leonora's courage when confronted by it, Hodgson's hopefulness at what he thought he saw.

Across the desk lay the Fowler file, waiting like the sullen water behind a dike. Calling. Luring. Clamping the cigarette between his lips, he squinted through the smoke raking the file toward him with his fingers. He opened it and took out the initial inquiry conducted by Waterman and himself.

"Studies That Point to the "woman" Being the Real Miss Fowler."

"SAINT"	"WOMAN"
-poor health, little appetite; insomnia, neurasthenic	-healthy, good appetite; sleeps well, no discernable illness
-chronically depressed	-strong-willed, optimistic
-morbidly religious, obsessed with church,	-indifferent to religion, rarely attends church, free

claims to experience Visitations	from delusions
-dresses in black and other dark colors	-fond of bright, vivid colors
-dependent on others	-self-reliant
-mentally unstable	-psychologically stable; able to perform activities requisite to day-to-day living

For a time, the doctor pondered, puffing his Chesterfield, then drew the second, most recent, inquiry from the file. A drill of bile worked its way up from the pit of his stomach.

"Studies That Point to the "Woman" Not Being the Real Miss Fowler"

"SAINT"	"WOMAN"
-patient	-most impatient
-considerate of others	- considers only herself and her personal convenience
-even-tempered, compliant, never angry	-quick-tempered, prone to rages
-weak-willed, easily influenced, yielding	-indomitable and obstinate, rarely influenced by others
-mentally unstable; unable to live normal life due to ill-health and ephemeral nature	-physically stable; behavior often rash and erratic, may preclude ability to function in everyday life

Prince stared unseeing, the smoke from his cigarette rising like whispered curls of doubt. Based on the findings of the first inquiry, he and Waterman had worked together, suppressing the "saint" and thwarting the "demon's" existence with ether, while allowing the "woman" to establish herself. But lately he had his doubts about their strategy. True, by all psychiatric standards, the "woman" was a full-blown entity with discreet thoughts, emotions, and opinions. Yet, like the itch of a phantom limb, uncertainty tugged at the periphery of his resolve. As often as not, her behavior was erratic, even hostile; her childhood memories—vague and incomplete—seemed the recollections of an observer rather than a participant in Miss Fowler's life. Also, he discerned inconsistencies in his own logic. If Miss Fowler's consciousness had been shattered by Forest's assault, how could the "woman," the *real* Miss Fowler, remain intact?

Prince dropped back into his chair, devastated by the implications of his latest findings. He recalled the letters, demon-to-Clara, that James had referenced. *"There are messages in its writing like a voice calling out from the distant past. The demon is trying to tell Clara something; some dark secret, and in doing so is calling out to us along with her."* The secret, he had assumed, was Forest's assault, but was that it? Was there something more yet undiscovered? To Prince it was like unlocking a safe. If he turned the knob to all the right numbers and in the right order, the door would open. But what would he find? What was the "dark secret" that even the demon dared not reveal?

The question passed through his mind like a runnel of dread. He rested a brow on quavering fingertips, head jerking up at the sound of three hard raps on the door as William James stormed into his office.

"What you did was unfair, Dr. Prince! *Caesar's Gallic Wars*, indeed! A 'trick,' by God, that is what you played on us!"

"Waterman knew about it," he answered. "Besides, what's 'fair'? Three years of work leading to one blind alley after another in this damnable case."

"You made a fool of Hodgson, not to mention Mrs. Piper and myself!"

"Calm yourself, Will. And, for God's sake, try not to shout. I have a headache a forest of *spirea* couldn't remedy."

The professor dropped into a chair, the flash of anger dissipating.

"I don't understand you, Morton," he said, shaking his head. "This isn't a contest of wills. There is no 'right' or 'wrong.' Can we at least agree that what we call Miss Fowler's disorder is secondary to the restoration of her health?"

Prince met his gaze boldly.

"I'm sick and tired of Hodgson and his Spiritualism," he erupted. "I find the man exasperating, eccentric at best, juvenile at worst. And now we have the esteemed Mrs. Leonora Piper to contend with. I don't know why I took them on in the first place."

"They are involved because you need them. There are seven million Spiritualists in the U.S. and Europe, some of them the brightest lights in science: *Nobel Laureate* Pierre Curie, physicist Sir Oliver Ambrose; perhaps even myself since I believe in an immortal soul. Without a Spiritualist perspective, the paper you deliver at the Paris Conference will never achieve the acceptance it deserves. Besides, Hodgson raises serious questions about the Fowler case, questions that demand answers. What we witnessed today was remarkable."

"There is no 'demon,' Professor James. We both know that, so what's the point in going on with this charade? The 'exorcism' I performed was purely for effect. A theatrical performance that begot a theatrical performance." He stabbed his cigarette into an ashtray. "For the love of God, Will, we're physicians, not gypsies and soothsayers!"

"I didn't come here to argue, Morton, only to ask that you give Hodgson and Piper the respect they deserve." He ran the palm of his hand over his beard speculatively. "Have you read Planck's paper on "Quantum Discontinuity" in this month's issue of *Nature*? He proposes a new perspective concerning our understanding of space and time based on the existence of a 'subatomic' world. The desk you sit behind," he asserted, rapping the wood with his knuckles, "though it appears solid, is a motion of particles. 'Fluid in flux', he calls it, and not solid at all. If true, Planck's theory will turn Newtonian physics on its head!"

"And your point, Professor James?" Prince asked. "The one you didn't come here to argue?"

"My point, Dr. Prince, is that once the vestiges of arrogance and pride are stripped away, we know almost nothing about the nature of human existence."

"Call me 'Thomas, the Doubter', but what I see I believe. As for Planck, Hodgson, and the rest—interesting speculations—but none that I take seriously."

"Well, then, let's discuss an aspect of the Fowler case that even you cannot ignore. The subject of murder—*serial murder*—as practiced by John Fowler, Holmes, and the Ripper." James fixed his gaze upon him. "Morton, I need you to believe there's something malignant in the air around us. It takes on many forms, but has been around for as long as anyone can remember. I started peeling back the layers. It's a pattern—not only the number of murders, but the barbarity of the killings. Things are changing before our eyes, *right now*, as we enter the new century. I fear we are on the precipice of something massive. Death and suffering on a scale we have never seen before!"

Hands trembling, Prince tapped out a cigarette from his pack. He lit it, inhaled, then let out a stream of smoke that encircled him like an incandescent cloud.

"I'm sorry, Morton, I've upset you. Are you all right?"

He took a nervous puff.

"Insomnia?" James asked, concerned. "The nightmares we spoke about?"

Prince passed him a wan smile.

"I'm having second thoughts about our strategy. Two weeks ago, Clara took a job as a waitress at a local canteen. After working the better part of the morning, the "woman" awakened. Horrified at the prospect of waiting tables, she threw down the tray she was holding, stomped to the manager, and quit on the spot. Then, there's this," he murmured, taking a letter from the Fowler file. He pushed it across the desk. "It seems the "woman" has decided to confront the "demon" head-on."

Eyes riveted on his longtime friend, James took the letter and began reading.

> 'Dr. Prince,
>
> I shall never recognize the "demon" as anything but mental delirium, nor treat it with any more consideration in the future than in the past— with less for I propose killing it, and wish neither you or Mr. Hodgson to interfere. You must leave me alone, and send me away if, as that monster, I appear before you. I begin treatment at once.'

"*I propose killing it*," James uttered. "Exactly what the "demon" wants."

A knock sounded at the door. Waterman entered.

"How is she?" Prince asked, urgently.

"Hodgson and Mrs. Piper are still at the hospital. Miss Fowler was resting soundly when I left."

"Thank God!" Prince gasped.

At 3:00 a.m., the "woman" awoke in hospital room 401A, wondering how she got there. She sat up in bed, set her bare feet on the floor, and walked to the sink. She switched on the faucet and splashed cold water on her face. Eyes clamped shut, she reached for a towel and dried her face, then glanced into the mirror, and her heart froze.

She blinked at the mad-staring face grinning back at her. The cracked, parched lips, the eyes glistening with venom.

Then, screamed until she fainted.

THREE

Danvers State Lunatic Asylum
September 9, 1901

There was something bone-chilling about Danvers asylum, Bassett was thinking as he approached the Kirkbride Building. Its Gothic spires reached out into the arborescent gloom like something enormous and deformed. The gargoyles perched atop it grinned at the forest pressing in on it; fog curled up from rotted leaves like departed souls. But it was what was rumored to go on inside that caused the Marshal's flesh to crawl.

Originally designed for four hundred patients, Danvers housed three times that many with reports of sexual abuse, naked patients wandering the corridors covered in their own filth, and experimental surgeries like *topectomy* where an ice pick was inserted above the patient's eyeball into the *frontal lobe* of the brain ablating parts of the *parietal cortex* to keep inmates under control once ensconced behind its stone walls.

The Marshal passed through the main lobby into the "open" ward, then into the outmost "disturbed" wing reserved for the most hostile patients. Behind the charge desk, a squat, short-haired man with a weightlifter's physique waited.

"Conway's the name," he greeted, firm and straightforward. "Some call me 'Joe,' but most call me 'Champ'," he explained, turning to a portrait hung crooked on the plaster wall, "and, yes, that is a photochrome of the great John L. Sullivan. Do you follow the sport, sir?"

"Some."

"Then, perhaps, you recognize this ruggedly handsome countenance with cauliflower ear and flattened proboscis. A classic 'Roman' nose, sir. Roamin' all over my face, I tell 'em."

"You're a pugilist."

"Was, sir. Ranked number five in the country 'til John L. put his mitts to me." He extended an open palm. "Identification, please."

The Marshal handed him his badge and credentials.

Conway glanced at the .32 Colt holstered inside his long coat.

"I'll take that revolver, sir."

Bassett shook his head.

"No, thanks. I think I'll keep it."

"They told me a Marshal from Fall River would stop by today. You're here to see 'Fowler, John, Cell Thirteen'."

He nodded.

"Will you be wantin' me present during your visit?"

"Unnecessary. I can handle Fowler."

"Better you than me."

He handed the badge and ID back. When Bassett met his gaze, his eyes held an uneasiness that hinted at something like fear. The Marshal had seen it throughout the staff. A creeping silence like some unspoken terror had descended on the hospital. He looked down the corridor. Figures dressed in white moved like phantoms on a ghost ship.

His eyes narrowed.

"Why did you say that?" he asked. "Does Fowler frighten you?"

Conway thought for a moment, then jutted his chest out in something resembling a boxer's stance.

"In the ring, I can see what I got in front of me. Big. Small. Tough. Sissified. In there," he said, gesturing toward the corridor, "in that world, I don't know what the fug goes on in his mind and that scares the bejesus outta me."

He picked up the keys from the desk and walked. Bassett followed him and he was soon unlocking Cell Thirteen. The Marshal looked up at the corridor ceiling. As he watched, a lightbulb went dim then flicked-out completely.

"Go on in."

Bassett said nothing, just stared at him.

"Want it locked behind you?"

"No."

Conway held his gaze for a moment, then left. A cold, shadowy feeling washed over Bassett as he watched his squat frame disappear into the darkness.

He stepped into the cell. His body threw off an enormous shiver as the door slammed shut behind him. Eyes wide and alert, he searched the small, padded cell—a commode, a sink, a canvas cot where Fowler sat hollow-eyed, stroking the curly black hair of a ventriloquist's doll sitting on his lap.

"Bassett," he said in a toneless voice, nothing like his own. "I've been waiting."

Prominent in the background, the Marshal could hear the steady drip of water into the basin, plop, plop.

"For me?"

He nodded with certainty.

The lights flickered. Bassett's stare did not waver.

"Then you know why I'm here."

Again, he nodded, still stroking the doll's head. Then, he stopped and put his ear to the doll's lips.

"Isabella says she knows how you found us. It was the Pinkerton."

The Marshal approached the cot where Fowler sat, smiling. How could he know it was Frank Goyer who directed him to the asylum?

"Yes," he said. "How did you know?"

Plop. Silence. Another plop.

Bassett's tongue became thick. He was sweating. Though Fowler had shriveled to no more than one-hundred-twenty pounds, he sensed he was facing something monumentally powerful.

"The Evil One told me," he answered, eyes gleaming with intelligence. "He said you'd appreciate it."

"It?"

"The display of prescience. Isn't life theater, after all? Players on a stage and all that." He giggled into his palm. "He doesn't like you. You should know that. Call it a warning."

"I didn't come here to play games, John. You are John Fowler? Wife beater? Murderer? Member of the Fall River cult?"

The contour of his expression, drawn and sallow, suddenly brightened.

"Bottom fact is, those two—Charlie and Bess—was the pulse a me heart!" he exclaimed in Fowler's Irish brogue. "Banshees in hames! Bollox all of it!" he mimicked. "He's off his chump, I tell ya!" He shook his head, laughing. "What a fool our John Fowler!" he declared, voice returning to that of the stranger.

Bassett stared into his eyes; eyes like the claws of an eagle, impossible to escape.

"If you're not John Fowler, who are you?"

"The Master is a Traveler! He loves to travel," he prattled, stroking the doll's head excitedly. "Says it's the gypsy in him!"

"You killed them, didn't you? Charles and Bessie. Your own flesh and blood. Strangled the life out of those babies and used their bodies as an offering to Satan!"

"Not nice, Marshal Hilliard," he chided, wagging a finger at him. "Not nice at all." Then, putting his ear to the doll's lips, "Yes, that's right. No doubt about that," he affirmed. "Isabella says you are judgmental," he advised, looking up to him. "Says the Master doesn't like you. She doesn't like you, either."

"So, you killed them."

"Not exactly," he temporized, turning the doll's head around to face him, watching Bassett's expression change from curiosity to horror at the sight of the doll's visage: eyes plucked from the sockets, cheeks slashed, nose, ears, mouth removed, face smeared with blood and feces. "You see, our communication is rarely direct. Understand, the Evil One has a million things on his mind—disease and murder, imminent war, the dawn of a new century, *his* century. And so, he requires intermediates. A doll will do in a pinch, though he much prefers humans. Takes delight in bringing down the 'holy' ones. A nice girl, a 'saintly' girl, like our Clara. But I'm not the object of his affection, few are, so I communicate through Isabella. And, trust me, it works. You're here, Marshal Hilliard, are you not?"

Bassett felt the hair prickling up on his hands as he listened to the dripping.

"Yes," he conceded, darkly. "I'm here."

"But why did you come?" he asked, sprightly. "To hear my confession? 'Bless me, Father, for I have sinned—' Forgiveness? Mercy? Those are the sins, Marshal Hilliard. It's chaos and blood we pray for. Humiliation to the righteous! Desecration to the sacred!" he sang-out madly, then stopped, face writhed with distaste. "But what would you know about that?"

"I know what is right and wrong—"

"Do you?"

"—what is sick and evil," he continued, "and what is just. I am here, John Fowler, or whoever the hell you are, to right the balance; to avenge the murders of Charles and Bessie. I'm here to send you and Holmes, the Ripper and all the others back to the molten pit you crawled out of!"

"But I didn't do it," he said blithely, stroking the doll's head again.

"What?"

"I did not kill them."

"Liar!" Bassett shouted.

"You're a man of the law, a detective of sorts. You, above all, should know I didn't kill them—not those squalid little fucklets and certainly not Forest. How could I? It's your theory that whoever murdered Charles and Bessie also murdered Forest. But I was here at Danvers, locked in a cage, bound up in a straitjacket. Check the logs. I could not have killed him, or skinned him, or watched him die, because I was here in Cell Thirteen! From the bottom of my heart I tell you, I could not have murdered Forest and I did not strangle those babies though—to be fair—I drank their blood with the others and, yes, I was the one who cut them to pieces, *after* the life was wrung out of them, *after* they were dead."

"Then, who? Who killed them?"

In the small, padded cell his words sounded distant, otherworldly, as if someone else had spoken them.

"C'mere, Marshal," Fowler promised with a nod and a wink, "and I'll give you a clue."

Bassett stared at him strangely. Time seemed to stretch-out before him. A minute could have been an hour, an hour a day. He felt suspended between the seconds on a clock.

"C'mon, lean in, Hilliard," he said, waving him forward, "and I'll whisper it so no one else can hear."

He took a step forward, listening to the dripping, *plop*, *plop*, like the pounding of a drum in a death march, egging him on until, finally, he put his ear to Fowler's lips.

"You know 'im. The one what did it," he rasped, "and he knows you. It was a friend a yours who killed them babies. It was he who snuck into Forest's room, put 'im out with a dose, and skinned 'im alive!"

Bassett's eyes grew wide. As he pulled back, startled, Fowler slipped his hand into his long coat, snatching the Colt revolver from its holster. Then, with a high-pitched laugh that pierced the cell's gloaming silence, he held the gun up and took aim.

The Marshal gathered his strapping frame, furious and unafraid.

"Go ahead. Shoot, you son of a bitch!"

And he did. Fowler put the gun to his temple and pulled the trigger, a miasma of blood and white brain tissue splattering the wall behind him.

FOUR

Rooming House

Two Days Later

The "woman" spoke from the depths of her soul when she vowed to kill the 'thing' inside her. At first, the "demon" could only access her thoughts fleetingly and assumed her existence was inconsequential. But once in tune with her innermost feelings, it was shocked to discover the "woman's" enmity knew no bounds.

Unlike the "saint," who it could torment without reprisal, she was determined not merely to hold her ground, but to destroy the "demon." Almost immediately upon discovering its control over her, the "woman"—proud, self-reliant, determined—rebelled. At first, by resisting its coming. Then, in premeditated attacks, designed to destroy it.

While in the hospital, the "demon" appeared spontaneously. She had looked into the mirror after washing her face to find it glowering back at her. It was a shock, she admitted, but that was because she was unprepared. This time, they would meet on her terms. She would lure the "demon," duplicating her actions, inviting it to appear and stand up to it. Why was it here? What did it want? What right did it have to put her life at risk? But it wouldn't end there. As rightful owner of the body, she would demand that the creature leave or be cast out by whatever means necessary.

At precisely 9:35 p.m., the "woman" splashed water on her face. She reached for a towel and dried herself, then glanced to the mirror, exactly as she had done forty-eight hours earlier. At first, there seemed no more than her own reflection. But, then, in the swimming fog, she discerned something peculiar. The eyes that stared back at her were glinting. A smile curled the corners of her lips in an expression totally unlike the emotions she was feeling.

She brushed her fingertips across her cheek. The image did the same. Or did it? She lifted her right hand. It replicated the gesture, but sluggish and out-of-synch. She whipped her head around to the left and her heart skipped a beat. The image reflected no motion at all, its expression molded into a mocking smile—sinister, diabolical—the 'thing' that possessed her.

"Who are you?" she asked, warily.

No answer. Just the smile, frozen like a clown's painted grin.

"What do you want?"

Again, no response. The eyes glowered.

"Why do you hate me?" she asked, then stopped, realizing the absurdity of her method. How could she speak and answer at the same time?

The two eyed each other with cautious surmise as the "woman" reached for a pencil and paper.

"I am going to ask you questions and you are going to write the answers. Do you understand?"

The "demon" nodded.

"Who are you?"

Again, that wintry grin, eyes black as coal.

"Answer when I talk to you!" she screamed, stomping her boots on the floor. "Why do you not answer!"

Ponderously, her hand lifted.

"I am Spirit," it wrote.

"Nonsense!"

"Do not test me," the "demon" warned.

She thought for a moment, then spoke.

"What happened in Fall River?"

"Forest hurt you and you died."

"Is that all?"

The hand glided across the page.

"Ask Prince."

"Something else happened," she said, straining to remember. "What was it?"

The "demon" drew a crude sketch of a girl engulfed in flames.

"Tell me!"

"I won't."

"You will!" she insisted.

The "demon" drew a second picture. This one of a girl surrounded by figures dressed in dark, hooded robes.

"You are an idiot!" the "woman" huffed.

"Ask Prince," it scrawled. "He knows."

"What does he know?"

"Babies," it wrote, suddenly agitated, *Dead! Dead! Dead!*", pressing the pencil down so hard it broke, then hurling it across the room.

The "woman" snatched another pencil from the drawer.

"What does Dr. Prince know?"

Devil! Devil! Devil!" it scribbled, followed by a raft of wild scrawling impossible to decipher.

"Wait! You can't leave! Not now!"

But it was no use. The "demon" had left. Their second encounter was over.

Vexed and angry, the "woman" changed into a nightgown and slipped into bed, thoughts of her confrontation with the "demon" spinning like pinwheels in her mind until, exhausted, she settled into granite sleep.

Hours later, drenched in the room's crawling darkness, she awakened to the sound of scratching—*scraping*—like fingers clawing from within the surrounding walls. She sprung up in bed. Her eyes prowled the four corners of the room, listening, then stopped, spellbound, and that is when she saw them. Like shadows, dark and grim. Creeping toward her.

They arrived in a cluster. Surrounding the bed. Pulling tight around her. Cowled in dark, hooded robes, faces hidden, they reached out at her.

Grabbing her arms. Slamming them down onto the mattress. Then, her legs. Clamped down and spread open. Convinced they had her secured, their heads turned to the hulking figure rising behind them. Looming over her: the One.

"You want to know what happened?" the creature demanded. "You want to know what they did to you?"

Suddenly, she was twelve years old again, sensing a sudden change blind with revulsion as she watched the men line up in front of her. Some wore the heads of pigs. Others, the masks of jackals, or wolves, or goats. One at a time, they edged forward, between her legs, spread wide by the others. The first mask lifted. It was her father, John, pie-eyed drunk, thrusting his erection inside her. Stinging. Ripping. Pain tearing through her body and soul while the others swarmed. The Reverend Parker, dressed as a harlot, performed an invocation, brandishing an excrement-covered crucifix over the devirgination. Next, Doc Landry. Then, Richard Forest, and a parade of others.

Body writhing, the "woman" lashed her head to the left where Charles' torso lay, his severed skull beside it. Then, to her right, where Bessie's defiled corpse rested, appendages stacked in a pile, head removed, staring marble-eyed, atop it.

"You want to know what happened?" the worshipers demanded, passing a blood-filled chalice one to the-other. "You want to know what we did to you?"

"THIS IS WHAT HAPPENED!" the One roared, red-veined eyes drilling into hers, thrashing a machete down into the altar. "THANK ME! ADORE ME! ALL OF THIS," he proclaimed, "MADE YOU WHAT YOU ARE TODAY!"

"Hail to the Master! Hail Satan!" the worshipers clamored.

"Oh, how the mighty hath fallen," the One sniffed, rearing its body upward, jamming its phallus into her.

Overcome, the "woman" fainted, still whimpering in a state beyond consciousness.

She would not awaken the next morning. Nor the one after that.

FIVE

Old Corner Bookstore
Washington Street
Boston, Massachusetts

Morton Prince perused the rack of magazines on the wall of the Old Corner Bookstore, surrounded by shelves stacked with volumes dating back to the store's founding in 1828. Its history as a meeting place for authors like Hawthorne, Emerson, and Dickens was almost as enticing as its selection of periodicals, Prince was thinking, as his eyes swept over copies of *Argosy*, *Scientific American*, and *The Atlantic*.

He picked up the *American Review*, John Sargent's portrait of TR with the caption "Theodore Roosevelt, 26th President of the United States" on the cover. He paged through it, flicking a furtive glance beyond the plate-glass window to Washington Street, where he expected to see Bassett any time now.

His gaze dropped to a photo of President McKinley lying on his deathbed. Nicknamed the "Human Iceberg," he had been shot twice in the abdomen by Leon Czolgosz, a twenty-eight-year-old anarchist, after giving a speech at the Pan American Exposition in Buffalo, New York. Now, it was up to the "young firebrand," TR, to lead the nation the *Review* declared alongside a photo of the Vice-President being sworn into office.

The article was informative, McKinley's assassination shocking, but where was Bassett?

He looked at his pocket watch: 2:05 pm. It was Bassett who requested the meeting, but Prince who chose the location, off-site from his office, where the Marshal wouldn't be recognized.

"Dr. Prince!" he heard a voice ring out above the hushed commotion of book buyers and sellers. It was Dr. Putnam, bespectacled with Van Dyke goatee, beaming a greeting as he approached. "I see you're reading *The Review*. Forty-two years old," he decried, referring to Roosevelt. "Never liked him much myself. But he's president now."

"Yes," Prince deflected, eyes darting to the window.

"First class portrait," Putnam admired, glancing at the cover. "Chartrand?"

"No. Sargent," he replied.

"I thought about telephoning last week to inquire about the Fowler girl, but never got around to it. Has her condition improved?"

"Yes, but slowly," Prince answered, frowning as he spied Bassett parading toward the entrance.

Dressed in a black, vested suit, leather boots and long coat with handlebar mustache and white hair swept to either side of his steed derby, he looked like something between a Dodge City lawman and a riverboat gambler.

"I'm not prying, mind you," the doctor chundled on, "but I understand she was hospitalized last week."

Prince watched Bassett enter. The Marshal acknowledged him with a wink and stepped discreetly behind a row of bookshelves.

"An overnight at Mass General for observation. Nothing serious," he advised, then, turning to him, "would you excuse me, please? I'm here to meet someone. I think he just arrived."

"By all means," Putnam agreed. "Regards to Fanny," he called out, watching him disappear behind the book racks.

"Come with me," Prince said, ushering Bassett toward the staircase leading to the second floor.

The Marshal looked at him steadfastly.

"Why are we meeting here and not your office?"

"If you must know, it's because Fanny is afraid of you. You frighten people, Bassett!"

Upstairs, they sat in a private reading room with portraits of Longfellow, Melville, and Thoreau hung on the walls.

"You wanted to meet," Prince said, an edge of irritability creeping into his voice. "You said it was important."

"Fowler's dead."

"Dead?"

"Yes, 'dead,' as in no longer living. I tracked him down to Danvers Lunatic Asylum. He shot himself through the head with my gun," he said, patting the revolver inside his long coat. "I wrote the Colt Company in Hartford and thanked them."

"My God, Bassett, it's not a joking matter! A man is dead, but at least the murders are solved, and this nightmare is over."

"Not nearly."

"I don't understand. John Fowler murdered Charles and Bessie, then killed Forest for revenge for breaking from the cult and taking his daughter. No need to go into your theories about Holmes and the Ripper. You got what you came for. Fowler is dead, if not by mandate of the court, by his own hand."

"I checked the logs. Fowler was trussed-up in a straitjacket, Cell Thirteen, at Danvers on the night Forest was murdered and for three months before that."

"But the infants, surely—"

"No," he said, cutting him short. "There was a cult and the babies' bodies were sacrificed in Black Mass ceremonies, but before he blew his brains out, Fowler swore he had nothing to do with the murders."

"He's lying!" Prince blustered. "If not him, it was the doctor. As family physician, he had the opportunity and the means. Poison, or asphyxiation, like the coroner reported. As for Forest, Chief Homer is assuming one of his business partners carried the murders out. It seems Forest was what the Chief calls a "confidence man," luring investors with forged city contracts for construction projects, then making off with their money."

"Not likely."

"Why?"

"A disgruntled investor would use a gun, not a knife. A knife is personal. And if it was a knife, no sane man would kill him like that—cutting, then peeling the face from his skull, leaving him to suffer for hours on end. No only a maniac kills like that. This was no business partner. This, Dr. Prince, was a monster, and it wasn't about money. It was about annihilation—"

He grunted, "—and your theories about Holmes and the Ripper, I suppose."

Bassett pulled a flask from the inside pocket of his long coat. He held it out to Prince, who declined, then sat back in his chair. He took a leisurely swig and deposited it back into his coat pocket. He stood, stretched his long, muscular frame toward the ceiling and sniffed at the air.

"That odor," he said, "that scent you carry in the fabric of your clothes. I noticed it before in the consulting room where you conduct your sessions. What is it?"

"It's ether, infused with lilac," he answered. "A proprietary formula I have blended at Robinson's apothecary. The raw chemical is pungent." He chortled. "Fanny complained it made the house smell like an infirmary."

"Ether? That's an anesthetic, isn't it? Used by surgeons during amputations?"

"And other procedures."

He flashed a quick smile.

"But you're not a surgeon."

"If you must know, Miss Fowler is subject to changes in personality, some of them violent. I use the ether to facilitate her therapy."

"The 'demonic' episodes Hodgson talks about?"

"Yes."

"And how is Miss Fowler? Since that incident at Harvard Bridge, I worry about her."

"No change."

"I'm sorry to hear that," he lamented. Then, looking up from the floor, took note. "You used the word 'violent' to describe her personality changes."

"'Acute' is a more precise term. The alternations in her demeanor can be intense. It's symptomatic of her condition. Think of a normal individual's disposition given the requisite circumstances—sadness, joy, anger, contentment—multiply it ten times and that will give you some idea of what I'm describing. But the 'ether'?" Prince asked, puzzled. "Why the sudden interest?"

Bassett shrugged.

"An observation. I meant to ask before now but didn't."

"No," Prince insisted, "you asked for a reason. What was it?"

"Forest's room, at the Parker House, where I found him that night. It reeked of what I mistook for perfume. Strange, I thought then, that the air would be filled with the scent of lilac. But now I know. It wasn't perfume. It was ether." He stopped and thought for a moment. "Did anyone other than yourself have access to the ether in your household? A patient? A visitor?"

"Cody, I suppose, but what use would he have for it?" Prince felt the skin of his face contract as if something repulsive had touched him. "You're not suggesting Cody had something to do with Forest's murder?"

"No," he said, shaking his head, convinced. "What motive would Cody have? And if the murders—the one in Boston and two in Fall River—are connected, how would he fit into the picture? Still, you might ask him where he was that night," he suggested, then, thinking past that, added, "You mentioned Doc Landry, who was at the Fowler house at the time of both murders. So far as I know, his current whereabouts are unknown. If you could ask Clara—"

"I'll see what I can do," he replied. "Is that all? Is there anything else you wanted to see me about?"

The Marshal eased himself back into the armchair and lit up an Old Judge. He crossed his long legs, one over the other, exposing the black leather of his spit-shined boots.

"No, there is something else," he said, tense and careful, as he drew on his cigarette. "Something even more puzzling, that eats at me."

"Yes?"

"That night at the hotel, I was sure Forest had left his room. I watched someone leave through the School Street exit dressed in Forest's overcoat, wearing Forest's brown fedora," he explained, "but it could not have been Forest because Forest was bound to a chair, dying."

"That's easy to explain. You were mistaken. There must have been two hundred people in the lobby that night."

The Marshal leveled a sullen stare at him.

"You were one of them."

Prince felt the earth shift under his feet. The rambling conversation had made a sudden turn toward interrogation.

"Along with Fanny, the James, and Lowells," he answered. "You were there, too, Marshal. In the lobby. And the first to discover Forest's body. Now that you mention it, I've often wondered why you left before the police arrived. Did you report it? You never said."

"*Touche,*" Bassett said, blowing a stream of cigarette smoke into the air. "I see the doctor is as handy with words as he is with a scalpel." He laughed. "I did report it to the police. Check with Chief Homer, he'll tell you."

"And your presence at the Fowler house, June 11th and August 24th," he remarked, getting up from his chair to leave. "Doc Landry wasn't the only one there at the time of Charles' and Bessie's murders. Good day, Marshal." He smiled, a glint of satisfaction in his expression. "Let me know if there's anything else I can do to help."

"The ether, Dr. Prince," he called out after him, "with the lilac scent? I checked at the apothecary. Seems he blends it exclusively for you. There are no other users."

The doctor digested the remark for a moment, then swung around to him.

"You can go to the Devil with what the alchemist told you, Marshal. Take your gun, your badge, and your flask of whiskey, and go to Hell!"

Bassett watched him storm out of the room. He crushed his cigarette out on the floor with the heel of his boot, ran his fingertips thoughtfully over his handlebar mustache, smiled, then laughed.

SIX

Prince residence

12:30 a.m.

It was the doorbell ring, followed by three taps on the front door, that brought Dr. Prince out of bed, down the staircase, and into the foyer. Annoyed that anyone would call on him at this late hour, he slung the door open, prepared to vent his irritation, but stopped at the sight of what confronted him.

It was the "woman," but unlike he had ever seen her. Dressed in a cotton nightshirt, shivering amidst the low-hanging fog, her face was blue-gray from the cold, her eyes misty and remote. But there was more. Something dark and desolate that forced the juices of fear through him. Beyond physically beaten, the "woman," once proud and confident, seemed psychologically broken, fearful of everything around her.

"Miss Fowler—"

She took a mincing step forward.

"I did good, didn't I?" she asked in a faltering voice. "I fought hard as I could to rid myself of the devil. And I was strong—at least for a while. Isn't that so, Dr. Prince? Didn't I do good?"

"Come in out of the cold!" he urged, shepherding her into the house.

"Morton, who is it?" Fanny trilled.

She drifted down the staircase, then stopped abruptly, seeing her husband looking up from the foyer, Miss Fowler shuddering beside him. She bustled down the stairs.

"My poor dear," she said, taking her into her arms, wrapping them tight around her.

She stood unsteadily as Fanny clutched her to her breast. Then, sensing some quaking agony inside the woman she held, examined her at arms' length.

"Look at her, Morton! She's covered with bruises!"

The doctor stepped toward Miss Fowler as Cody rushed to join them.

"Sorry, Dr. Prince," he apologized. "I was downstairs in me room sleepin'."

With those words, the "woman" collapsed into the doctor's arms.

"Help me get her upstairs!" he said, turning to Cody, Fanny trailing in their wake as they climbed the staircase.

Their footsteps sounded hollow on the uncarpeted stairs, little Claire watching, hand-to-mouth, from beyond her bedroom door.

"Go to bed," Fanny demanded.

"But, mama—"

"Get back in your room now *and close the door!*"

Fanny collected a blanket and some dry clothes from the hallway closet, sensing a sudden change in the atmosphere. The house boiled with nervousness. The walls vibrated unease.

She entered her husband's office as he and Cody rested the "woman" down onto the davenport. Half the room was in shadow and the grayness from the outside washed the rest in pale spectral light.

"I believe she's comin' to, Dr. Prince," Cody said, looking up from the protracted body.

But Prince had already stridden to the cabinet where he kept his medical supplies.

"Look at this, Morton," Fanny declared, aghast, "cuts covering every inch of her body and—bite marks! Who, in God's name, would do such a thing!"

"Perhaps, she did it to herself," he suggested, splitting a spirit of hartshorn capsule and fanning it under her nose. "Possibly, an attacker or gang of them."

"'To herself'?" Fanny asked, incredulously. "Look at her back, Morton. Her legs! Her thighs!"

Fanny put a blanket over her. The "woman" bucked up from the couch, terrified. Her flaring eyes searched the room, her mind picking up pieces and fitting them together—Dr. Prince, Fanny, Cody—with one thought plowing through the delirium.

"Kill me, Dr. Prince," she begged. "I want to die, do you understand? Please promise you will do it!"

"What happened, Miss Fowler?" he implored. "Who did this to you?"

She shook her head, a frenzied animal look in her eyes.

"I don't belong here! Can't you see that? I must go back to where I came from. Please help me! I want to die!"

"Miss Fowler," he exhorted, seizing her by the shoulders. "I can't help you, unless I know who did this and why!"

The "woman" looked him full in the eye. An amalgam of terror and rage rose within her.

"I know what happened now. All of it!" Her voice trailed away. Her eyes grew troubled and distant. "They needed a virgin, Dr. Prince. A virgin like Mary, the mother of Jesus, to—" she started to explain but stopped mid-sentence, burying her face in her hands.

"To do what, Miss Fowler? You must tell me!"

She looked up to him, helplessly. The glistening of tears stained her cheeks.

"To defile the Virgin. To have their way with her. To have their way with me! All of them. My father, Dr. Prince. He was one of them. And my mother. Doc Landry. The Reverend Parker! They needed Charles and Bessie for their ceremony. Cut them to pieces, drank their blood, and they raped me!"

With that, the "woman" broke down, Prince watching as Fanny raced to her.

"You remembered what happened," he whispered, a slow-burning fire lit in his brain. "The 'catastrophic trauma' that tore you apart, shattered you as a whole person into fragmented pieces of yourself." His head snapped around to Cody. "I want Dr. Waterman here at once. Hodgson, too!"

"But, sir—"

"I don't give a damn what time it is. Get them!"

"Professor James?"

"Yes."

"Mrs. Piper?"

His face flushed crimson.

"All of them, here now!"

"She needs to go to the hospital, Morton," Fanny worried, turning to him as he prepared a *paraldehyde* injection.

"No, she shall stay here, until the others arrive," he said, administering the needle. "There is nothing the doctors at Mass General can do that we can't do here. In the meantime, I'd like you to prepare a kettle of tea for Waterman and the others. If what I'm thinking is correct, we have a grueling day ahead of us."

With the "woman" sedated, the doctor returned to his desk euphoric at the prospect of identifying the 'catastrophic trauma' that triggered Miss Fowler's *dissociation* and the insight it provided. If neither the "saint" nor the "woman" were real individuals, was there an alternate possibility hidden in plain sight?

He put one hand on the "saint's" character study and the other on the "woman"s.' He pushed them together. As expected, they fit like two pieces of a puzzle. The positive characteristics integral to the "saint's" persona—patient, even-tempered, considerate of others—counterbalanced the negative characteristics of the "woman"—impatient, quick-tempered, obstinate. Likewise, the positive characteristics of the "woman"—healthy, resolute, stable—counterbalanced the negative characteristics of the "saint"—neurasthenic, depressed, mentally unstable. Perhaps, more compelling, Prince surmised, was the pairing of memories. When hypnotized, the "saint" remembered Miss Fowler's current life, but almost nothing about her childhood. When hypnotized, the "woman" remembered Miss Fowler's childhood, but nothing about her current life.

Prince scrutinized the two studies, turned into one. What if the hypnotized "saint" and the hypnotized "woman" could somehow be fused together into a unified consciousness? Might that combination restore the fractured Miss Fowler to her original self? More, would it eliminate the "demon"?

He dipped his pen into the ink well on his desk and drew a schematic of the process.

$$BI (``saint") + BIII (``woman")$$
$$- BII (``demon")$$
$$=$$
$$BIV (Miss \ Fowler \ restored)$$

For more than a decade, the psychical catastrophe that caused Miss Fowler's *dissociation* was locked away in a vault deep within her subconscious mind, unreachable by either the "saint" or the 'woman.' At last, she had confronted the horror that haunted her; a tectonic shift in the lonely journey that was her life. With the vault's door open, this was his opportunity to fuse the two entities, cure her, and claim his rightful place among psychology's pantheon of icons. He would not let his moment pass!

Hidden beyond the specter of a gas-lit street lamp across from Prince's row house, Rufus "Bassett" Hilliard observed with a recording eye. Through the window shades, he watched the doctor working late into the night, Mrs. Prince busying herself in anticipation of visitors, and Cody, their servant, bolt from the house.

He slipped his watch from out of his vest pocket, 2:15 a.m. Over the next ninety minutes, he would see Dr. Waterman, Mr. Hodgson, Professor James, and the medium, Leonora Piper, arrive at the Prince residence.

None of it made sense, the Marshal ruminated. Unless something massively important was about to happen.

VI: RESURRECTION OF THE DEAD

*"The greatest trick the Devil ever played
was convincing the world he does not exist."*
–Charles Baudelair
The Flowers of Evil

ONE

Prince's Home
November 2, 1901

9:15 a.m.

The team gathered in Prince's office, Fanny having taken Miss Fowler to the guest room where she slept, a smile as archaic as the Egyptian gods stamped on her lips. The viciousness of this latest attack appalled the doctor. Whether self-inflicted or paranormal, he knew he had to change tactics. Bereft of alternatives, fusing the "woman" and the "saint" seemed his last chance to cure her.

Despite the impromptu nature of the meeting, everyone attended, each believing the Fowler case was important, if not historic. Fanny fortified them with strong coffee and hot tea served in stout, ceramic mugs, but with the team already locked in furious discussion, the gesture seemed superfluous. Understanding the deadly crossroad Miss Fowler was facing, they sat in chairs arced around Prince's desk.

"Though we may disagree on the identification of her disorder, I think we can assume the trauma Miss Fowler experienced from the Fall River cult is responsible for her condition. In short, we have at last uncovered the 'catastrophic trauma' that caused her *dissociation*." His gaze shifted to Hodgson. "Now, I realize, Richard, that you and Mrs. Piper see last night's assault as a manifestation of the demonic, but I ask that we put our differences aside and find a path forward. I have proposed mine."

"Pardon me," Hodgson reminded, "but wasn't it just two months ago that we identified Forest's assault as the 'catastrophic trauma' that triggered her condition?"

"Let me be clear, the shock of the Satanic ritual cleaved the bedrock of Clara Fowler's psyche. It was on that night that her single consciousness split, creating the 'saint" and the 'woman.' One that lived in our current world, the other frozen in the past. Forest's attack jarred those memories and, though buried deep in her subconscious, the "woman" awakened. Finally, last night, unable to suppress those memories any longer, she was forced to face the reality of what happened. So, to answer your question, Richard, it was both. First, the splitting of the original Miss Fowler when she was twelve. Second, Forest's assault, at the age of eighteen. Simply put, these two events represent the 'psychic catastrophes' that lie at the heart of her disorder."

William James drew on his Meerschaum pipe.

"What about the demon?"

"Yes," Prince sighed, "the most problematic. The so-called "demon" is the only one of the three that possesses all of Miss Fowler's memories, including both attacks. If the original personality split in two to escape knowledge of them, what might the third be like, the one carrying with it the horror of both abominations?"

"A demon—" Waterman whispered loud enough for the others to hear.

"No, no," James objected, "my question runs deeper than that! Even if the "saint" and the "woman" can be fused it still leaves the "demon" to plague the surviving entity. That is no cure!"

"May I respond?" Waterman volunteered. "In fusing the two entities, Dr. Prince—we," he amended, "are trying to squeeze the "demon' out. When the "saint" and the "woman" are combined they will restore the original Miss Fowler—physically strong, mentally stable—the one who, prior to the Black Mass experience, suffered no delusions and knew nothing about demons."

"Yes, that sums it up nicely," Prince commended, turning to a black board set beside his desk. "I have drawn a schematic of the procedure."

He scribbled, 'BI +BIII-BII=BIV' on the board with chalk.

"What you are proposing, Dr. Prince, is reckless," Leonora Piper's voice rang out amid the roiling silence. "You ignore the fact that every pathology you have described is deeply rooted in the spiritual. The possession of an individual is often brought on by opening a door to the spirit world, sometimes intentionally, often without forethought. Here we have a young woman and two innocent babes sacrificed to Satan on an altar as heathens might sacrifice animals to their pagan deity. I ask you, what could be more enticing to the devil than a Black Mass inviting him to appear, if not in carnal form, then in the person of a spirit that invades another's body. Don't you see? What you are proposing, Dr. Prince, is as dangerous to Miss Fowler as it is to those around her. You are challenging a dark and powerful enemy with psychology when it is God's wrath it fears!"

The doctor smiled condescendingly.

"And what would you recommend, Mrs. Piper?"

"An exorcism, authorized by the Catholic Church, and carried out by an ordained priest!"

The doctor's smile died. His eyes narrowed.

"Let me be frank, Mrs. Piper. There is nothing mysterious or mystical about the Fowler case. Of all the medical records I have studied, nearly all had histories of childhood incest, torture, or other abuses. Clara's condition is a manifestation of an inner conflict caused by trauma, so we try to get at it. The best procedure is *hypno-therapy* or *narcosynthesis*, a treatment that uses drugs. In Miss Fowler's case, we chose the former and despite how it may appear, we are making progress."

"When forced to decide between two choices, I resort to the law of chance and probability. In my opinion," she answered in a burst of fury, "it is far less fanciful to believe an alien entity has taken control of Miss Fowler than to believe that each of the paranormal phenomena we have witnessed is likely to occur in one individual through purely natural causes!"

Professor James tapped out his pipe and lifted a book from the table in front of him.

"Mrs. Piper, Mr. Hodgson, you talk about the Catholic Church and exorcism. Let me read a passage from the *Acts of the Synod of Rheim* given as instruction to would-be exorcists. 'The too credulous,' the Church forewarns, 'are often deceived, and lunatics often declare themselves to be possessed and tormented by the devil, but these people are far more in need of a doctor than an exorcist.' That statement was written in 1583." His dark, deep-set eyes swept over each of them, one at a time. "I see no point in arguing. I propose we take a vote between Dr. Prince's fusion procedure and Mrs. Piper's exorcism."

He looked across the desk to Prince.

"Fusion procedure," he stated. "I shall always believe in science over superstition."

"Waterman?"

"Fusion procedure."

"Mr. Hodgson?"

"Exorcism."

"Mrs. Piper?"

"Exorcism."

"It seems the decision comes down to my vote," James pondered, brushing his hand over his beard. "Me, a proponent of abnormal psychology who, to the core of his being, believes in life everlasting." He chuckled at the irony, then spoke. "Fusion procedure."

A dim and lacy sunlight penetrated the doctor's office from the window facing Beacon Street, then dissipated to semi-darkness as the team dissembled.

Miss Fowler would be escorted to the consultation room shortly. The fusion experiment was about to begin.

TWO

Consultation Room

They walked into the consultation room like primitives entering a dark cave, never knowing what to expect. Once inside, Prince broke from the group. The others fell back to the four chairs in the rear of the room.

Miss Fowler sat on the sofa she often used during sessions. The doctor approached. It was the "woman" who sat before him.

"How are you feeling?"

"I am embarrassed about last night," she confessed. "Dr. Prince, will you ever forgive me!"

He took a seat across from her. Almost immediately, he had an imminent sense of danger—something untouchable, beyond his reach.

"You needn't be embarrassed. Perhaps you'd like to tell me how you got those cuts and bruises."

She hung her head down, sobbing.

"You know what happened," she blurted, her face mottled with anger. "I told you last night." She shook her head as if to dispel the memory. "I don't want to talk about it!"

"Was it the "demon"?" he asked.

"It happens late at night; sometimes when I'm awake, often when I'm sleeping. I keep telling myself it's only a dream, a 'night terror' as you call them, but it isn't a dream. Look at what they've done to me!"

"'They'?"

"You know who 'they' are. You know what 'it' is. The One and his surrogates. Monsters that creep into my room like shadows in the dark. Sometimes I can see them, but never clearly as last night. Dr. Prince, I need to go back to where I came from! Can you not see that? You've got to help me!"

"Please, Miss Fowler, calm yourself. You are in a safe place now. Whatever happened last night is over."

"No, it is not over! You know that. And the others back there," she said, pointing a quavering finger. "Look at them, gaping like hyenas at a freak show. You're all as lost as I am. Wasting your time searching for a cure that doesn't exist!"

"I can see that you're upset and I don't blame you. But working together, I believe we can find a cure," he promised. "There is a procedure that may give you a chance at a happy, productive life. The life you've been trying to live for so many years. But I can't do it without your help. Will you?" he asked. "Will you help me?"

She nodded, brushing tears away with a handkerchief. "I shall try."

Prince looked pityingly at her ravaged face. And for a moment, time stood still.

Mrs. Piper was correct in warning him about the danger of the procedure, but the risk came, not from the spirit world, but from the procedure itself. In order to fuse BI with BIII, he had to retrogress both to face the trauma that had fractured one consciousness into three. The "woman" had already confronted it with cathartic results while the "saint" knew nothing about it. Given her fragile disposition, Prince wondered if retrogression was a mistake.

He started with the "woman," who sat before him. As expected, she recounted the Black Mass with soul-crushing agony: from the time her parents took her into the forest, to the discovery of Charles' and Bessie's dismembered remains, and the serial rape that followed. Afterward, it was essential that he keep her entranced simultaneous with the coming of the "saint", in order to fuse the two entities.

He shifted a furtive glance to his colleagues. Then, summoning the scattered forces of his mind, probed the silence in a low, strained voice.

"I am talking now to Clara Fowler. Do you hear me, Clara?"

"Yes."

"Do you see me?"

She opened her eyes, "Yes."

Satisfied she was hypnotized he began the retrogression.

"Relax and stay calm," he instructed, "and listen to me carefully. I want you to return to the time when you were a young girl of twelve. Back and back, still farther. What do you see?"

"I am reading a book in bed. I don't want to go into the other room because my father is there and I'm frightened of him."

"Why does he frighten you?"

"Because he is big and strong and brings out the strap for most anything I do."

The doctor contemplated his next question, then spoke.

"Do you go to church on Sundays with your father and mother?"

"I go to church, but not on Sundays."

"When do you go to church?"

"We go at night. It is dark. Especially in the forest."

"Is that where the church is, Clara, in the forest?"

"Yes."

"Very good," he encouraged. "Now, I want you to go back to the forest. You are with your father and mother. What do you see?"

"Fire. A big one."

"What else do you see?"

"Men dancing wearing horns and masks of animals. I'm scared. Shivering in the cold."

"What are you seeing that frightens you?"

"Behind the fire I see an altar, but not like the one in regular church. This one is made of wood, flat on top, like a table. Candles are burning on it."

"Yes, but what is it that scares you? What else do you see?"

"I am walking toward it. Mama is holding my hand. Several women join her, laughing and giggling and making a fuss over me."

"Is that what scares you?"

"No."

"I want you to look more closely and tell me what else you are seeing."

"I can't."

"Why?"

She closed her eyes, clapped her hands over them.

"It's too horrible to talk about."

"You must open your eyes," he commanded, "and tell me what you see."

"I see Charlie, my brother, and Bessie, my sister. Only it is not them, not anymore. Their bodies are cut up like in the butcher shop. Their heads are cut off and lying next to their arms and legs and chests. No!" she screamed. "I don't want to see! I want to go home!"

"Calm yourself, Clara. Take a deep breath. You are in a safe place. No one can harm you here."

She took a deep breath. Then, another and stopped, looking dazedly at Prince.

"Why are you doing this to me?"

Prince started to answer.

"I don't mean you. I'm talking to the animal men standing in front of me. I don't know how I got here, but I'm lying on the altar. The women are singing songs, dancing naked around the fire. My shoes and socks are off. My dress, too, and it's very cold."

"What else do you see?"

"I see my father. He is without clothes and the men pull my legs apart and he lies on top of me and it hurts like a fire burning inside me. I want to go home, but they won't let me!"

She squirmed in her chair, struck out at the air with her fists.

"My head feels like it is exploding. Suddenly, I am not there, but watching as the men force themselves into my mouth and vagina."

"You say you felt like someone else. Was this the first time you watched as if you were another person?"

"No," she said, shaking her head sadly.

"There was another time, is that right?"

"Yes," the voices of the "saint" and "woman" resonated in unison.

"I want you to go back to the first time you felt like another person. Do you understand what I am asking?"

"Yes," they replied.

"Tell me what you see."

"We are in the house with mama. Father is yelling. The baby is crying. Mother is sick in bed but gets up to hold Charlie. She nurses him. We all go back to sleep."

"Tell me, what are you seeing now?"

"We are in our bed. Mama is sleeping and Charlie starts crying again, loud, and he will not stop. Father is sleeping. Mama is too sick to get up. So, we go into the room. The baby's face is red and he is screaming. We pick him up. Take him in our arms and hold him to our breasts like mama does and that is all we see," they explained in strange, lilting voices. "We see black now. Nothing else."

The doctor sat forward in his chair. Something cold and shadowy rustled within him.

"Did you hurt the baby?"

"No," they answered.

"Did someone else hurt Charlie?"

"Yes."

"Who?"

"We can't tell you."

"Why can't you tell me?"

"Because he told us not to."

"Who told you not to?"

"We can't say anymore," they squalled. "He swore he would kill us if we did."

"Wait!" Leonora Piper shouted, racing toward the front of the room, Hodgson in tow. "Something is wrong!"

"Who?" Prince asked, rising from his chair, looming over her.

"Stop!" Piper screeched. "Stop this now!"

"Who threatened you?" Prince demanded.

"Morton!" Hodgson cried out. "You don't know what you are doing!"

"Who did it?" he screamed, shoving Hodgson aside. *"Who killed Charlie!"*

Then, silence.

Waterman and James drifted slowly up to join the others. Prince hovered over Miss Fowler, perspiration streaming down the sides of his face, physically and emotionally spent. Her head was bowed. Her face was hidden. At last, both entities had confronted the psychic trauma that lay dormant within Miss Fowler. Was it possible, the doctor's mind churned dream-like, that he had succeeded? That, at last, the "woman" and the "saint" had fused into one.

He cupped his fingers to the point of her chin and gently lifted it to see her face. Finally, he spoke.

"Who are you?" he asked prayerfully.

She looked up to him, her eyes shimmering with the blighting desolation of the crucified.

"Help me," she whimpered. "I am Miss Fowler," the "saint" entreated. "No, I am Miss Fowler," the "woman" countermanded. Then, with lips fleered back from her teeth like a wolf at the kill, "And I am the Devil!" the "demon" proclaimed, its massive, terrifying voice bounding through the room. And now the eyes were those of the One—eyes shrieking—eyes waiting. "Did you really think it would be that easy?"

The earth shuddered like a reflection in the water. Whether objectively real or a hallucination, what Prince's team saw was as beautiful as it was alien: red eyes beaming, mouth curled upward into a smile, both vengeful and exquisite, lips spread slightly to expose its cuspidated teeth, glistening white.

A dark and ugly quiet crept into the room.

"What business have you here?" Prince breathed.

"Why do I do the things I do? Is that what you're asking? An appropriate inquiry for an intruder into the minds of others." Still, the question amused it. "Sometimes for fun," the demon answered. Then, its smile died, its eyes narrowed. "But mostly, I'm all business."

Hodgson looked around him. The dim room seemed a chimera swarming with particles of brilliant light whirling like clouds of gnats. He stepped from behind Prince, eyes lit with wonder.

"Where do you come from?" Hodgson asked, edging toward it. "If you exist, there must be life on the other side. The body is flesh and bone, but the spirit lives on, isn't that so?" He drifted closer. The demon leered at him. "There was a young woman who I loved deeply. My Darling looked like a little girl when she awakened. Her skin had a lovely scent, like new-cut grass. The most comforting scent I know. But she died. Now I simply want to talk to her, do you understand? It has been so long and I miss her terribly." Hodgson gazed into its reptilian eyes. "Is it possible to contact the dead? To talk to them? To see them?"

"You want to know what awaits you after death?" the creature asked, lifting him by the throat with one hand. "Darkness awaits you. Eternal torment awaits you. I await you," it seethed, slamming him against the wall, upending a table, shattering a lamp. "As for your 'darling' Jesse? She is in Hell with the other whores sucking cocks; fucking our friends—the worst of the lot, I can assure you—scores of them, for all eternity." It smiled, eyes shiny and cold as a snake's eyes. "And to think, you never touched her!"

Outside the Prince residence, Bassett watched shadows flickering, voices screaming. His eagle eyes fastened on the second-floor window, brows pulled tight with apprehension, as he stalked across Beacon Street to investigate. Then, seeing a light go dark, broke into a mad dash.

"Want to know a secret?" the demon asked Prince. "While you are here playing psychiatrist, Cody is talking to your daughter, Claire. Moments from now, he will kill her. Did you know that?"

"Don't listen to him, Morton!" Leonora Piper cautioned.

"Shut your mouth!" Prince shouted at it.

"Of course, he'll start with ether. Your ether, from the medicine cabinet? Next, he will remove her clothing, shoes, socks, dress. Then, the corset waist—"

"Shut up!" Prince demanded.

"—and once she's stripped naked? That's when the fun begins. Surgical tools like this," he said, holding up a Liston amputation knife, long and razor-sharp. "You don't use it much anymore, and that's a disappointment, but Cody is using one right now. On your daughter. First Cut: sternum to pelvis. Second Cut: let's go for the throat—"

"Morton," James urged, grabbing him from behind as he marched forward in blind fury. "It is not true! It lies! It coerces!"

"—and if the proper surgical instrument is selected like the knife Cody has in his hands this moment, the throat can be slashed, and the spinal cord severed. Not easily, mind you. Not without a lot of blood. Then, and only then, can the head be removed." Its eyes burned into him. "Did you know that decapitated heads can continue to see for about—oh—twenty seconds?" the demon marveled. "So, when I have one that's gawking, I hold it up so it can see its body splayed open and eviscerated. A little extra I passed along to Cody."

"You are a mutant sent from Hell," Prince muttered.

The demon's eyes sparkled with amused arrogance.

"Easy to get someone to kill. Anyone can become a murderer. How do you get an ordinary 'Joe' to slaughter people in war? Of course, it helps if the enemy looks different or talks different. But, in the end, one simply has to get used to killing things. A man can get used to most anything. Slaughtering or undertaking, or even execution. Rack and pincers is just a job once you get used to it." It chuckled amiably. "Christ on the cross, I do go on! But let's get back to the neighborhood, upstairs in this household, where Cody is carving up little Claire—*cut, cut cut*—"

Prince threw James' grip off him.

"You demented son of a bitch!" he cried out, charging the demon, seizing it by the throat.

"Please don't hurt me, Dr. Prince," the voice of the "saint" bleated, her expression remolding to the "woman". *"How dare you lay hands on me!"* she chastised; then, the "demon" growling, snarling. *"You hypocrite. It's because of you she's like this. You'll never live up to the Prince family name. Ask your father. He'll tell you!"*

In the squalling madness that followed with Prince's fingers locked tight around the demon's throat; the demon struggling, cursing, howling, Prince caught glimpse of its face and was horror-struck. Its blackened tongue flicked in and out rapidly, its head weaving slowly back and forth like a cobra's.

"I want to kill you. I want to bite out your throat!" it seethed, hurling him to the floor, leaping atop him with the quickness of a panther. "Say you love Satan! Worship me! Adore me!" it hissed, drawing the knife up into the air, ready to plunge it deep into Prince's heart, when two claps like the cracking of a bull whip shattered the mayhem!

Bassett stood at the room's entrance. His Colt revolver pointed at the ceiling, lowered as he took aim.

"Freeze," he growled, "or I will put a bullet between your eyes."

The demon's head turned around to face him.

"Bassett," it yawled. "I've been waiting for you."

Slowly, it rose to its feet, Prince lying unconscious on the floor beside it.

"Marshal Rufus 'Bassett' Hilliard," it announced, taking a step toward him, amputation knife in hand. "Oh, that's right, I forgot. You're not a Marshal anymore, are you? Not since they put you on 'sick leave.' A nervous breakdown. Isn't that what they called it?" The demon thrust a jagged smile across the room. "How about a drink, Marshal?"

Bassett tightened his grip on the revolver.

"Go ahead, shoot! Is your hand steady enough to kill the saintly Miss Fowler? Do you have the stomach for it? Afterall, she is me and I am her, or haven't you figured that out yet?"

"Stand back," the Marshal swore, "or I will shoot."

"No, you won't," it said, moving three steps closer. "You're a homeless drunk, rattled in the head, chasing spirits. How's your investigation going so far?"

"It was you who murdered the Fowler babies," Bassett accused. "It was Clara Fowler's body, but you who did the killing."

"It was me," the demon sang out, blithely. "It is me. It will always be me," it bragged, and in its voice a whole lost world moved. "Yes, I strangled the Fowler fucklets. Squalid little things. Wrung their necks and took them apart piece by piece. Like a doll's parts. Forest, too. Carved him up. Watched him endure excruciating pain. But credit where credit is due. I could not have done it without Clara."

The gun quaked in Bassett's hand. He licked the corners of his dry, cracked lips

"Borden and Corriero," he said. "The others, too."

"Yes! We've met before, Marshal. At the Borden house. I was Lizzie—timid and shy—a schoolteacher. We split her mother's skull open with a poleax. Do you know what human brains look like weeping out of an old woman's head? Then, the father, Walter. No loss there. A real bastard. Was it seventeen or eighteen whacks we gave him? I don't remember. And let's not forget Corriero. Pleasant man. Loved dogs. So I became one. Next, he knew he was mounted on Ol' Bertha's chest, beating her brains to mush. Shall I go on? Would you like me to describe the Ripper's *modus operandi*? Crude, but effective. Slice off a breast or two. Cut out the heart for safekeeping. Remove the uterus and place it beside her head. Like I said, crude," he explicated, taking another step forward. "It took Holmes to perfect it. Oh, we were a team. Murder with penache! Lock the kiddies in a trunk. Pipe in a liter of hydrofluoric acid. See what that does to flesh and bone eating away at it from the inside. Ah, the wonders of modern science! And, Christ on a cross, we were close! Right up to the end. So proud was I of our work together that I gave him a legacy. Kept him alive for weeks after he was hung by the neck and buried under ten feet of concrete. I can still hear him screaming."

Its icy glare riveted on Bassett. It took two more steps toward him. Then, stood perfectly still.

"A handy sticker, this one, don't you agree?" it asked, tossing the amputation knife back and forth, one hand to the other.

"Stop where you stand," Bassett threatened.

"No, I think I'll just keep coming forward until I'm close enough to stab this into your heart and turn it in circles." It grinned, still tossing the knife in front of it. "But fair as I am, I'll give you a choice. Either I kill you or you kill the sniveling bitch inside this body with me. Which will it be, Marshal, you or Clara Fowler?"

Their eyes locked: the demon's with scorching contempt for all that was human, Bassett's with righteous loathing for the destruction of all that was sacred to him.

It winked monstrously at him, still edging forward.

"Godammit! Drop the fucking knife!" Bassett shouted, finger tightening on the Colt's trigger.

It took one last step toward him, raised the knife, about to plunge it into him when, with eyes, deadly and determined, the Marshal pulled the trigger—*click!* He pulled it again—*click!* Then, three times in succession—*click! click! click!*

The demon grinned toothily at Bassett, who, towering over Clara's emaciated body, stood frightened to the marrow.

It slapped the gun out of his hand with a powerful swipe. It skittered across the floor.

Not a word was said. Not a word need be spoken. The force of the blow, itself, signaled the enormous strength the ninety-pound body held, if not in muscle and sinew, then in the massive energy that possessed it.

It cast a dismissive glare at the Marshal, who John Fleet, his deputy, once said would stay cool and effective with his throat slit. But not this day. His eyes quivered in their sockets. His muscular, six-foot-one-inch frame seemed fragile as if a modest shove would send him crumbling to the floor.

The demon's eyes touched all four corners of the room. Everyone—Hodgson, Waterman, James and Prince, still not recovered—looked on in a weird state of calm.

Satisfied that all was as it should be, it snapped its head around to the medium.

"Leonora Piper," it said. "You saw this coming, didn't you?"

Her head bobbed timorously.

"You needn't be afraid. Look at me. Haggard and frail with a temperament as delicate as the dust on a butterfly's wing."

It tromped up to her, touched the side of her face. She jerked her head away, palsied with fear.

"No," it assured her, brushing its fingertips over her cheek, "I wouldn't harm you. We are kindred spirits."

She shook her head 'no.'

It snickered, half-turning from her.

"The problem with you is that you think you can communicate with one-half of the spirit world and not the other. Women no different from you can commit barbarous atrocities. I know. You can trust what I tell you."

"W-why?" she sputtered.

"Why do I bother with a pathetic bitch like Clara Fowler? I do it because it's my job. God is dead!" it bellowed, suddenly inflamed. "Jesus is in Hell! Yet, moment-to-moment we fight for the souls of humans. Sometimes by the thousands. Often, one at a time. Each a small or momentous victory. And we celebrate those victories," he swore, "truly we do."

"G-god," she uttered.

"A tired General! Incompetent! Blithering! Angels have lost confidence in him, knowing the power of the forces I command." It lowered its voice and spoke with scorn. "I think the English would say 'he let his side down'."

It crept toward her.

"Another secret," it croaked, "most are borderline, but occasionally we come upon a 'special' case: Borden, Holmes, the Ripper—countless others whose names you will never know—and these, by their own choosing, *become me*, evil incarnate prowling the earth with one purpose: to reduce god's so-called 'creations' to the brutish animals I know them to be."

The notion leaped up in Bassett's mind, full-blown and ugly.

"I should have bashed your brains in the day I recognized it was you who murdered Abigail and Walter Borden. I should have killed you and lit the body on fire so there would be no place for you here, not on this earth."

"Ah! At last, Marshal Rufus Hilliard has decided to stand his ground." It paced the floor as silent as a shark circling. "It's been fun observing you over the years, Bassett. Like watching meat tenderize. You know you're insane, don't you? Nellie will never take you back, nor will anyone else outside a lunatic asylum."

It strutted now, ready to put its psychic powers on full display.

"You, Waterman," it said, turning to him as he looked up from behind his horn-rimmed glasses, "you shall live a long life, but spend it sleeping with the devil! And you, Psychic Researcher," it called out, whipping around to Hodgson, "you will see your precious Jesse sooner than you think, but not the way you wanted, not the way you imagined."

"And me?" William James spoke up, his deep-set eyes searching, as always, for answers to the impenetrable.

"You, Professor James, will live a life of questions without answers, chasing shadows of the truth, pretending they are knowledge, until death leaves you feeling your way through the corridors of Hell!"

"My daughter," Prince moaned, crawling toward the demon, a smear of blood tracking behind him.

"'Hail Mary, full of shit'," the demon mocked, "'the Fucker is with thee—'"

"Claire," he murmured.

"Your daughter is dead!" it shouted, the words shot into the air like a cannon blast. "You have only to pray that we never get our hands on her!"

"Monster," was the word that passed through Prince's lips, until again, he shrieked, *"Monster!"*

"Yes, I have been called that: Satan, Lucifer, the Evil One. My favorite is 'Angel of Light' for it is I who illuminate the pathway to Hell. Shall I tell you what little Miss Claire looks like. Now, as we speak? Pretty, even on the inside."

Leonora Piper started to cry, sporadic, soul-shaking sobs.

"Leave him alone! Haven't you caused enough pain already?"

"'Our Father, who art in Hell,'" it began praying again, "'hallowed be thy cock—'"

"Enough!" Waterman shrieked. "I can't bear to hear another word!" He pointed a quavering finger at it. "Craven! What you've done to Claire! What you've done to Miss Fowler. For God's sake—"

"A few boos from the gallery, I see. Very well. I can take criticism. I shall try to liven things up a bit."

Slowly, Prince rose from the floor, his expression blank and uncomprehending.

"I am her doctor," he said like a man discovering an artifact on an unknown shore. "I am Miss Fowler's physician."

"How splendid! The renowned Dr. Morton Prince—man of science, man of unquestioned integrity—has graced us with his presence!" It frowned. "But does anyone know the outer fringes of others? What are you like in there? Dr. Prince, do you hear? Who are you in there?"

A smothering stillness hung over the room. The demon's gaze locked tight on him.

"Hypocrite!" it thundered. "Liar! Scum! It is your indifference that killed your daughter, Claire! Your ambition that turned a beautiful young woman into this," he reviled, opening his arms to expose the ravaged body. "Look! Feast your eyes on her! See what you have done with your hypnosis and crackpot experiments. But not without design, isn't that so, Dr. Prince?"

"I care deeply about Miss Fowler. I wanted to help her!"

"Faker! Cheater! Deceiver! You don't give a whore's fuck about Miss Fowler. Admit it. Tell everyone the truth. It's about you. It's always been about you. You wanted to write a book about a case so shocking it would overshadow anything Freud had done and so you created one! In your book, you will call evil the product of a diseased mind. Sin a delusion. Me? A metaphor for the bad things people do. I like that! People do not see what they do not understand. But real, I am!"

James looked at Prince in disbelief. His eyes got glassy. His lips trembled with rage.

"So, it was you, Morton, who extracted the "saint" and the "demon" from within Miss Fowler," the professor excoriated. "You took a traumatized young woman already suffering from schizophrenia and delusions and reinforced those tendencies through hypnotic suggestion, until they were self-actualized, until they became real!"

Prince mopped his icy forehead with a handkerchief.

"Calumny! That 'thing' standing beside you is a liar. You said so yourself!"

The demon's eyes flicked over Prince, its accusations planted like a stake in his heart; then to Waterman, his anger turned to disbelief; then, James, intense as he pondered the withering power of unbridled ambition; Hodgson, perched precariously between two worlds; and, finally, Piper, quiet and stolid-eyed.

"Do you want her?" leered the demon. "I have no use for the bitch! Besides, there is work to be done," it said, staring out into glorious desolation. "A world to re-shape. A future to create!"

It scanned the faces a final time, then let out a high-pitched scream, piercing and hideous, as the body went limp and crumpled to the floor.

Breaking loose from the shock that gripped them, Leonora Piper ran to Clara and fell to her knees, Prince limping forward to join her.

"The girl!" Bassett spouted, the specter of horror knifing into his awareness as he bolted into the hallway with Waterman and Hodgson alongside him.

They arrived, panting, at Claire Prince's room. The door was locked. Inside, they could hear Cody ranting. Wild. Incoherent. Then, a piercing cry of terror! The Marshal yanked the Colt revolver from its holster, adrenalin surging through him as he kicked in the door and stormed into the room!

His raging eyes shot from the bed, where Claire sat quietly sobbing, to the bedroom windows shut tight, to the room's far corner where Cody, with teeth gritted, drove the blade of the amputation knife repeatedly into the speaker of the demolished Gramophone.

Bassett lowered his gun. Cody, knife raised over his head, stopped abruptly, and turned to him.

"It was talkin' to me, sir!" he blurted, unhinged. "Horrible things it wanted me to do." Then, looking up to him pleadingly, "To little Miss Claire," he said, composure crumbling. "The voices, sir. *They were wantin' me to kill her!*"

In that instant of recognition, the wrenching dread that gripped Bassett receded in a welter of pity and relief. He stepped toward Cody, shattered and inconsolable.

"Yes, the voices told you, but you wouldn't do it," he whispered, gently lifting the knife from his hand.

The Marshal's baleful eyes drifted from the would-be killer to the bed where Claire lay, head touched down on her pillow, Hodgson and Waterman consoling her as Fanny entered the room. She cringed, shrinking back in incredulous terror, then flying to her daughter, gathered her up in her arms, clenching her body to her.

Down one flight of stairs in the consultation room, still teeming with the residue of the unimaginable, Leonora Piper stared deep into Clara Fowler's eyes.

"Are you all right?" she asked, urgently.

Calm and composed as if awakened from a dream, Clara spoke.

"Yes, I am fine," she said, regaining her bearings. "What happened?"

"That's not important now," Piper said, brushing Clara's hair back from her forehead. "What's important is that you are safe here in Dr. Prince's office."

Eyes lit with anticipation, Prince studied Clara's demeanor, encouraged by the words she had spoken, the way she had said them.

"Who am I?" he asked.

"Why, you're Dr. Prince, of course."

"Where were you born?'

"Fall River, why do you ask?" she wondered, laughing.

Then, finally, with a sense of hopefulness that, once crushed, seemed alive again.

"Who are you?"

"You know perfectly well who I am!"

"Who?"

She shook her head, perplexed.

"Dr. Prince, you have been my physician for nearly five years now. I am Miss Fowler!"

Prince's gaze met Leonora Piper's. A smile, subtle and triumphant, crossed each of their lips, convinced that for the first time, they were in the presence of the real Clara E. Fowler.

EPILOGUE

Harvard Bridge
Boston, Massachusetts

February 2, 1902

A low-hanging fog curled up from the mud-silted river shrouding the steel girders of the Harvard Bridge. Bassett squinted against the keening wind that blew off the water from the east. He dug his hands deep into the pockets of his long coat, drew a breath, and watched it vanish into the ravening air.

It did not matter to him where he met Prince. They were going to meet. That was certain. But it mattered to the doctor. Rather than convene at his office or even a reading room at the Old Corner bookstore, he opted for this, the midpoint of the bridge, halfway between Back Bay and Cambridge.

The Marshal stopped at the line of demarcation separating the two cities. He clasped the steel railing with two gloved hands, and stared out at the river, fast-moving, below the swirling rafts of fog. The bulky stern of a barge emerged like a ghost ship then vanished beneath the bridge below.

Abruptly, his head jerked away from the river, more by intuition than by the sound of someone approaching because there was no sound, just Prince's sudden appearance from out of the fog. He wore a Notch lapel overcoat, Cahill hat, rose-colored necktie and soft-collar shirt with fashionable tooth-pick shoes, and it struck Bassett immediately: the doctor's attire had shifted from Brahmin conservative to garishly flamboyant.

His lips molded into a smile.

"Hello, Bassett," he said.

"I have got to talk to you."

Prince shrugged.

"Let's talk."

They strolled along the walkway toward Cambridge.

"It's about Clara Fowler," Bassett said. "The murders."

"The case is settled. Miss Fowler strangled her siblings. That's clear. But without the moral judgment requisite to accountability. She had no conscious involvement at the time and has no memory of it now."

"There's Forest."

"No different."

"Three human beings are dead, Dr. Prince."

"So, you intend to arrest her?" He chortled. "A jury would laugh you out of the courtroom!"

The Marshal stopped walking and turned to him.

"It's not my job to judge Clara Fowler, or anyone else. It's my job to bring her to Fall River where a jury will decide her innocence or guilt."

Prince nodded curtly and began walking, Bassett alongside him.

"You know, I've grown rather fond of you, Bassett. I admire your tenacity, but you know there is no evidence against Miss Fowler, not really. I told you what Chief Homer had to say about Forest's murder. She is not a suspect."

"But she is the murderer."

"You can't prove that."

"She was the only one in the room with him prior to the murder. And we both know the enormous strength the demon wielded."

"Do you want to put her through the ordeal of a trial? The police. The investigation. The cross-examination in a courtroom." He clutched at the folds of his overcoat more tightly against the wind. "I know you better than you know yourself, Bassett. You're an honest cop, not a monster."

"Maybe Clara is as much victim as murderess," Bassett remarked.

"Don't be melodramatic." He turned to him. His face was bright as a freshly minted coin. "Listen, I'll be coming into quite a large sum of money in the next few months—"

"The book."

"And a moving picture, by God, with the kind of celebrity no one would want to see tainted by a volley of charges against her. We agreed we would be partners. I could cut you a percentage."

"I don't want your money."

"What about your career? I assume you're headed back to Fall River now that the case has been solved. You'll need a job. Your wife, Nellie, will expect it. I can help."

"How?"

"The mayor—Coughlin. He was a friend of my father's. I could talk to him. Explain your situation. I'm sure he would listen and reinstate you as Chief of Police."

He shook his head.

"I'll take my chances. Besides, I think you know what I meant when I called Miss Fowler a 'victim'."

"I do not."

"Clara Fowler strangled Charles and Bessie; carved up Forest, too. But a question is still unanswered. From where did the "saint" and the "demon" derive?"

"Isn't that clear to you by now? As I've said all along, *dissociation* catalyzed by a catastrophic trauma. The cult. The murder of her siblings. The rape that followed."

"In her demonic state, Miss Fowler claimed—"

"Blasted man!" Prince said, turning on him. "Have you not listened to a word I've said? The "demon" was a fragment of the real person, an aberration. The things it did, the words it said, had little to do with Miss Fowler and nothing to do with the truth!"

"Professor James argued—"

"Professor James is not her physician!"

"—he believes it was you who cultivated both the "saint" and the "demon" through hypnotic suggestion, that those implantations, self-actualized, became real to her, but not to you, isn't that so, Dr. Prince?"

A pause came between them. The doctor's hard gray eyes glared at him.

"No," he answered resolutely, "there were no hypnotic implantations, self-actualized or otherwise."

The Marshal looked at him as though staring at a stone.

"You're not in a moving picture now, Dr. Prince."

"And you're not in a courtroom."

Bassett's mind began feverishly to thresh, to probe its fingers deep into the corners of logical doubt.

"Then, I fear, we shall take the identity of the murderer to our graves."

"You've decided—"

"For me, the case is closed. I'm going back to Fall River to start my life over. I saw Miss Fowler, saw what she became once possessed by that—*creature*. It wasn't her that killed those babies or Forest. It was something monstrous, something real and powerful and aligned with whatever is opposed to love. Now it has left her and gone back to some dark and forsaken place, the place where it belongs."

The Marshal pulled his steed derby tight down onto his head, fixed his eyes on the narrow walkway, touching the steel-slat railing with one hand to steady himself against the wind.

"Bassett!" Prince called out to him.

He turned.

"What made you change your mind?"

"The demon said it would re-shape the world and create the future," he shouted back at him, plucking the wooden effigy he had come upon at the Fowler house so many years ago from his pocket and hurling it into the river. "I know now how to prevent that. How to fight the demon with the only weapon we have."

The doctor stood waiting.

"Acts of kindness, Dr. Prince. Acts of kindness."

THE PERSONAL HISTORIES
THAT FOLLOWED

Dr. Morton Prince achieved a level of celebrity unknown to other psychologists of his time. His book *Dissociation of a Personality* (1905) chronicling the Clara Fowler, a.k.a. Christine Beauchamp, case inspired a Broadway play, *The Case of Becky* (1912), a silent movie of the same title (1915) and a remake featuring actress Frances Starr (1921). While fame followed him for the rest of his life, he would never achieve the stature nor the acceptance within the scientific community of his arch-rival Sigmund Freud.

Richard Hodgson would spend the rest of his life trying to contact his deceased lover, Jesse Dunn. He maintained his belief in Leonora Piper's psychical abilities until his sudden death, December 21, 1905, at 50 years of age.

Rufus Bassett Hilliard returned to his wife, Nellie, in Fall River, where he assumed his role as City Marshal. The "Hilliard Papers" documenting his investigation of the Borden and Corriero murders are archived at the Fall River Historical Society, along with the letter purported to come from Jack the Ripper.

Clara Fowler and Dr. George Waterman were married June 22, 1912. The couple spent most of their married life living at 410 Beacon Street, one block from Prince, where Waterman maintained a lucrative medical practice. Going by the name Claire Norton (Forest) Waterman, she and her husband thrived among Boston high society, eventually retiring to their summer home in Brookline, Maine. Clara died May 31, 1954 at age 77. George Waterman passed on six years later.

Leonora Piper gained the attention of many well-known scientists and psychical researchers prior to and after the Fowler case. Dr. James Hyslop believed her séance sittings could be explained only by spirits or telepathy, while others, such as psychiatrist G. Stanley Hall, flatly rejected her claims. In a statement made to the *NY Herald*, she announced, "I must truthfully say that I do not believe the spirits of the dead have spoken through me when in a trance state." She later claimed that she was misquoted, but faced a storm of skepticism that followed her to the grave.

Professor William James, author of the landmark work *Principle of Psychology* (1890), is credited with the founding of modern psychology in America. His relationship with Morton Prince remained cordial until his death at the age of 68, June 22, 1907.

"The devil might be a presence from another universe.
We might be fighting an implacable enemy out there and the devil might
be an agent of that implacable enemy with God as the tired general fighting
that war with his own agents of hope."
–Norman Mailer
David Frost Show
November, 1992

ABOUT THE AUTHOR

Ron Felber was educated at Georgetown University. He has written fiction and non-fiction books including *Il Dottore, The Double Life of a Mafia Doctor*; *Mojave Incident*; and *A Man of Indeterminate Value*. He began his career writing stories for True Detective magazine while working as a deputy sheriff transporting federal prisoners. Ron teaches creative writing at Drew University's Caspersen School of Graduate Studies.

NOTE FROM RON FELBER

Word-of-mouth is crucial for any author to succeed. If you enjoyed *The Unwelcomed*, please leave a review online—anywhere you are able. Even if it's just a sentence or two. It would make all the difference and would be very much appreciated.

Thanks!
Ron Felber

We hope you enjoyed reading this title from:

BLACK✸ROSE
writing™

www.blackrosewriting.com

Subscribe to our mailing list – *The Rosevine* – and receive **FREE** books, daily deals, and stay current with news about upcoming releases and our hottest authors.
Scan the QR code below to sign up.

Already a subscriber? Please accept a sincere thank you for being a fan of Black Rose Writing authors.

View other Black Rose Writing titles at
www.blackrosewriting.com/books and use promo code
PRINT to receive a **20% discount** when purchasing.

Made in the USA
Middletown, DE
22 July 2024

57834016R10146